Salem's Legacy

Vengeance Trilogy: Book Three

Aaron Galvin

Aames & Abernathy Publishing

Salem's Legacy
Vengeance Trilogy: Book Three
Copyright © 2015 by Aaron Galvin
Published by Aames & Abernathy Publishing,
Chino Hills, CA USA

Edited by Annetta Ribken.
You can find her at *www.wordwebbing.com*
Copy Edits by Jennifer Wingard.
www.theindependentpen.com
Cover Design by Greg Sidelnik.
www.gregsidelnik.com
Book design and formatting by Valerie Bellamy.
www.dog-earbookdesign.com
Cover photo by villorejo/Shutterstock and
Baimieng/Shutterstock

ISBN-10: 1516982207
ISBN-13: 978-1516982202

Printed in the USA

Also by Aaron Galvin

<u>Vengeance Trilogy</u>
Salem's Vengeance
Salem's Fury
Salem's Legacy

<u>Salt Series</u>
Salted
Taken With A Grain of Salt

The Grave of Lainey Grace

Find out more about Aaron Galvin
www.aarongalvin.com

for Everett

to Mary Ann
Hope you enjoy the ending.
Thank you for reading
my books! :))

"*H*istory is the story of events,
with praise or blame."
—COTTON MATHER

one

-January, 1728-

Sudbury, Massachusetts

THE WINTER CHILL GRANTS LIFE TO MY ESCAPING BREATH. IT floats skyward, ghostly in the moonlight, and vanishes. Snow crunches under my weight as I flit to the next tree, embracing its bark, hiding in its shadow. I peek around the old oak.

A lone farmhouse sits not three hundred yards from my position, smoke drifting from its chimney in curled, white tendrils. These past few days, the same chimney spit healthier, stronger smoke—white men's smoke, one unafraid of giving away the maker's location. The chimney will belch more of the same come the dawn, if I judge rightly.

Another phantom breath escapes into the night air, yet this one hails from further ahead. Did I not know better, I would think the tree itself exhaled.

I offer up a bird's whistle at my approach.

The sentry does not stir, though I take residence behind a neighboring elm. Like my own attire, the furred skins my brother wears blends with the darkness. His gaze never wavers from the home of Susannah Barron.

"Why have you come?" George whispers from his solace of shadow.

"You have held the watch since night fell," I say. "I thought to relieve you."

George scratches his beard. "I came not this far to lose sight of our prize now, Rebecca."

"I am Red Banshee—"

"No," he says. "In the wilderness, perhaps. Not here."

My heart sinks at the rightness in his claim, words that echo those Creek Jumper mentioned months ago upon our departure. I am Red Banshee in spirit, but must learn from my *manitous* and wear the mask white folk would have of me, especially while traipsing in these stolen lands.

"Go back, sister," says George. "Rest while you can. I will keep the watch."

"George, I—"

"*Go.*" He growls.

There be no words any may utter that will stir him from his post. As one hunter recognizes another, only the sight of our quarry will call George to action.

I leave him to his angry patience, fuming that we did not take Susannah Barron and her family days ago. Had George listened to my counsel then, we should all sleep near a warm hearth fire this night rather than freeze in the woods.

The wind picks up, howling through the woods, clacking tree branches against one another.

I pull my furred robe around me tighter and continue on.

The small, leather pouch round my neck hangs heavy.

I clutch it with my left hand, drawing courage from its contents.

My companions stir at my return, all huddled together beneath our lean-to. The largest of them, Mary Warren, scarcely glances at me before shielding her face in the furs we gifted her.

Ciquenackqua alone moves to grant me some little space to sit. "He will not come?"

"Of course not." Andrew answers for me. "George is a stubborn ass. And always has been."

"Aye. But we here have all supped on some little vengeance for ourselves." I look at Andrew. "George has not."

Anger glitters in Andrew's eyes. "My love did not betray us," he says. "Or else not knowingly, at least. It were my fault alone that Mercy tracked us."

"The truth of that matters little now," I say. "Knowingly or no, Mercy claimed it were Susannah's words that led her to find you, and from there to hunt us."

"Mercy ever was a liar," says Mary, her voice muffled by the robes. "And a cheat, and a whore, and a thousand other black marks the Lord damns sinners to Hell for."

My lip curls at her argument, our months of travelling doing little to quell the rage in me at her abandonment in the battle for my brother's trading post. And while I do not think Mary's claims unfounded, I am not yet convinced Mercy Lewis lied entirely—especially in her mentions of Mary's turncoat nature.

My gaze shifts to Andrew, noting he sits closer to her than me now.

"Mercy Lewis is dead," I say to Mary. "As are all those who followed her to hunt us. Her mention of Susannah Barron is all we have to learn the truth of it."

"You hold to an enemy's words as truth." Andrew spits. "But I ask again, why will you not consider mine? I have long loved you and George both, Rebecca. Aye, and bled beside you."

"Your actions—"

"Were mine own," Andrew's voice rises. "Your own true

father wrought death and suffering upon us all by his actions. Sarah, Hannah, the people in your village, even mine own sister, Ruth—did they deserve death for Simon Campbell's sins?"

"No."

"Aye," says Andrew. "No more than Susannah deserves to die for my drunkenness. Do not deal her pain on account of my failings."

I shake my head. "Andrew—"

"Speak to George, Rebecca, I beg you," says Andrew. "For he will not heed me. Your brother has ever been a better man than I, but let you hear me now—it will be murder if he slays Susannah come the morn. Not vengeance."

I feel Ciquenackqua's eyes upon me. The look he gives mirrors my own twisted feelings on the matter as Andrew continues his plea.

"If ever you had some little love for me, Rebecca, convince George," says Andrew. "Your words alone can repel the darkness in him now. Susannah is a goodly soul. I know in my heart she would never betray or wish ill upon any person. Do not allow the loss of Hannah to damn George's soul for this grievous sin he plots."

I weigh his words, despite the knowledge that convincing George be a lost cause.

"Let your god determine whether my brother's actions be sins or no," I say. "I will not dissuade him should he choose to take vengeance for his wife—"

"Rebecca—"

"But I will hear truth from Susannah's lips ere he claims it."

Andrew's shoulders sag at my words. "She *is* an innocent, Rebecca. On that I swear my soul."

"Perhaps," I say. "And we shall discover the truth of it come the dawn."

I bury my face inside my furs, as Mary did, to warm my cheeks. Sleep does not come easy and, when it finds me, brings naught but night terrors and the faces of murdered loved ones. Always my dreams include the vision from my dream fast—one of Father coated in darkness. He reaches out for me, blackness dripping from his hand onto my skin. It feels hot to the touch, near scalding, and bids me cry out.

I do not relent, even when he takes hold of my shoulder and grips it hard.

"*Rebecca.*" Ciquenackqua wakes me, his face blistery red with cold.

Blinking sleep from my eyes, I notice Andrew gone.

I start to my feet.

"Rest easy." Ciquenackqua whispers. "He waits with your brother outside."

"Why?"

"Perhaps their god heard Andrew's prayers."

I chew on his words and cast my gaze to the heap of furs shielding Mary Warren from the cold.

"I will stay and guard her," says Ciquenackqua, his hand clutched tight around his father's war club.

"Do not trouble yourself with such thoughts that I might run." Mary lifts her head. "These lands are filled with Mather spies and my face well known to many of them. Trust me when I say—"

"I do not."

I clasp forearms with Ciquenackqua then sling my bow and quiver across my back before exiting into the sharp, winter cold.

The wind kicks snow in my face, swirling and howling like the banshee the Wyandot named me for, limiting my sight.

Andrew's deep tracks leave an easy trail for me to follow, especially with the approaching dawn to light my way. His strides be longer than mine, but they aid me speed through the woods to find both my companions halted near the edge.

A violet hue creeps across the horizon. We must abandon our woodland safety if hoping to surprise the Barron family. Already stronger smoke fuels out their chimney than when last I visited George.

"What be your plan, brother?" I ask, settling next to him.

George scarcely looks at me, his gaze trained on the Barron's barn. "These past few morns, it were Susannah who worked the chores. We will await her there."

"I slept in that barn many a night in secret," says Andrew. "Her father oft came out first."

George turns his sharp eyes on Andrew. "I watched her father leave yesterday from this very spot," he says lowly. "And overheard men at the pub say Benjamin Barron were soon off to New York to visit his associates."

Andrew's face pales.

"They are alone," says George, casting his gaze back to the Barron homestead. "Or so they believe."

"George, please," says Andrew. "Spare her. Let me go and speak with her."

"Aye, I intend you to," says George. "Do you truly believe me so cold-hearted that I would slay an innocent woman on the claims of a traitorous witch?"

Andrew's expression proves telling to my mind.

"You wrong me again, old friend," says George. "I will have

you go and speak to this woman you hope to marry, but Rebecca and I shall be there also, listening in the shadows. Let you inquire on the words Susannah and Mercy Lewis last spoke to one another. Pray I find her answers pleasing."

Andrew clutches my brother's shoulder. "You shall," he says. "I swear it, George. She is a pious woman, as you will come to understand."

George nods. "Then let us be off. You lead."

Andrew obeys, springing from the snow, bound toward the barn.

"You think me a fool?" George draws my attention.

"He will give the game away," I say. "Whatever she think of him, he loves her true."

"Lust only." My brother sneers. "Andrew knows little of love, and lesser still the bond between man and wife."

I choose my words carefully. "Still, I believe he means to save her, no matter the cost to himself. We should have left him with Mary and brought Ciquenackqua instead. No doubt we three could have taken the Barrons while they slept."

"Perhaps," says George. "But our father oft told me a man catches more flies with honey than vinegar. If she be innocent, it might be we learn more secret truths through Andrew's affections than all the fearful lies your blade's edge would fetch from her."

My brother claps me on the shoulder then pushes me to follow Andrew's lead.

I sprint through the snow, racing for fear someone might catch sight of me and ruin George's plot. Andrew waits at the barn, his head peeked around the side in careful watch.

I fling myself against the side to join him, panting and shuddering as the frigid air invades my lungs.

George joins us a moment later. He takes hold of Andrew's cloak and pulls him near. "Lead on," he commands Andrew before turning to me. "Keep watch. Knock three times should anyone leave their home."

At my nod, George pushes Andrew toward the pigsty, both of them climbing the fenced enclosure and crawling through the small entry space. I lean around the barn's edge enough to grant a sightline on the Barron home.

My heart thuds against my chest as I wonder what answers Susannah Barron may give us, or if such knowledge could sate my brother. Aye, and what actions might need be taken to bid her give over such answers if we find her unwilling.

The wind picks up anew, shrieking past me, kicking snow in my face. Blinding me. When it dies, I see a shrouded figure staggering toward the front of the barn.

I rap my knuckles against the barn siding then slog through the drifting snow to reach the pigsty. The scent of half-frozen swine muck fills my nostrils as I poke my head through.

Pitched into darkness, I rely on my other senses until my eyes adjust. Warmth coats my hands along with bits of sticky straw. I snort the foul stench away and continue on. Several pigs grunt at my invading their home and flee to the opposite end as I crawl, feeling my way around.

A familiar whistle calls my attention.

I follow its sound, my head thumping against a fence post. I duck beneath it, slinking to firmer ground and promises of sweeter smells—hay bales and cows, oats and horses.

Movement on the wall opposite me draws my attention— a massive shadow shuffling in its pen. Two figures crouch near it—George and Andrew.

The rattling of the barn door latch opening calls me to flee.

I tread back, thinking to leave the way I entered. Instead, my hand grazes a ladder. I test its sturdiness, then fly up its rungs and roll onto the landing, scattering loose hay and dust, frightening cats and rodents who made the loft their respite from the bitter cold.

Hinges squeak. A wooden door slams against the barn side, then silences the outside winds when closing again.

I crawl to the edge and look down on the barn's newest visitor.

She strikes a flint to her lantern. Scattered light illuminates the barn and banishes the shadows to flee high into the rafters where they lie in eager wait for darkness to return.

The woman knocks the bits of snow off her person then takes down the shawl from her hair and face.

My stomach twists.

George and Andrew cannot see what I do. The woman joining us in the barn be no maid at all, but a lady near old as Father to judge by the greyed lines in her elsewise red-gold hair.

I gnaw my lip when Andrew rises in the stall and steps into the light, making himself known to her.

"Susannah—"

The woman gasps, drawing back. But even at my high vantage, there be no mistaking her true feelings for Andrew Martin once past her first shock.

"What brings you here?" she demands of him.

Andrew also seems startled, to my mind, though slower to recover. "I...I—"

The woman steps forward. "Why have you returned?"

Quiet and slow, I unsling my bow from across my back.

"Where is your daughter?" Andrew asks. "I-I must speak with her."

"If anyone, you'll speak with my husband—"

"Your husband is gone," says Andrew, some little bit of his courage regained. "Off to New York, or so I heard tell."

"My husband—"

"Where is Susannah?" Andrew asks, his tone deeper.

"It matters not," says the woman. "We have no want of you in this family. I too have heard tales and know of the black company you keep, Andrew Martin."

I nock an arrow to my bow and hold the end of it between two fingers, my body rigid in wait.

"An unspeakable name," she continues. "One I had not thought to hear again in this life, nor the next, if God grants me His mercy."

"Pray, tell me what you have heard," says Andrew. "And of who would speak such lies."

The woman draws on her shawl anew. "Let you be gone from here and beg me that I do not speak with the other men in town. You will have no answers from me."

I rise in the loft as she makes to leave and let fly my arrow. It shoots through the hem of her dress and *thunks* in the barn floor.

She shrinks at the sound, spinning like a startled cat.

"Perhaps you will speak with us." I call her attention and nock another arrow.

Her eyes draw wide at the sight of me, calling a smirk to tease my lips.

"Wh-who are you?" she asks.

"I am a banshee. Would you hear my song?" I lower my aim

to her heart. "Or will you sing for me all the secrets I would have from you?"

"*Rebecca*—"

My brother's voice draws my focus as he makes himself known to the woman.

"—cease your threats."

At the sight of George, the woman screams in such a manner that I swear she will wake the whole countryside. She leaps toward Andrew, cowering behind his body.

"Away with you, foul spirit!" she shrieks. "Away!"

I relax my bow arm at her reaction.

George opens his palms to her, approaching her slow. "Peace between us, Goodwife," he says, his voice calm and soothing.

The woman falls to her knees, trembling. "God in Heaven, pray show me Your mercy. Please, Lord, I beg You. Do not allow this devil ensnare me a second time."

I share a concerned look with George as Andrew kneels to hold the frightful woman.

"What fears you so?" Andrew asks her.

"It is written...th-the Devil make take any form." She clutches Andrew closer.

"There be no devil here," says Andrew.

"You lie! He stands before us now," she cries, her eyes mad. She raises a quivering hand, pointing her finger at my brother. "And in the guise of Dr. Simon Campbell."

-two-

"SIMON CAMPBELL IS DEAD," I SAY TO THE WOMAN. "MURDERED near sixteen year ago by Abigail Williams."

She looks on me as one in disbelief. "He need not be living for his spirit to haunt me."

"My sister speaks truth, Goodwife Barron," says George. "I have heard it said by others that I bear my father's likeness, but I assure you, I am my own man."

"And a far nobler one," I say.

I do not miss the look my brother gives me for the last remark, but he does not scold me for it as he once did. Or at least he will not in present company.

The woman blinks, casting her gaze between George and I. "You are the son and daughter of Simon Campbell?"

"We are," says George.

His easy admission surprises me at the first. Then I think back on our time in the woods and wonder what deeper game my brother plays.

"Did you know our father?" George asks the woman.

"Little enough, though he haunts my dreams to this day," she says. "God be praised, my father sent me away from Salem to shield me from the evils he foresaw marching upon its doorstep. Near all I learned of Simon Campbell were told me by Mercy Lewis."

My hand turns to a fist at her mention. "I should like to hear of what Mercy said."

"You know Mercy?" she asks.

I ignore her question. "Would you hear more, brother?"

"Aye." George coughs. "But not here. I tire of this blasted cold, and hunger for more than words alone. You, Goodwife Barron," he says to the woman. "You have naught to fear should you answer us honestly. We know your husband is gone away for a time. Be there anyone else in your home?"

I smirk at my brother's test, knowing she and Susannah alone occupy the home this day.

The woman glances at Andrew. "M-my daughter, Susannah, only."

"And have you food enough for us and others in your home?" George asks.

Her eyes wander throughout the barn. "How many others?"

I laugh at her question. "This one is no fool, brother."

"No," says George. "She is not."

His tone bids me think we should be warier still of this woman.

I fidget in studying her. Despite her early surprise at mistaking George for our father, her relative calm since unsettles me.

"Andrew," says George.

"Aye?"

"Let you fetch the others and bring them to the Barron home. This woman knew our father." George glances at Susannah's mother. "It seems we have much and more to discuss outside of your would-be bride."

Andrew looks up at me as if expectant I will volunteer to take on his task.

I give him no such hope.

He and George share a silent exchange, one reeking of an

alpha willing its subordinate to make a claim. Andrew relents without another word. Only when he has gone does my brother speak again.

"What is your name, Goodwife Barron?" he asks the woman.

"Betty, sir."

George coughs again. "Carry on with your chores, Betty. We will wait."

I finger my bowstring when she does not move.

"Please, sir," she says. "I must ask, do you mean my daughter harm?"

"No," says George. "We seek only truth and a warm meal before moving on."

He says it in such a way that even I am inclined to believe him. Still, I cannot forget the harshness I have witnessed overtake him since Hannah's death. His easy tone belies the relentlessness with which he drove us through wild and open country to reach this moment.

As Betty Barron carries out her tasks, I mark the coldness in George's eyes, his gaze following her around the barn. I think if I am the hawk circling the rat, my brother is the tomcat in the bushes, eager to steal my prey and play with his meal ere devouring it.

I sling my bow across my back then descend the ladder to join George. Once at his side, I lean close, whispering. "Why did you send Andrew to fetch the others rather than me?"

"Andrew asks me to trust him again," he replies, his tone mindful of Betty near the hen coop. "How he carries out this task will be telling if he be worthy."

"Another test?"

"Aye," says George.

My stomach turns at this stranger before me. I ever thought George cunning as our father, but more and more he reveals the darker side, as Andrew warned. And, in my heart, I wonder how I might save George from such a fate, or if I am meant to.

We wait in watchful silence as Betty carries out her tasks. Only at the last does George step forward to carry the milk pail for her. He takes the lantern from her and gives it to me, bidding me lead.

Opening the door and stepping outside grants me a quick reminder how thankful I ought be of the warm relief of the barn. I trudge through the snow, carving a new path to the Barron home.

I reach the front door without consequence and stand aside to allow Betty first entry. It pleases me when she does not hesitate to pull at the latch. I swing to follow her, finding blessed heat awaits us inside, and I breathe deep of the scents wafting through the home—porridge and crackling bacon, burning wood, and spices I cannot rightly name.

The hearth burns bright, its fire glowing beneath a small cauldron hung over its flames. A slender young woman dressed in green stands beside it, stirring the contents, her hair red-gold, like her mother's, unbound and spilling over her shoulders.

The girl turns at hearing us enter and drops the stirring spoon at the sight of me.

My hand drifts to my side, grazing the hilt of my father's dagger. Before I can speak, George urges me forward to rid us of the cold. He slams the door still faster, shutting out the wind.

"Mother," says the girl. "Who are these?"

"Guests," says Betty. "Aye, friends of Andrew Martin."

"Andrew?" the girl's voice rises. "Pray, where is he? Where is my love?"

"Are you so eager to see him?" I ask. "Or do I mark surprise in your tone that he might well be with us?"

She steps back, her green eyes quizzical. "Y-you are Rebecca Kelly, are you not?" She looks past me. "And you must be George."

Anger seethes through me that she calls our names so easily and could only have learned of us from Andrew's tales. George halts me ere I can make toward the girl and learn what other songs Andrew sang the scrawny sparrow that stands before us.

"We are." George steps closer. "And you must be Susannah."

"A-aye," she says. "Andrew has spoken of me to you then?"

"Often." George replies.

"Too often," I say lowly. "Indeed, it seems Andrew shares all our names with little regard for we might keep them to ourselves."

"*Rebecca,*" says George. "We are guests here."

I think to remind my brother of our true purpose, one of vengeance rather than being taken with a young maiden, as he seems to me now. I wish to think better of my brother, yet womanly instinct warns few men could look on Susannah Barron's face without it captivating them.

"Aye. You have the right of it, brother." I look to Susannah. "Forgive my impatience. I am weary of nights spent upon the road and with little to sup on."

Susannah smiles at me, though her demeanor remains meek. "We have plenty here and to spare," she says. "Especially for friends of my husband-to-be."

"Andrew Martin will be no husband to you." Betty Barron

steps past me and walks to the cauldron. "Your father will not permit it. Nor will I."

Though Susannah bows her head, I do not miss her lingered gaze on my brother's face.

I move between them.

"Sit," says Betty, from the hearth. "And eat, if you will."

"Aye, we shall," says George. "You have our thanks for it."

My brother clenches the upper part of my arm as he passes by. The gesture confuses me—I know not whether he means to calm me to our surroundings, or does so in warning to let his game play out.

The pair of us sit at opposite ends to keep apprised of our surroundings. Memories of the life before rise within me as I settle onto the wooden bench, the sights and smells of the Barron's home bidding me recall a time when I, too, lived in such a place. All before Cotton Mather sent his witches to steal it away.

I glance at Susannah and wonder if I, too, should have been such a meek and delicate creature had Father and Bishop not rescued me from such a fate. Had it been such a humble life alone taken, perhaps I could have forgiven Hecate and her ilk.

But the faces of those I buried not six months past linger in my mind also. The blade at my side reminds me of a blood debt owed.

My fingers close around the hilt of Father's dagger as Betty Barron approaches me with a bowl of steaming porridge. My muscles tense in wait to learn if she means to spill its boiling contents on me.

Betty does not hesitate to study my face. She places the bowl before me. "You look tired and dirty, child. Shall I heat a bucket of water for you to bathe with?"

My stomach grumbles at the smell of piping hot food. I fight the hunger away, not wishing to seem desperate for my first taste of a warm meal in weeks.

"No," I answer her, then look to George. Anger swells within me upon finding him more mindful of Susannah than her mother at my side. "We have little time for baths. Do we, brother?"

George glances up. "I should like a bath. My sister may prefer the grime and smell of the wild, but I would shut my nose of it." He grins at Susannah. "And her."

Susannah smiles in such a manner that I would smack from her face if given the chance. "I shall fetch some water for you then, sir, if it please you."

"It would," said George. "My thanks for your kindness."

As she rises from the table, I note my brother's gaze follows her. No sooner is she gone than George looks on me, his eyes turned hollow again. A wolfish grin teases his lips, one to let me know he only sports with this young maiden's affections.

"Why have you come here?" Betty Barron places a bowl of porridge before George. The *thud* it makes upon the table speaking she did not do so without purpose. "Truly?"

"We have told you—"

"You and your sister have both said I am no fool," she says. "Must you persist in treating me as one? I am not so old and blind to see you look favorably on my daughter, sir."

"Her face is fair, I grant you," says George. "A gift from her mother, by the look of you."

"So you have come for her then?" Betty steps back.

"Aye," says George. "To speak with her."

Her eyes narrow at his reply. "If your purpose were true, why wait until my husband were gone from our home?"

"You name me liar, woman?" George rises, as I do in following his lead.

Betty earns not a little of my respect when she does not wilt before us.

"I said naught of lies," she answers. "Only inquired of you, sir."

"You may not like the answer," I say.

"I will hear truth," says Betty. "Even if I despise it. I have heard enough of lies in my life." She looks on George. "Speak truth to me now then, son of Campbell, I beg you. Did Andrew Martin tell you we would not accept his proposal?"

George coughs, deep and hoarse. He winces. "Aye."

Betty's shoulders quiver. "And now you come to steal my daughter whilst my husband is away?"

My brother's face tightens at the strain in her voice. Yet, like me, I gather she has impressed George too with her elsewise steely manner.

"As I said in the barn to you, Goodwife Barron, I too seek answers," says George. "Much as I fear that *I* will despise them. Whatever you may think, or know, of my father, he learned me truth harms less than a lie."

"What truth could my daughter know that brought you all this way if not for ill purpose?" Betty asks.

"Mercy Lewis mentioned Susannah's name before her death," I say.

Betty gasps. "Mercy is dead then? You are certain?"

"Aye," I say. "Killed by mine own hand for her lying tongue and evil ways."

The tears welling in Betty's eyes take me aback. She runs at me before I recover from my shock.

Her body trembles upon embracing me.

"Thank Heaven for you, child," she cries. "May God bless you for ridding this world of her malicious ways."

George looks on me, his face puzzled as I suspect my own seems to him. "You knew her then?"

"Aye." Betty pulls away from me, lifting her apron to wipe her face. "All too well."

"In what time?" he asks.

"Since I were naught but a girl of nine," she says. "When I lived in Salem."

I pull away, staring into tear-stained eyes. "Who are you? Truly?"

Pain flushes across her face as Betty opens her mouth to speak.

The door behind me slams open and a cold blast of wind chills my backside.

"Mother, look! Andrew has"—Susannah stops short inside the entry, holding a bucket of snow in one hand, and clutching to Andrew with the other—"returned."

She approaches the table, her gaze flitting betwixt Betty and I.

"Mother, why do you weep?"

Boots stomp upon the wooden floor and the door shuts again. Ciquenackqua escorts Mary Warren around the corner. Their cheeks flushed from the cold, their hair and furred robes covered in snow.

"*Mary Warren?*"

Betty's voice draws my attention.

"Can it really be you?"

Scorn flames across Mary's face at the question.

"You know this woman?" I ask her.

"Aye," says Mary. "And by your tone, I gather she has not been wholly honest with you as to who she is."

"No," says Betty. "I have not. No more than I reckon you were, Mary. We Salem sisters find it hard to shed the stain of our past, do we not? Though I were about to tell them of mine."

Mary grimaces. "Aye. Convenient that you should do so only at the sight of me."

More lies. I cross the distance between us, grabbing Betty Barron by her arm, yanking her to her feet. *More secrets.*

Susannah's screams ring in my ears as I draw my father's dagger and hold it to her mother's throat.

"Keep your bride quiet, Andrew." I glare at Betty. "Who are you? You question our honesty and lie to us—"

"Please," she says. "Please, I beg—"

I silence her by lifting her chin with the edge of my blade. "Speak one more untruth to me and I open your throat as I did Mercy Lewis's."

Betty trembles in my grasp.

I draw my blade away but a little, enough for her to look me in the eye. "How do you know Mary Warren?"

"W-w were Salem sisters, she and I," she says. "Along with Mercy Lewis."

George coughs so deeply it forces him to sit. He clears his throat and blinks. "You were a witch then?"

"I-I thought to be," says Betty. "But my father saved me from such a fate, thank God."

"Aye." Mary steps toward the hearth to warm her hands. "Saved you and condemned the rest of our souls to hellfire."

"Cease with these riddles," I shout, silencing them both. "I would—"

"S-she speaks true," says Betty.

I draw back.

"My father sent me away before things turned darkest," says Betty. "And he abandoned the others to the whims of evil men."

"Your father was one of those evil men," says Mary. "No better than Thomas Putnam and Dr. Griggs."

"A-aye," says Betty. "I will not deny it, though my father loved me with all his heart."

"*Who are you?*" I ask her through gritted teeth. "I will not ask again."

Betty wets her lips. "M-my maiden name were P-Parris. I am the daughter of the Reverend Samuel Parris." Her eyes find mine. "Your father and mine worked their evil on Salem together."

I glance from George to Mary.

"She speaks true," says Mary. "Though she has said naught of another person who may be of some little intrigue to you."

"Who?" I ask.

Mary's gaze falls on Betty, her lip curling. "Betty is kin to the woman who slew your father." Mary turns her icy stare on me. "The cousin of Abigail Williams."

three

"PLEASE," BETTY SHOUTS AT MY TIGHTENED GRIP. "HAVE MERCY on me..."

"Rebec—" George coughs several times over. "Rebecca, stop."

I squint at my brother. "Why should I? This snake has fed us lies, as Mary Warren said."

"I never lied," says Betty. "Only—"

George pounds his fist against the table. He sits, harder than I believe he aims to, and rubs sweat from his forehead. "I would hear her story. God knows she is not the lone snake in this pit."

Mary snorts when our eyes connect. "Think what you will of me," she says. "But I have ever been honest with each of you on my cowardice. I betrayed you when I ran for fear of my life, as I have ran since cast out of Salem. But this one"—Mary waves at Betty—"she has never known fear as we here have. Protected all her life."

Betty's green eyes offer no denial in them but fear aplenty.

"Let you ask yourself why she felt no need to run nor hide after Salem," Mary continues. "How has she lived so long within the reach of Cotton Mather when all other Salem sisters were either swayed to his service or silenced."

"I have been both swayed and silenced, Mary," says Betty quietly.

"*Bought*, rather," says Mary.

"Aye." Betty casts her gaze on Susannah at the table with Andrew. "My loyalty fetched for the same price Dr. Campbell had from my father."

I lower my dagger. "You love your daughter."

"All my children, aye," says Betty. "But Susannah has ever held my affections most."

"Oh, Mother," says Susannah, her words choked as she scurries into Betty's embrace.

I find it hard for their apparent love not to sway me, reminding me of bonds I once shared with those now dead and gone. I clutch the leather pouch round my neck.

"How do you mean our father bought yours?" I ask.

Betty places her hand atop Susannah's head, stroking her hair. "What goodly parent would not sacrifice themselves for their child?"

Mary chuckles. "I recall your father and Putnam both were not so inclined. Both gave the lot of you over. Abigail, Mercy, and Ann Putnam too, all lent to Campbell's plot with little regard for their souls and safekeeping."

"Let you not speak ill of my father," says Betty, a raised tone in her voice that I had not recognized before.

"I shall speak all that I desire," says Mary. "You hold no power over me any longer."

"You wrong me, Mary," says Betty. "Let you remember it was never I to exert power over you."

"No?" Mary asks. "How is it—"

"You were among the oldest of us, older even than Abigail and Mercy. Tell me true, if you could not withstand their willfulness, how should the girl of nine that I were then refuse them and my father both?"

The hearth fire seems to pull Mary's focus, keeping her tongue.

George clears his throat. "You claim your father loved you." He spoons a bit of porridge, chewing it thoughtfully before swallowing hard and coughing again. "Why then would he force you into such an evil plot?"

"I would let you ask him," says Betty. "Had he not passed on near eight year ago now, God rest his soul."

The reverence in her tone matches the same George shares for our own true father. Still, it be one I have little respect for, safe in the knowledge the man I called Father, the Black Pilgrim, would have never subjugated me to such a ploy.

"The Lord will not save your father's soul, Betty." Mary jeers. "God abandoned us the moment we lied on our neighbors and saw them hang for truth."

"You speak blasphemy, Mary," says Betty. "Does it not say in the good book the Lord our God is merciful and forgiving, even though we have rebelled against him?"

Mary smirks. "I see you have your father's gift for scripture, though I suppose it be little wonder a reverend's daughter learned to quote word and verse as it please her. Was that not your father's part to play in Salem? To use the good book and his knowledge of it to sway the minds—"

"Cease your prattle, Mary," says Betty. "Let you count your own sins before speaking on my father's."

The outburst takes me aback, as does the fire in her words.

A grin teases the corner of Mary's lips as she looks on me. "You see?" she asks. "My words strike home with her."

"Aye, I admit they do," says Betty. "How should they not when a traitorous wench denounces my father? And that when you, more than any, ever played one side against the other." Betty glances at me. "Has Mary Warren been honest with you of her works?"

"Somewhat," I say. "The rest we learned from her actions."

"And yet you have not condemned her?" Betty asks.

I step closer. "Let you be thankful we have not condemned you yet."

"Forgive me," says Betty. "But I do not think you will pass ill judgment upon me. Not when you allow one such as Mary Warren in your company."

"She be no company to me," I say. "But my prisoner only."

"Why?" Betty asks. "What good could she provide you?"

"Who better to learn of rumored witchcraft, than from a witch herself?" I cluck my tongue, eyeing Betty up and down. "And now I have two."

Betty straightens. "I am no witch."

"No, you are not." I grimace. "They all hanged in Salem, if the stories are to be believed."

"Aye, stories only. The righteous dangled from those gallows," says Betty. "And my father learned me they now sing with all the angels in Heaven for their sacrifice."

Metal scraping across the floor draws my attention. Mary Warren stands by the fire, a poker in hand. "My own father taught me but one lesson," she says, staring on the cold bit of iron. "And that one furthered by my master, John Proctor."

Mary stokes the fire, scattering the logs and sending bright plumes into the air.

"Speak all you will on the chains of love, Betty." Mary spits the words as she sets the poker back in its place beside the hearth. "I should gladly bear such shackles all the rest of my days rather than live with the fear men like your father instilled in me."

"Our father played a part in that also," says George from the table. "And yet I only ever knew him as a goodly man. People can change."

"Aye." Betty acknowledges his claim. "As you say, sir."

"Believe what you will then," says Mary. "Betty played a role in Salem as much as I."

"Nor will I deny it," says Betty. "But I have begged God forgive my transgressions—"

"And not asked the public for theirs," says Mary.

Betty stiffens. "What good should that do me, but land me in the same grave as Ann Putnam? The Lord knows my heart, Mary. I pray daily for His mercy."

"I cannot speak for God," says George, groaning as he rises from the table. "But I do not hold one guilty for their father's sins, or most of us here should be damned for it."

"No," says Mary quietly. "No, I will go to Hell for my own faults."

I sigh. "I care little for which of you will be damned when and where. There be only one soul I wish to send from this world."

"Whose?" Betty asks.

My eyes narrow at her response. "Why should you concern yourself with such matters?"

"*George!*" Andrew's voice calls my attention, as does the crashing chair and Susannah's screams.

George lay sprawled upon the wood floor, shuddering. Beads of sweat drip down his forehead and his chest wracks with a deep cough akin to a grumbling bear.

I stand rooted as Andrew falls to his side, feeling his head.

"His skin burns with fever," says Andrew, more to himself than any of us in the room. "George...stay awake, my friend."

"*Witch,*" says Ciquenackqua in our native tongue, drawing me from my trance. He approaches Betty with his father's weapon in hand—the long-handled war club bearing an eagle's talon clenched round a wooden ball. He puts the ball at Betty's chest and backs her against the wall.

"No," says Susannah. "Leave my mother—"

I snatch her by the arm and pull her back to me.

"Please," Susannah cries. "Why are you—"

I silence her mewling voice with a jerk of her hair.

Ciquenackqua looks from George to the tabletop, then to me. He motions his head toward the spot George previously sat. "*Poison.*"

Rage seethes in me at the sight of George's half-eaten bowl of porridge while my own remains untouched. "You dare poison—"

"No," says Betty. "No, please, I did no such thing!"

Her claims fall deaf on my ears.

Mary and Andrew argue over George's condition—Mary backing Ciquenackqua's claim, Andrew stating it matters not what we believe and that we must fetch cold cloths to bring down the fever.

I shut their voices away, all my focus on Betty. "Will he die, witch?"

"Pl-please," she says. "I am no witch."

"Liar! No sooner do we arrive and my brother alone eats from your table then he falls ill. What say you to that?"

Betty glances around the room, her eyes frantic and wild.

She settles upon the table where George sat. "Allow me eat from his bowl…"

"What?"

"If you truly believe I poisoned him, allow me eat from his same bowl."

I study her face, searching for any tell of a lie. "A test, then?"

"A-aye," says Betty.

Ciquenackqua turns to me, his face questioning.

"A true test it will be then," I say to Betty.

Susannah squirms in my grip and she shouts when I lead her toward the table.

"Wait!" Betty calls.

I force Susannah's face toward George's bowl and feel her flinch. I glance back to Betty. "Will you allow your beloved daughter to eat of your concoction?"

"Mother!" Susannah cries.

Betty's mouth works wordlessly open and closed as she takes in my actions.

"Rebecca, let you stop this now!" Andrew shouts.

"No," I answer, my sight never wavering from Betty. "What will it be?"

"It…it be porridge only," says Betty, her voice barely above a whisper. "I swear it."

"Then she will not hesitate," I say.

Susannah whimpers. "Mother?"

"*Eat.*" Betty says through her tears.

"Aye," I say to Susannah. "And quickly."

The spoon rattles against the bowl as she dips into the remaining porridge then brings the food to her mouth. The spoon wavers.

"Eat," I say. "Unless you would rather breathe porridge."

I steel my emotions at Susannah weeping.

She takes the spoon in her mouth then swallows.

The spoon falls from her grasp into the bowl and her body heaves as she sniffles.

"More," I say.

"Rebecca, cease this folly!" Andrew yells from the floor. "She ate of the porridge. What more would you have from her?"

I glance down at the half-eaten bowl. "She will finish it."

"Please," Betty cries. "It be porridge only."

"Then let her eat the lot!" My grip tightens on Susannah. "For I will be sure of your claims, false or otherwise."

"R-Reb-Rebecca..." George's weak voice calls me. I find his eyes glazed, his hair wet and slick, face pale. Slowly, he lifts his hand toward me. "N-no...no more."

I forget Susannah when George's hand drops to his side and his head lolls upon Andrew's shoulder.

"George!" I cry.

Mary rushes to his side, falling next to the pair of them. She paws at his clothes. "We must rid him of these," she says. "I fear his nights in the snow have soaked them through and his skin with it."

"Take him to my bed," says Betty. "You will find blankets and a change of my husband's clothes in the trunk. There be a hearth also, though it sits cold and empty now. I will fetch wood—"

"No." I say. "Let you stay here and allow Mary fetch the wood. Andrew and Ciquenackqua will move my brother and strip him of his clothes."

"Rebecca," says Andrew. "These are goodly people who mean no harm. Let them help us."

"*No.*" I hear the weakness in me as I tear my gaze away from George's face. "They have yet to earn my trust." Rage burns through me at the sight of Betty. "Liar, witch, or neither at all. She and her daughter will not touch my brother until I learn the truth of them."

"Rebecca, I beg you—"

"Andrew, if ever you loved George, help him now," I say. "I will keep watch of these two."

For a moment, I think us at an impasse. Then Ciquenackqua leaves his guard of Betty and moves to lift George's feet.

"Aye, I will fetch the wood," says Mary, fracturing the stare between Andrew and I. "But if there be an evil spell on him, I know not how to break it."

"There be no spells here, Mary," says Betty. "As you well know."

Mary gives me a curious glance. "See George stripped before placing him into the bed."

My brother's body and build be larger than either man struggling to lift and bear him into the next room. Both waddle backward, their faces red.

I fight the rising panic in me at the sight of George swaying between them.

The howling winds bid me take note Mary exits out into the cold, shutting the home of winter, leaving me alone with the Barron mother and daughter. For a moment, I think my plan daft—if ever Mary wished to again abandon us, she could so now.

My mind races with whether I should call for Ciquenackqua to follow her, or no. I take comfort in Mary's earlier claim that she has a face known to many in these lands. Despise her as I do, even I recognize she should be a fool to leave our company now.

"I did not poison your brother," says Betty, her soft voice drawing me from my conflict. "I swear it on my daughter's soul."

I forget my distrust of Mary, focusing rather on the Salem sister in my midst. "Perhaps not," I say, picking up the silver spoon and placing it back into Susannah's hand. "But we will all know the truth of that before long."

"Why do you distrust me without cause?" Betty asks. "What have I done to deserve such ill treatment?"

I rest my palm on the hilt of father's dagger, and watch her eyes drift toward it. "I have lost near all my family to Salem sisters, Betty Barron. My brother is all that I have left in this world. If he dies in your home, whether poisoned or no, I swear it will be the end of you also." I focus on Susannah. "You will eat all that remains in my brother's bowl."

"Aye, let you do as she commands," says Betty to her daughter.

Susannah dips the spoon quick, swallowing the porridge without second thought.

I step back. "Why—"

"And when Susannah yet lives," says Betty, standing. "Will you trust us then, daughter of Campbell, and allow us help you in your quest for vengeance?"

My fingers close around the dagger hilt. "What would you know of my vengeance?"

"Nothing of your own," she says. "But by your brother's tone, it strikes me the events in Salem changed both our fathers for the better. And I well know what it is to be a daughter living with such secret guilt."

Her words stir a chord in me.

Susannah spoons the last bit of porridge into her mouth and places the silverware upon the table. She forces a smile as she looks on me, and, for a moment, I swear there be more playful devilishness in her eyes than first I noticed.

"I have no guilt," I say, inching my blade from its sheathe as Betty approaches me.

"No," she says. "But vengeful thoughts aplenty. I too harbor much of that in my heart for the man who brought low my father's name."

"My father—"

"I do not speak of Dr. Simon Campbell now," says Betty. "I speak of the evil one who sent him to Salem. The blasphemer who walks blameless among the people, safe in the knowledge his honor goes unquestioned and untouched, unafraid his legacy will live on long after we here are dead and gone."

"Speak his name then," I say. "If you be so unafeared of him."

Betty's face sours. "The Reverend Cotton Mather," she says. "You journeyed all this way risking both the wild and the savages to reach him, did you not?"

I raise my chin at the easy manner in which she marks my people. "The wild is my home and the only savages we encountered came when stepping into these stolen lands. But what care you for that which I have risked? You who have lived long in Mather's shadow and done nothing to claim this vengeance you desire?"

"The good book teaches patience is a virtue," says Betty. "I have long hoped for a means to fulfill the wish my father asked of me on his deathbed. Today, the Lord answered our prayers, bringing me those of a similar mind." She looks on my dagger. "And one better suited to the task."

"Your god did not bring us here," I say.

"He did." Betty clutches the wooden cross around her neck.

"The Lord works in mysterious ways. We should be fools not to see the signs lain before us."

"Does your god teach you to follow bad omens?" I glance to the room where my brother lay. "I can think of no worse sign than my brother falls ill before we reach the end of our path."

"Your brother shares your father's face," says Betty. "Others from Salem will recognize it as well as I did. Perhaps he was not meant to go further and give you away."

The mere thought brings rage to my heart. "If he dies—"

"I cannot speak to if he will or no," says Betty. "But I did not poison him, as you will see when my daughter does not share his sickness."

Susannah steps around me to join Betty. She stands tall, her face flushed with life and bearing no trace of the evil spell that George suffers.

"Perhaps soon you will trust us and see we share a similar goal," says Betty, her green eyes transfixing me.

"And if you speak true," I say. "What then?"

Betty studies me up and down. "Your guise and face hold little secret as to your true nature. Believe what you will when first you catch sight of the Reverend Mather. He speaks all manner of religious zeal, but he is a monster who learned his tricks from the Devil himself. He will see through you."

I cluck my tongue. "He is still a man of flesh and blood, no?"

"Aye, I believe so," says Betty. "For time has not been kind to him. I heard it said he suffers even now."

"I will end that suffering." I draw my father's dagger, its gleam a reminder of the glint in Father's eyes for those who trespassed him in life. "If it be the last act I do on this earth."

"You speak like a man." Betty chuckles. "It may have served

you well in the wild, girl, but here you must learn the ways of a devout woman. Aye, and of her secret tricks."

Her words bid me think of my dream fast, the vision of my *manitous* and the masks it would teach me. A shiver runs up my spine as I look between the mother and daughter, recalling Mercy Lewis once echoed similar words.

Betty steps closer. "In the good book of Matthew, our Lord savior reminded us we should not suppose He came to bring peace to the earth, but a sword. You brought the blade," Betty says. "I will lead you to a shield."

-four-

SUSANNAH BARRON MEETS MY STARE FROM ACROSS THE ROOM. Three hours passed and she has yet to show any sign of the sickness that overtook George. Indeed the only thing she reveals is affection for Andrew. Despite her mother's presence, Susannah whispers secrets with him like children playing at a foolish game.

Andrew looks a dog, to my mind, lapping for food and approval whilst his master sports with him.

I turn my attention instead on the room where Mary and Ciquenackqua stay with George. My heart would have me go attend him also, but I fear what the sight of him expiring may do to my soul. I cling to each cough from beyond the closed door and pray to the ancestors for my brother not to quit this life.

A creaking bench draws my gaze—Betty rising from her chair near the fire. She walks to join me at the table, approaching as one unafraid even when my hand drifts to my side.

Betty grimaces as she sits. "My daughter remains well."

"Aye, so it seems."

"And yet you loathe to trust us."

"Trust be a delicate thing," I say. "Strengthened with time, yet easily broken."

"I wish my daughter knew as you do," says Betty. "Susannah has ever given of herself with little thought she might be taken in by others. My husband believes it a mark of her goodliness."

"And you?" I ask, noting she holds to the wooden cross around her neck. "What do you think on such matters?"

"I pray she learns wisdom before life teaches her otherwise. Still, her innocence gives me hope."

"Does it?"

"Oh, aye," says Betty. "Even when broken, trust can yet be mended and made near whole again. But innocence..." She toys with the wooden cross. "The Lord may wash our sins away, but nothing in this world can restore innocence once stolen."

"Your words remind me of another," I say. "My sister, Sarah."

"There is another of you?" Betty asks. "A third child of Campbell?"

"No longer. Your friend Mercy Lewis sent her from this world."

Betty casts her gaze to the floor. "Mercy was no friend to me, as I have told you."

"I have been told many things this past season." I glance to her bedroom door wherein Mary Warren sits with George. "Few of which I know to be true."

"I am sorry for your loss." Betty takes my hand in hers then kisses the back of it.

I recoil.

"Forgive me," says Betty. "I too know what heartache the loss of a sister brings."

"What could you know of my pain?" I ask, bitterness thick in my throat. "Did a witch raid your village and take your sister's scalp while she yet lived and screamed your name to save her?"

"Not a witch." Betty looks on me, her eyes shining. "A fallen angel. I heard it said she were a most beautiful and terrible sight to see, her skin singed from her descent, and her hair afire. Those who witnessed claimed it could only be God sent her from heaven to rid this world of she who I once named sister."

My mind recalls a memory of that fateful night. I remember the cold blade pressed against my throat in an attempt to lure my sister from the flaming barn.

"The sister you speak of were Hecate," I say. "Abigail Williams, no?"

"Aye," says Betty.

"But Mary Warren claimed you were family."

"Cousins by blood," she says. "But sisters in spirit, raised alongside one another in my father's home. For a time, I desired nothing more than to be like Abby. I followed her every whim until Father sent me away."

Her small smile tempts sympathy from me, as I too recall the struggles only a younger sibling may know—half desiring to walk in the footsteps of our elders, the other wishing nothing more than to carve our own path.

"Aye," Betty sighs. "Sent me to save me."

"And now the men who gave us life are gone," I say. "Leaving us to play out the evil sport they crafted."

"Abby painted fate a cruel mistress," says Betty. "I oft wonder what fate may have dealt us had our situations been reversed. Would I have turned to evil means, as Abby did—"

I note her long stare at Susannah and her fingers again clutching to the cross.

"Or did I yet hold some child's innocence that should have shielded me?"

My mind drifts to Sarah, lingering in our *wikiami,* watching her spirit fade, all while doing naught to revive the liveliness she once held.

George's coughing from the other room draws my focus away from the past.

"Who can say?" I ask. "We must live in the here and now."

"Aye, you have the right of it," says Betty, turning again to face me. Staring in my eyes in such a way that I might see her pain lives there also. "There be no way for you to trust my words, but you will soon understand I am a true friend to you and your brother."

"If you were, you would speak plain with me about this shield you have mentioned. What power does it hold to hide us from the Reverend Mather's sight? How it has kept you safe in his reach all these years? You have said naught of how this shield will help us."

"And I will say no more for now," says Betty. "Nor lead you anywhere so long as Mary Warren is near. Only when you send her from your company will I agree to help you."

"Strong words." I saunter toward Susannah. "But I think you will take me to this shield if you love your daughter well."

"No," says Betty. "I owe my life and Susannah's, aye, the lives of all my children and their children to follow after, to this secret. I will not risk its safe-keeping with a traitor in our midst."

Betty's conviction tempts me to believe her, though my mind bids me not let her sway me. Her earlier words of tricks and guises give me pause to study the former Salem sister with renewed interest. Unlike Mary Warren, Betty does not flinch to meet my gaze.

Squeaking hinges distract my attention.

I stand when the door to Betty's room opens.

Ciquenackqua crosses the threshold, his eyes finding mine. The silence hanging between us forces me to hold my breath.

I thank the ancestors at my brother's cough, and slump back to the table.

"He would speak with you," says Ciquenackqua to me, his gaze flitting to Andrew and Susannah. "And her alone."

Andrew's hurt slaps me from across the room, the lovesick mongrel I thought him now glancing away like one kicked by its owner. His gaze follows me to the bedroom door, his pain turned scornful.

I halt outside the room, my feet hesitant to carry me but a bit further.

Ciquenackqua squeezes my shoulder.

The markings of our people on his face embolden me. He seems a man grown, though I know him younger than all who occupy the Barron home. And while George lay ill, the look Ciquenackqua gives me in return proves I yet have a brother beside me now.

Ciquenackqua turns his gaze on the Barrons and Andrew. "*I will keep watch of them,*" he says in our native tongue. "*Let your heart stand with your brother now rather than worry of these.*"

I clap his arm then step inside the smaller room.

The warmth of the hearth near forces a gasp from me no sooner than I walk near the bed. George lay covered to the neck with checkered quilts piled upon him. Though his face is blocked from my sight, the rise and fall of the blankets sets my heart at ease.

Mary Warren stands near the corner, wringing a bit of wet cloth over a bucket. She swaps the sopping cloth for the used one upon George's forehead at my approach.

George glows with defiance, though his face is pale and his breathing labored.

I rush to his side, placing my hand upon his feverish cheek. "Brother."

"Aye," he says. "I-I yet live, sister."

"Not for long, should you risk the cold again," says Mary. "Fool."

George forces his cough to become a chuckle. "H-Hannah often said the same of me. But you will see, Mary Warren." He coughs anew, the sound of it deep as the drums my people beat for the war dances. "Th-that same stubbornness will save me from this illness now."

"Rest will save you," says Mary, turning to me. "He cannot leave here, unless we would risk death upon him."

"How long?" I ask.

"I know not," says Mary. "A few days at the least, perhaps a week."

George falters in his attempts to sit up. He falls back, coughing anew. "You do not speak for me—"

"No," says Mary. "Your body speaks. Believe me, I would have us gone from this place now if you were able. I am not yet convinced Betty did not work some spell on you, George."

"She did not," I say. "Susannah ate of the same bowl and has not fallen ill."

"Aye." Mary snorts. "And she need not, if her mother did not wish the illness upon her."

"Mary," says George, his voice soft. "Give me a moment... with my sister."

Her demeanor gives no indication she wishes to grant his request. Then she fetches up the bucket and used cloths, taking them from the room without another word spoken.

"She is angry with me." George's grin fades to more coughing.

"I care little for her happiness," I say. "Let her glower all she will. It will not sway my feelings."

"You wrong her," says George. "Mary Warren means us no harm."

"She need not mean us harm for her to cause it," I say, my voice shaking. "Let you remember she abandoned us in our time of need—"

"And yet she cares for me now," he says quietly. "Staying by my side all this while with a tender and guiding hand."

I shake my head. "I think she does so only to not share a room with Betty."

"Perhaps," says George. "Or mayhap not to share a room with you."

His words tease a grin from me. "Am I so difficult?"

"Aye," he says, wincing as he closes his eyes, adjusting his head upon the pillow. "As is your nature."

"You would not speak so candid if you were well," I say. "You say so only now, safe in the knowledge I would not risk harm upon a sickly man."

He smiles. "Believe what you will, little sister. When this sickness has gone, I will yet speak the same to you."

"Then may you hurry to be well," I say, sporting with him. "I would not wait for spring to arrive."

"Aye." George's eyes flutter open, fixing a stare on me. "And you will not...you must keep on without me, Rebecca."

"George...no—"

"Aye, you will," he says. "I know not how long this sickness will plague my spirit. In truth, I cannot say if it will not be the death of me."

My heart plummets. "George, let you not speak so and

instead recall how stubborn you truly are. The words spoke to Mary and me."

"Hopes and half-truths." He coughs again. "Yet I am not so stubborn to neglect the harsh ones. I will fight this, Rebecca, but no man can withstand God's will. If He call my name, then I must go."

My eyes sting. "I do not believe in your god."

"And yet truth exists whether we believe in it or not," says George, struggling to sit.

I reach to hold his hand.

"Betty Barron's husband will return," says George, resting his head against the wall. "And when he arrives, you and the others must be gone from here."

I lean toward George. "When Benjamin Barron returns, we will hold him hostage until you are well."

"No. This is his home, Rebecca, and he did not wrong our family."

"But his wife and daughter—"

George waves me silent. "Let you cease this hate, sister." He licks his cracked lips. "God save you, but let you listen to me for once in your life."

"Perhaps I would, if you spoke sense," I say. "The more I hear, the more I believe Mary has the right of it. An evil spell has been worked on you."

"I yet keep hate in my heart," says George. "But not for any folk here in this home." He squeezes my hand. "Nor should you."

"How can you say these things?" I ask, drawing my hand from his. "It were you beside me these past months, driving us hard to reach this place."

"Aye," says George. "That I might hear from Susannah's lips the truth or lies of such things as Mercy Lewis told. Did Susannah knowingly sway Andrew and betray us with such knowledge as she learned of us from him?" George shakes his head. "I needed to know. Aye, and see it in Susannah's eyes."

"And you believe her?" I deride him. "After but an hour in her company?"

George nods. "My life's work has been in fair dealing with all manner of folk who would war on one another. Trading with rival tribes, the French and English, be a dangerous game, sister, as you well know. I should have been dead long ago had I not learned to spot truth in the faces and words of others."

"I do not doubt in your skills," I say, "only that this illness blinds you."

"Perhaps, but you are a warrior thirsting for vengeance. Mayhap your lust for it blinds you." George again reaches for me. "Believe me, sister, when I say we have no enemies here. Not unless we make them."

I rise from the bedside. "We are surrounded by enemies."

"The Reverend Cotton Mather does not live in this home," George says. "Nor has he walked beside us all the way from the wilderness."

"You came all this way—"

"I learned the truth I sought." His voice rises. "Now let you understand it also."

"What truth be that?"

"There yet be goodness in this world, sister," says George. "We knew that in the wild for a time before it were stolen again from us. Indeed, darkness has so long loomed over our family I think we scarce recall what life means without it."

"Aye, and we have come to strike that dark away for all time," I say. "Do not ask me to do so without you."

"I would ask many things of you," George says. "And the first will be the hardest. I cannot force it on you, but hear my plea, Rebecca. Do not let this hate consume you. Unleash it upon the man who earned it of his own actions. Not those he has likewise hurt."

George grips my hand harder.

"We have a common enemy," he says. "Let our hate for him bring us together rather than divide us."

I wish agreement with George that he might know his words are not lost on me. But the bitterness living in our sister, Sarah, lingers in me also.

"Why, George?" I ask. "Why do you trust these people so?"

"Because those I love have told me I can," he says. "Ciquenack-qua left not only his people but his world behind to follow you, even when you cautioned against it. Do you doubt him?"

"No," I say. "But Andrew—"

George silences me with a wave of his hand. "Those first years in the wild, you and Sarah looked to each other and Priest for solace." George sighs. "I had Andrew."

"George—"

"He is my brother, Rebecca," says George. "And for all his faults, I love him still. Look you no further than the next room if you would yet mistrust him. He knew I would make good on my promise to harm Susannah if she were dishonest and yet he never halted me."

"He did," I say. "He said—"

"Aye, words only. But had I raised my hand against her, I have no doubt he would have risen against me. Andrew spoke with the hope I might hear truth." George fights another coughing fit. "I needed look into her eyes to learn it true. Now I understand Susannah is indeed a goodly woman. Aye, as good as Hannah."

"Do not compare your late wife with the blushing girl in the next room," I say.

George grins. "My wife were a blushing girl once also. It were only life with me that hardened her, just as life with Priest hardened you."

I shake my head. "And what of Mary Warren? You believe in her now too?"

"Aye," says George.

"Why?" I ask, my voice dripping. "How can you—"

"Hannah trusted her," he says, his eyes watering. "When first Mary came to our post, I doubted her husband's intentions, but it were Hannah who convinced me otherwise. She spoke that Mary were a goodly, if frightened, soul whom we should show kindness."

"Hannah is dead, George," I say. "In part on account of Mary Warren."

"No," he says. "She is gone because the Lord called her home. And if my wife were here now, she would ask you forgive Mary for this sin you wrongly heap upon her shoulders."

"How can *you* ask this of me?" I clench the blankets upon the bed. "What do we have left to us if not claiming vengeance for those whom we loved?" My jaw clenches. "I cannot forgive her, George."

"Then you wrong yourself also, sister," says George. "We must trust in others, if we hope to bring our enemy to his end."

"But how?" I cry. "How am I to accomplish that without you?"

"You will find an answer. Priest learned you his secret ways. I have little doubt you came all this way without a plan to see your own stubborn will carried out." George smiles weakly. "Now allow me rest, sister, if you would see me rise from this bed again."

I remain by his side, listening to his rasped breathing and the crackling fire. Though I recall our father were a large man, George stands in my mind larger still. The sight of him laid so low at the sickness coursing through him weakens my soul.

George's words race through my mind, my love for him and what he would have of me toying with the mistrust I hold for the Barrons and Mary and even Andrew. I know not how long I sit at his side, only that I keep close watch of the rise and fall of the blankets upon him.

I clutch the pouch around my neck, feeling its weight, praying its contents keep my brother safe. After a time, I slip the pouch off my neck and place it over George's head, resting it upon his chest.

Then I lean close to his ear, hoping even in sleep he will hear my voice.

"You asked of me many things, brother. I will work to do them all, if you but grant me one wish of mine." I clutch at his hand, making no effort to halt my tears. "Do not quit this world, George, I beg you. Do not leave me alone to mourn your loss with all the others gone before."

My brother stirs, his fingers gently grasping mine.

-five-

A SOFT RAP AT THE DOOR BREAKS ME FROM THE WAR WITHIN. Ciquenackqua enters the room.

Wax pools around the nubbin of candle that yet remains. I blink my sleep away and rub my eyes.

Ciquenackqua gently closes the door behind him to not wake George then pads toward me. "The others grow restless," he says in our native tongue.

I nod. "And what do they say?"

"Little, with their words," says Ciquenackqua.

I grin, his speech comforting me as something Father might say. The sudden thought erases my brief respite, reminding me yet again of all that has been taken from me.

Ciquenackqua moves to the opposite side of the bed, forcing me to acknowledge his presence rather than dwell on George. "What are we to do now?" he asks.

"George wishes us to go on without him." My chin dips. "But I know not what to do. We have so long planned to hear what Susannah would say that—"

"No," says Ciquenackqua.

I look up.

"George wished to hear her words. You did not." Ciquenackqua lays his father's club upon the bed that I might recognize the eagle talons grasping the wooden ball. "*We* did not."

George shudders in the bed, the pouch slowly rising and falling upon his chest, his breath raspy.

"We came for vengeance and blood," says Ciquenackqua. "Not words. This is the way of *our* people."

"And we will have it," I say.

"When?" he asks.

The sharpness in his tone takes me aback.

"We have lost more than a few days to George's plan." Ciquenackqua reaches for the necklace his father carved for him as a gift on his naming day. "The turtle is my *manitous*, its path slow and steady, but even the turtle leaves its shell to bite when needed."

The fire in his voice bids mine to rise also, willing me to take up my father's dagger and make the war dance with Ciquenackqua.

"I did not follow your brother through the lands of our enemies to hunt these white devils," says Ciquenackqua. "I followed Red Banshee, the daughter of Black Pilgrim, and my friend. We have walked this path for months together, you and I. Do not wander from it."

"I cannot bring myself to leave George as he is now," I say. "Not when we draw so near to the end, nor among these folk."

"Your brother is a warrior," says Ciquenackqua. "As our fathers before us and we are now. Would you have George quit this hunt if you fell ill?"

"No..." I say quietly.

"Then see his wish carried out."

"I would," I say. "But I know not what to do."

"You do," says Ciquenackqua. "Your *manitous* did not choose you for meekness, but for your cunning and resourceful ways.

Were Creek Jumper here, he would urge you channel the ringed-tail now. Use those of us in this home as your *manitous* would have you do."

I think on my vision and the many masks worn by the ringed-tail, the same masks Creek Jumper bid me take up and wear as my own person. The plan I have held since leaving my brother's trade post burns in my mind alongside the pain I would deal Cotton Mather. The same torments he and his brood worked on my family.

I lean toward George, my lips burning on the heat of his forehead. "Sleep well and rest easy, brother," I say. "I go now to carry out your wishes, for better or worse."

I wipe my cheeks and steel my soul under Ciquenackqua's stern gaze. Then I rise from my brother's side, and leave the room with Ciquenackqua in tow.

The scents of venison and potatoes from the Barron table remind me I have not eaten in three days. Both Barrons and Andrew eat of the dinner, the scraping from their forks and knives cutting against the howled winds outside.

Betty watches Ciquenackqua and me, her face questioning.

"Have the pair of you ceased conspiring?" says Andrew.

"We have no secrets, Andrew." I snap.

"Then why not speak plain so Susannah and her mother might understand that also?"

His tone sets my temper to rage, though I do my best to cool it quickly in keeping to the promise I made George. "We ride for Boston on the morrow," I say. "George would not have us halt our plans on account of his illness. Indeed, he—" My voice catches in my throat. "He is not certain he will survive it."

Andrew places his fork down. "All the more reason we should wait. It would be wrong to abandon him now."

I cannot keep my lip from curling, feeling the mere presence of Susannah at his side emboldens Andrew. "We will go," I say. "My brother does not wish us to further intrude upon the Barron household."

"His company is no intrusion," says Betty. "The Lord bids us care for the sick and wounded. We will see him back to good health, if within our power."

My stomach turns at her last words. "No," I say. "You will see us to Boston."

"I will see you nowhere so long as Mary Warren be in your company," says Betty. "I will not risk my shield."

I glance at Susannah in hopes of witnessing some lie in her eyes, or else a clue as to the shield her mother speaks of. Yet for all my passing thoughts on her girlish nature, Susannah has her mother's gift for donning a stone face. She gives me nothing.

"When will your husband return?" I ask Betty.

"Who can say?" she answers. "The winter snow may keep him abroad, or else he may return tonight. I have no right to ask him of his business."

"*She lies*," Ciquenackqua mutters in our native tongue.

I keep my stare on Betty. "And what would your husband do, should he return to find...guests...in his home?"

Betty's gaze drifts to Ciquenackqua. "That would depend on the guests, I suppose, and what I would say of them." She then looks on Andrew. "In truth, I do not suppose he should be pleased at the sight of any of you."

"Perhaps," Susannah says quietly. "Perhaps if I spoke for them, Mother."

"Quiet, daughter," says Betty. "Despite the favor you hold in your father's eyes, he will be none pleased with you either now that this one has returned." She turns her hard stare on Andrew. "Your father has already cast his judgment on such a proposal. He will not change his mind no matter how much you and Andrew might wish it."

Her disdain is not lost on me, though my mind wanders back to George. Leaving him unattended with no one I trust dampens the fervor I once held to reach our goal and claim our vengeance. With war raging in me on how to placate all parties, I call my *manitous* to mind and think how I might play to each person's needs and wants.

"Andrew," I say. "You have been to Boston many times in your trading. How far till we reach the city?"

"A day's ride, perhaps," he says. "If the weather be kind to us, though I do not suppose the weather will be, to judge by the winds outside."

"And Mather," I say. "Do you know how to find him?"

"No," says Andrew. "I had not thought to search him out before. Still, we should have little trouble in finding someone who will know. He being a reverend, I suppose we should find him at church."

"You will not," says Betty. "He turned over his pulpit near Christmas and it has been said he will not take it up again. Old age and illness keep him abed."

"He must call somewhere home," I say, my mind recalling mine and Ciquenackqua's village, George and Andrew's trading post—both of them razed to the ground. "Someone will know."

"Aye," says Betty. "There will be those who know where he lives. But you will not find anyone he trusts to allow you enter inside his home without conflict." Her eyes glitter as she looks into mine. "Not without me."

"Your shield, rather," I say.

"Aye."

I step toward her. "And do I have your word, Betty Barron, that you will aid us if I banish Mary Warren from our company?"

Betty's head cocks to the side. "Aye," she says, after a time. "I swear it."

"Good," I say. "Then we leave at first light."

"Who leaves?" she asks.

"All of us here, save your daughter and George."

Betty eyes me with suspicion. "You mean to leave Susannah behind? Truly?"

"Aye, I would keep her safe from harm," I say. "Who better to safeguard and quicken my brother than Andrew's intended?"

Susannah blushes at my words.

The stern look Betty gives me warns she will not be won as easily.

"Rebecca," says Andrew. "Ciquenackqua should remain here also."

"No," says Betty immediately.

Andrew ignores her. "I attempted to sway his accompanying us before we left the trade post. I stand by that warning now."

Ciquenackqua glares at him. "No man tells me my place, or where I cannot go."

"That may be," says Andrew, glancing at me for help in this matter. "But it does not change the truth of my words. Boston is no place for a native, brother. Not even one brave as you."

"I am a Miamiak warrior," says Ciquenackqua. "We do not fear."

"I believe that," says Andrew, walking to Ciquenackqua and placing his hands about our friend's shoulders. "But I have seen how the fearful respond when one unafraid ventures into their company. For the shared love we bear this family"—he glances back to the table—"let you remain here and keep watch of George."

"No," Betty shouts. "He cannot stay. I do not trust a savage in my home."

I step toward her. "No more than I trust a witch upon the road."

Betty glares at me. "I am no witch."

"And he is no savage." I return her stare.

Betty seethes at my response, but she keeps her tongue.

Ciquenackqua looks on me, his usual stern face now hiding little mystery of his pride and loyalty. *"What would you have of me?"* he asks.

"Stand with me," I say. *"If you remain willing."*

He nods.

"Then we leave come the dawn," I say.

Betty strides from the kitchen into an adjoining room with Susannah quick to follow after.

"Mother, please," says Susannah, following her. "Can you not listen to them?"

Andrew glances at me. "And I half thought I alone had the power to displease her mother so."

"I care little for her happiness. If she did as I bid her, there would be little need for any of this," I say. Glancing around the room, my heart races. "Where is Mary Warren?"

"She asked Betty's blessing to visit the barn," says Andrew. "I think she wished to be alone with her thoughts."

"And you allowed her go?" I ask.

"Aye," he says. "Was I wrong to do so?"

"She is our prisoner," I say.

"Not ours," says Andrew. "Yours."

I storm toward the front door and fling it open, braving the cold, finding night has overtaken the day. The winds whip at my cheeks and nose, pinching them with what feels like tiny needles pricking at my skin. The snow gleams in the moonlight and casts the barn as a foreign object to my mind—a dark, hulking thing in an elsewise brilliant, frigid world.

I fumble at the door latch and lose hold of it. A gust aids in opening it, allowing me stumble into the barn.

The dim, small light of a candle casts long shadows into the rafters further to the back of the barn.

I close the door and latch it, then hear the rustling of straw.

"Who comes?" Mary asks.

"Rebecca." I kick the barn side, knocking clumps of snow off the leather boots Andrew salvaged from the trade post fires.

A horde of cats scrambles around me no sooner than I tread toward Mary, all of them mewling for scraps, a few near tripping me.

Mary nestles in straw, her broad back lain against an even broader heifer. She gives me no kind word, nor even acknowledges my presence, her sight transfixed by the pale light of the candle, perched atop an upturned metal bucket so the wax drippings cannot catch the barn aflame should she fall asleep.

A stallion neighs from the stables, frightening me for a moment. It kicks at doors holding it at bay.

For a moment, I believe closing my eyes might transport me back to my brother's trade post. A part of me wishes when I open my eyes again it would be no strange horse, but my father's stallion—the majestic beast waiting for some little affection.

But the stallion remains unfamiliar. And the candle flame, small and weak, reminds me near everything I held dear has been given over to fire and ash.

I run my palm over its flames, culling its heat to stoke the embers in me rather than give over to the somber.

"How fares George?" Mary asks.

"He rests now," I say, turning my attention to her.

"Good," she says. "The cold will not abandon his body so easily. I fear also the toll upon the road has dampened his soul." Her voice breaks. "Aye, and the loss of Hannah."

My chin dips. "She were a goodly woman."

"Never in my life had I met one so kind as she," says Mary. "In truth, I do not expect to witness such kindness again in my life. Nor after, if we are speaking plainly." She shifts against the heifer. "I know myself as one bound for Hell. Still, I thank God for allowing me meet one of His angels for a time."

The many memories with my sister-in-law flood within me— the way Hannah balanced my brother's calculative mind with her open and trusting ways, that she followed him into a life lived in the wilderness when few others would have done the same. All gone in an instant, due to the cowardice of the woman seated before me.

"The others told you I were out here, no?" Mary asks.

"They did."

Mary nods. "No doubt they believe I braved the cold to be shut of Betty's presence."

"Is that not why you are here?" I ask.

"In some small manner, aye. The larger truth be I wished to sit alone with my thoughts and take in the quiet." Her shoulders sag. "I know not the last time I were truly left alone to do so."

The wind whistles beyond the barn's wooden boards, shaking several.

"It is hardly quiet here," I say.

"It suffices." Mary strokes the heifer's back. "As a girl, I often wondered what it must be like to live as a hermit. But even then, I knew hermits must have courage to withstand both the wilderness and the isolation. In truth, I should have been content to live in such a barn as this. I ever enjoyed those chores most whilst living with the Proctors. No cow or swine ever mocked nor threatened me. They sought only food and care. Nothing else."

"Hannah once said the same of my brother." I grin.

Mary does not. "George, perhaps. Food and care alone never sated any man I had personal dealings with."

"Then they were no true men," I say.

"No, they were not," says Mary, her cheeks tightening. "But you did not brave the cold to speak of the ghosts in my past. You came to learn if I were still here, or else if I broke my word and ran off."

I settle down into the straw in front of her.

"Aye," I say quietly. "Those were my first thoughts."

"Were our situations reversed, I suppose I should think the same," she says. "I have given you no reason to trust me."

I will the words George would ask of me to come out. "And yet you earn it even now."

Mary snaps her gaze from the candlelight, her eyes interrogating me.

"The others said you were in the barn," I say. "And here I find you. I know not how long I spent at George's side, but you could have been gone from here by now if you wished." I open my arms to her. "And yet you remain."

"Where else am I to go?"

I lean closer. "To Boston with me?"

Her face pales. "I have told you George cannot travel."

"He bid me keep on without him," I say, noting her face darken at my words. "I leave at first light with Betty and the others."

"But not Susannah," says Mary.

"No," I say. "She will stay."

Mary scratches her cheek. "And were that your plan or Betty's?"

"My own," I say, though her question takes me aback. I look long on Mary's face, studying it for any trace she might have clued to my true plan. "George counseled me trust the Barrons."

"And yet you cannot."

"No..."

"Then you are wiser for it." Mary grimaces. "Did neither of you entertain the notion I should keep watch over George and Susannah?"

"I need you at my side," I say.

"Are we speaking truths still?" Mary chuckles. "Say rather Betty does not trust me alone with her daughter."

"Perhaps not." I grin at her for gleaning such truth of the situation.

Mary plays with a bit of loose straw. "And what did Betty promise you in return for her daughter's safe keeping?"

"Why should she have promised me anything?" I ask.

"Because you venture into the lion's den," says Mary. "And you would have a lioness lead you there."

"Should I take a lamb instead?"

Mary's face tightens in study of me. "What could Betty have promised to make you waver? Aid, I shouldn't wonder."

I flinch.

Mary grins. "And did she say more of the form this *aid* would come in?"

Her confident and mocking tone surprises me, one I have never heard from her lips. Still, the glint in her eyes be one I have seen before—the same I saw when the pair of us slipped among Mercy Lewis's followers and dispatched them from this world.

"She promises a shield," I say.

"A fitting reference." Mary chuckles. "Did she tell you the name of this shield, or the part he played in Salem?"

"He?" I ask.

"Aye, if he yet lives and I judge her rightly," says Mary. "She would lead us to Samuel Sewall, brother to the man her father sent Betty to stay with in waiting out the poison of Devil's powder."

"You know this man well then?"

"Aye, I should," says Mary. "He were one of the judges during the Salem trials and his ties to Cotton Mather be little secret."

My lip curls at his name. "You think she leads us into a trap then?"

"Perhaps," says Mary. "Betty were ever cunning as Abigail. I have little doubt the years have dulled her mind. And she said herself this very night she would do anything to protect her daughter."

I think back on Betty, and my dealings with Mary, my feelings hazy on which Salem sister to trust, if either.

"This Judge Sewall," I say. "What did you think of him? Were he a righteous man?"

"All men believe themselves righteous, girl." says Mary, twisting the bit of straw in her hand.

"But you have seen him," I say. "Been in his company and witnessed how he treated both the condemned and the accusers."

"Aye, and, in fairness, he did indeed seem a goodly man to my eyes at the time," she says. "I might have casted doubt on his judgment had I not also witnessed Mercy and Abigail's convincing acts."

"You would trust him then?" I ask.

Mary's face sours. "Hard to say. Time changes many things and it has been over thirty years since I saw him last." She sighs. "I heard it said Sewall begged public pardon for his part in the trials, though I cannot speak to if that be true or no. Still, if he truly did ask forgiveness from the public for his actions, then he were the only one to brave Mather's wrath and live to tell of it."

"But you once spoke to me of Putnam's daughter," I say. "You said she too asked forgiveness for her part in the trials."

"Aye, and I said also she were silenced for doing so."

"Then why not Sewall?" I ask. "How is it he could ask forgiveness and be left to live?"

"Because he is a man." Mary chuckles. "And the laws of men grant more weight to the sons of Adam than they do the daughters of Eve. Far more still when that man holds a powerful position other men be desperate to suckle at. The untimely death of a judge who asked forgiveness for his part in the trials would call questions. I doubt any cast little concern at all when Putnam's daughter were found dead."

Silence stands between us for a time. I wonder if Mary lies now, yet believe she has little reason—if we were found out by Mather, then she should be discovered also.

"I will say this on behalf of Sewall," says Mary. "Betty's father had many contacts of note throughout these lands, yet for all his choices, he sent her among the Sewalls. And of all my Salem sisters, Betty alone lives safe within Mather's reach, her life untouched and her daughter unclaimed. The Sewalls hold some sway, but whether they use it for good or evil I cannot say."

I nod at her conviction. "Then perhaps I will meet this man and take what lessons I can from him."

"Allow me caution this also," says Mary. "Betty were the youngest of us during the trials, and she never once hesitated to join in the sport."

My brow furrows.

Mary smirks. "That which all the powerless secretly wish to witness played out—to bring the mighty low and to heel. Aye, learn them but a little taste of what it means to know true fear, the same fright we lowborn live with all our lives."

"I did not come for sport," I say.

"Aye, but you play nonetheless. As Mercy once said, we few that remain are but the last pieces upon the board." Mary fixes her stare on me. "And let you believe me now, Betty has a talent for creating division. It be the same gift her father had."

"Betty will not divide us," I say firmly.

"She has already," says Mary. "Her promise of a shield has made you reshape your plot. In one move, Betty rids her house of us and leads the daughter of Simon Campbell into Boston. Who can say she does not lead you to your doom?"

"None, perhaps," I say. "But she would be a fool to think I cannot reap my vengeance from beyond the grave."

"Ciquenackqua is a lone warrior in white lands, and Andrew has no family ties," says Mary. "Strong and steadfast as both may be, they cannot withstand a host of witches swayed by Devil's powder."

"I do not speak of Ciquenackqua or Andrew," I say. "I speak of you."

Mary sits back. "Me?"

"You noted Betty a player in this game," I say. "Just as you once said of Mercy in the wild, but *you* yet remain upon the board also, Mary Warren." I reach into my robes, taking one of the long daggers from my belt. I toss it at her feet. "I trust you will do your best to alter the board should Betty betray us."

Mary looks on my dagger, though she does not move to take it. "Why do this?"

I think of my *manitous*, willing the convincing words it would have me speak to Mary that will bring her to my side. "I do not give my trust easily, but George spoke of his faith in your goodness," I say. "And of Hannah's belief in you also—"

Mary's eyes well, giving me pause.

"I have wronged you thus far and mean to make amends. You are no longer my prisoner. Let you be gone from this place, if you wish." I glance at the dagger. "It may be the lonely life you desire yet awaits you, but I would have you delay it a little longer."

Tears stream down Mary's cheeks as she reaches for the dagger and takes it up. "If there be any honor in me, it belongs to you and George. I will help you gain your vengeance"—she stares upon the blade's edge—"or else see Betty and Susannah join you in the grave for their trespass."

I rise. "Then I leave you the barn and to your thoughts."

My mind cautions turning my back to her so armed, yet my brother's words of trust and faith ring louder still.

I halt by the barn door, risking a glance back at Mary Warren.

She yet stares upon the blade, turning it to catch the candle-light, mumbling words I cannot rightly hear.

My conscience screams for such an act and warns me take back both the dagger and my words.

I open the door, embracing the cold and howling winds as doubt threatens to hold me in its sway.

-six-

I BREAK MY FAST TO MEAGER FARE, EATING OF IT HEARTILY AF-
ter witnessing both Susannah and Betty partake of the same.
While Andrew and Mary ready the wagon that will bear us to
Boston, I sit at George's side. My spirit wishes him wake that I
might speak with him, to provide me some small comfort before
leaving. My mind bids me let him rest.

A soft knock comes at the door.

"My mother and the others wait for you outside," says
Susannah, her head bowed. "All is prepared."

I give George one final kiss, his forehead cooler than last I
felt though the fever still rages in him. "Sleep well and rest easy,
brother," I say, rising to leave.

"I will take good care of him," says Susannah.

Her voice seems full of innocence, her words and intent pure.
Indeed, a small part of me would almost mistake her goodliness for Hannah's had I not cast doubt upon she and Betty the
night before.

Susannah wilts under my gaze, more intrigued by the
floor than my face. "A-Andrew spoke of you often," she says.
"Sometimes I wondered if it were truly me he loved and not you."

She glances up, expectant, I think, for me to ward off such
concerns.

I do not.

Susannah averts her gaze from me again, her fingers playing

at the waistline of her dress. "N-now that you stand before me, I know you for a wild beauty that I could never possess." She sighs. "If Andrew loves you, I know now he could never truly love me."

Only when her green eyes dare meet mine do I speak.

"Life has taught me little of the bond shared between a man and woman," I say. "But Andrew spoke on your goodliness often."

Susannah blushes at my mention, adding to the reasons I prefer leaving George in her company rather than Betty's. So do I notice my words give Susannah courage to lose some of her former nervousness.

"Andrew cares for George more than his own soul." I say. "If you love him true, you will take care of my brother as if it were your intended himself fallen ill."

"I will." Susannah weeps openly, her chin nodding. "You need not worry. My mother has oft said God gifted me a healer's touch. Your brother will be well again before you return."

"Aye, see that he is."

I stride past her. Worry keeps me from chancing another look upon George's face, fear that I will falter from my path and choose to stay at his side. I move quickly through the home, pulling my furred robes tight before stepping out into the cold.

The night winds have ceased and the sun has yet to peek over the horizon, but the sky provides enough light to know the dawn comes soon. I breathe deep of the cold air and stare out over the windswept and snow-covered lands.

My companions gather near a covered wagon. Ciquenackqua and Andrew load crates into the bed for Mary to stack. Steam flares from the nostrils of both draft horses at my approach.

They stomp their hooves in anxious wait, pulling at their yokes whilst Betty holds tight to the reins from her seat atop the wagon.

"What troubles you?" she asks.

"The last I rode in such a wagon were in the life before," I say. "When I was but a girl in Winford."

Memories of the man my brother and sister named father live in my mind, how he smiled when catching me as I leapt into his arms from such a wagon.

I grab hold of the bench and use a wheel spoke to aid me climb and join her.

"God be praised for quitting the winds," says Betty. "It should have been a long drive to Boston elsewise."

"We are not there yet," says Andrew. "Let you instead pray the weather keeps awhile."

I ignore their sparring, my attention turned on the bits of cloth poking through the wooden crates. I tease one of the strands out.

Betty slaps my hand. "If you intend to converse with those in Boston, you should dress as they do."

The cloth feels thin enough to rend with little regard.

Betty wears similar garb and already shivers, despite her wool blanket.

Though the temperature reddens my cheeks also, the rest of me remains warm and leaves no want to change them out for the light rags Betty donates. I tuck the cloth back in the crate as Ciquenackqua springs into the wagon bed, joining Mary.

"*This thing stinks of white men,*" Ciquenackqua says in our native tongue.

"*Aye,*" I reply. "*Though we should give thanks at least for the cover it gives upon the road.*"

Andrew stands with Susannah near the Barron home, the pair of them conversing in hushed tones, bidding their farewells.

Susannah wipes her cheeks with her sleeve as he takes his leave of her to rejoin us. Her gaze switches to my face, lingering in a way that unsettles me. Whether scorn we abandon her or envy that I should be in Andrew's company and not her, I cannot tell.

I move the leather flap aside to join Ciquenackqua and Mary in the wagon bed as Andrew climbs onto the seat. Though Andrew claimed Boston is but a day's ride away, he and Ciquenackqua have stocked the wagon near full up with supplies in the event a sudden winter storm should waylay us.

Mary sits near the back flap, as if ready to retreat at the first sign of trouble. Between her natural bulk and the furred robes, I cannot guess where she hid the dagger. Her confidence bids me assume she yet keeps it upon her person.

I sit beside Ciquenackqua with my back against the wagon front. My surroundings darken with the rustle of leather—Andrew closing the flap to shut us of the cold.

The closed flaps in both the front and back of the wagon prevent me from witnessing the countryside roll by, and I stir with entrapment.

A snap of the reins breaks the quiet and the wagon jolts beneath me to the neighs of the draft team. The snow crunches under the wheels and boards groan against one another as the wagon sways side-to-side.

My stomach soon lurches with each bump we strike upon the road and, after a time, forces me close my eyes. The darkness soothes my ailment, my stomach lurching with the wagon's uneven movement. When my head nods, I clutch the hilt of Father's dagger, waking me to my true purpose.

I think of my promise to George, how it conflicts with the plans I have laid since first leaving his and Andrew's trade post in the wilderness. Mary's distrust of Betty and her alleged protector, Judge Sewall, also weigh heavy on my mind. Everything in me wishes either Father or Bishop yet lived to guide me in the path to come and remove the burden from my shoulders.

I lean closer to Ciquenackqua, drinking deep of his comforting smell—a blended mix of the wild and home.

"Are you with me, brother?" I ask him in our native tongue. *"Truly?"*

"I am," he answers.

Though I know my question need not have been asked, his quick reply eases my spirit. *"I have spent much time dwelling on this moment and those to come,"* I say. *"Yet now we are here, I doubt. Do you fear, as I do, where this path may take us?"*

"Aye, but we must go. For your sister and father. Our people." His voice grows quiet. *"And my father also."*

Though I dare not open my eyes for fear of the moving sickness, I picture Ciquenackqua gazing upon his war club, as I lean on him for comfort.

"You need not have come all this way for your father alone," I say. *"You claimed your vengeance on Two Ravens for his death."*

"I did not follow you on his account," says Ciquenackqua. *"You once found me in the wilderness, lost to fear and with Creek Jumper near death. It was you that led me to hope again, and you that I made the war dance with. How might I name myself a man if I abandoned you to walk this path alone?"*

I smile at the memory, longing for the beat of drums and Creek Jumper's songs rather than being shut in a foul wagon. *"You are a good man,"* I say to Ciquenackqua, my gut wrenching with what I think to ask next of him. *"As a good man, do you recognize another?"*

"Who?"

"The one who rides with us now," I say, not naming Andrew for fear he might hear overhear his name and know we speak on him. *"Would you trust him to do any task that needs be done? Or do you think he should wilt at the last?"*

His answer does not come quickly. *"I cannot say without knowing the task,"* says Ciquenackqua. *"He loves you and your brother dear, yet he is a different man in the presence of women. And the two have grown close in our journey."*

"The two?"

I open my eyes, curious to gather his meaning.

He raises his chin in the direction of Mary Warren. Snoring, her head rests upon the leather gap between the wooden arches, riding out the wagon's rhythm in gentler waves.

"I know not why you kept her after her betrayal," says Ciquenackqua. *"But if she has a role to play in your plans, do not speak them to Andrew."*

My shoulders sag at his words, beliefs that echo my own. Though the flap prevents me the sights beyond its leathery borders, I picture Andrew seated next to Betty. The two have not spoken a word during our journey and her distrust of him bids me think they will ride the whole of our way to Boston in similar silence.

George's demand for me to forgive Andrew rises like a phantom in my mind, yet Ciquenackqua's words ring true also. I sigh at the war plaguing my soul, half wishing to recognize Andrew

Martin as the friend I have known all my life, the other urging me not forget the drunken fool he became when my family needed him most.

"And what of you?" I ask Ciquenackqua. *"Would you wilt at a task I asked of you?"*

His silence and stern gaze serve as his reply.

The wagon's sway bids me close my eyes again, or else allow the sickness overtake me. I scoot to the side of the wagon bed and follow Mary Warren's example, resting my head between the wooden arches.

The gap between the leather flap and wind outside bristles goose pimples up my neck.

I revisit my plan over and again in the hours that follow, safe in the knowledge Ciquenackqua will stand by me in the events to come. Without the pouch around my neck to cling to, I clutch at the hilt of father's dagger with one hand. With the other, I hold to the bone dagger I took from Mercy Lewis.

I fade in and out of sleep throughout the day, waking to a sudden bump in the road, the voices of those bidding Andrew and Betty good day as they pass our wagon on horseback, or else when we halt to answer nature's call.

Night falls before I risk standing in the wagon to peek my head out the leather gap.

Andrew sits hunched in the wagon seat, his head dipped low in his robes like a hawk resting upon a tree branch. Betty sways beside him, sitting taller, alert.

"How far?" I ask Andrew.

The sudden jerk his body makes bids me wonder if he had fallen asleep at the reins. "A few hours more," he says, his voice hoarse with cold. "Look yonder."

I stand upon my tiptoes in the wagon, gasping at the sight ahead.

A second heaven with a thousand stars burns in the direction we ride. The fires strike doubt in my heart, their sheer number speaking plain to the number of folk residing within the city's bounds.

Scattered homes and barns litter the surrounding area. They grow in number with each passing mile, echoing the expanded reach of white men, bidding me understand we drive into the heart of their territory.

I force myself not to look away and to drink in every sight the moonlight provides. My thoughts drift to the life before, warn I too would have lived in such a home were it not for Hecate and her brood. My father's voice cautions those who live in these houses are not my enemy and that many of them are likely innocent, as I were in my youth.

Then my mind warns some might be Mather spies.

That we ride under the cover of darkness comforts me somewhat. We meet fewer travelers upon the road the longer we ride. But always the shadow of Boston looms closer.

Andrew pulls back on the reins, slowing the wagon.

"What are you doing?" I ask.

"We are but a few miles from the city now," he says. "And the guards there inquire of those entering after dark. We will camp here until the dawn."

He and Betty both squeeze back into the wagon bed with the rest of us, our five bodies lumped as one in wait. Andrew falls to sleep quickly, his snores mixing with Mary's.

I sleep little, my mind restless with wonder of what awaits me, and warier still of the night terrors in my dreams—Father pitched in darkness, abandoning me to watch Sarah suffer and die at the hands of Mercy Lewis over and again.

At the first hint of our canopy brightening, I shake Andrew awake.

He wipes sleep from his eyes and yawns, then moves to unpack the crates.

"What are you doing now?" I ask.

He answers by throwing one of the cloth dresses upon my lap. Andrew then sheds his fur robes and exchanges it for a thick, lined jacket, dyed green and wool spun.

I grimace at the ugly heap of rags in my lap.

Andrew chuckles. "Best don that now," he says, packing his furred robe into the crate. "We are not much longer for the road and the folk of Boston will not take kindly to a girl warrior such as you look to me now."

"They will not look kindly on me in any manner," I say.

"Aye, they will not," says Andrew. "Not with the long face you wear. Let you change that also."

"How?" I ask.

He thinks on his answer and, for a moment, I think the answer is lost upon him also. When he looks on me again, it is not without some little pity. "Let you think of my Susannah and aspire to her manner," he says. His chin dips, his voice quiet. "Or Hannah."

"Or my sister," I say quietly, my mind recalling her once gay demeanor. "Sarah as she once was."

"Aye," says Andrew. "Think of Sarah."

He climbs through the gap, resuming his seat before shutting the leather flap to blind his sight of me.

Closing my eyes, I think of my *manitous* and the masks it would have me wear. Fixing the memory of Sarah in my mind,

I turn my back to Ciquenackqua and shed my furs and the belt my daggers hang from.

The cold nips at my bare skin.

I dwell on the laughter Sarah and I once shared. The way she smiled whilst crafting the straw dolls for me, or else when we played scotch-hopper. I stir the muscles in my cheeks from a position long kept, forcing them practice at the memory.

I clutch for my belt and clasp it around my bare waist, needing the weight of my daggers at my side. Then I slip the dress over my head, push my arms through its sleeves.

"That were a dress of mine once," Betty whispers.

The muscles in my cheeks relax, finding the familiar sternness quick and sure.

Betty eyes my body up and down, nodding. "It fits you well, though your hair needs doing." Betty motions to the wagon floor in front of her. "Sit."

There be no malice in her eyes or voice, but I do not sit without first waking Ciquenackqua.

Betty shows no sign if my actions displease her. Her fingers work deftly through my hair, soft as she gathers it behind my shoulders, then gliding down, tugging to work out the knots binding the strands together.

I welcome the slight pain, Sarah's face fixed in my mind, recalling the days when she fashioned my hair. All the while, I think how it must be Sarah's essence that I channel while entering these enemy lands.

"Live within me, sister," I pray in the native tongue of my people. *"Lend me your spirit and your goodness."*

Betty calls me from prayer by tying my hair tight in a bun that pains my scalp.

I turn to snarl at her, but the gentle touch of her hand upon my back bids me take no offense.

"You look a wolf in sheep's clothing if ever I saw one," she says. "You must work harder if hoping to fool anyone."

The wagon floor bounces beneath us, clattering loud.

"Could you unlearn a lifetime as a wolf in a single day?"

"Even a wolf lowers his head to track a scent." Betty glowers. "And a righteous woman casts her gaze upon the ground. She does not meet the stare of others in public, especially men."

Her words ring true in my ears, though I do not wish to hear them. "And what other lessons would you give, Betty Barron?"

"Turn back now," she says, her tone low. "Allow your brother's good health return and then leave off to the wilds from whence you came. The good book says damnation waits for those with a vengeful heart. Let you forget your hate and forgive—"

"I cannot forgive the wrongs done against my family," I bristle at her pitiful speak. "Nor would I."

"Aye, there be the truth of the matter," says Betty. "You will not."

"You would not either had you witnessed loved ones tortured and slain."

Betty *tsks*. "I well know the difficulty of what I ask. The hardest task of all is accepting none of us be worthy of God's love and forgiveness. But if we truly seek to humble ourselves before His mercy, He will grant it."

"And you believe your god has forgiven your past?"

"Aye," she says. "What I fear are the sins you would soon force me commit."

"Let you rest easy then," I say. "When the time comes, I will not leave you the task of claiming vengeance."

Betty turns silent at my reply, though, for once, her face speaks plain that she wrestles with our sparring.

Rather than remain with her, I stand and pull back the leather flap shielding us from the cold. Icy needles strike my face, warning me rethink my actions.

I brave them anyway.

"I have drunk my fill of hiding," I say, climbing aboard the driver's bench, joining Andrew. My gaze sweeps across the snow-capped hills, my breath given phantom life by the cold. "I would learn these new lands."

Andrew gives the reins another *slap*.

The wagon pulls faster as the horses heave in their bridles.

"You have yet to say anything of note on your plans to me, Rebecca," says Andrew.

I glance over my shoulder into the wagon bed at Mary Warren, her head dipping between her shoulders each time the wagon bounces beneath us.

Betty sits near her, though she hesitates little to hide her scorn for me.

"Aye," I say to Andrew, turning my attention back to the road.

"Will you share them now?" he asks. "We are soon to reach the neck of Boston. It would draw suspicion if you were to have us enter only to then retreat."

"What would you suggest?" I ask.

"You look to me for advice now?" Andrew laughs. "I should never have dreamed to see this day in all my life."

I redden at his tone. "Then forget my—"

"Peace, Rebecca," he says. "It were only some little sport. Surely you may allow me that after I have tolerated your angry nature these past few months."

We ride without speaking for a time, me preferring the wheels crushing snow and *thunking* of horse hooves upon the road to Andrew's mocking of me.

More people stir from their homes every moment we draw further up the road. Boys less than ten years of age bound for the wilderness with their father's flintlocks, men splitting wood in the yard, girls in thinner dress than mine cradling eggs between their arms as they wade through snowdrifts back to their homes.

We do not pass without they take notice of us. Several raise a hand in acknowledgment. Most do not.

Their dirtied and hardened faces putting me at unease and I shift in my seat.

"Rest easy," says Andrew. "These are but common folk, as we are. If these few here fear you—"

"I am not feared," I say.

"I were, when first I delivered furs to Boston." He casts a sidelong glance at me. "You have never seen such sights as you will this day, Rebecca. That I swear you."

"Would that I had seen them already." I mutter.

"Aye," he says. "But as you have not yet, let us speak of where your thoughts lie on our lodging. This blasted cold seeps me to my bones. I long for a fire and a full belly."

"Did you not store enough provisions to last us?" I ask.

"Aye, provisions," he says. "But none of us should sleep another night under this cold, unless you would have us all laid ill as George."

"We have no money or trade for an inn," I say.

"No money for *most* inns." Andrew grins. "Think of me as a drunken fool if you will, Rebecca. You may yet find much of my time spent in inns and taverns a boon to our cause."

I keep my silence rather than debate with him on the worth of such claims.

We ride for near another hour before the dawn. As we reach the precipice of a hilltop, the sun frights the night away, affording me my first glimpse of the city and something far greater still—a place where the earth turns bluish-grey and stretches into the horizon, moving in grey ripples crested white.

The ocean. A memory of the life before reminds me.

My eyes glaze at the sight, one I have not seen since I were a girl in Winford. I recall the stories Bishop oft told me by the fire of his many crossings, both as a slave and a free man. My heart near breaks at the thought, wishing he were at my side to hold my hand and tell me grand stories again in such a way as only he could tell. I swallow hard against the lump in my throat.

Andrew slaps the reins again as if the sight beckons him speed faster also.

My gaze shifts to the uncountable hulking, wooden beasts riding out the waves, rocking in the gentle wake, their canvases stretched from pole to pole like white sheets of laundry hung upon the drying line.

Ships, scattered memories of the life before whisper. *Ships from beyond this world.*

We draw closer and the ocean, ships, and city swell larger. All while I grow smaller, weaker in their looming shadows.

"There." Andrew points to a small strip of land separating the ocean, the lone bridge connecting city and countryside. "The Neck."

I think it aptly named—the thin, earthen tract teems with people, livestock, and carriages, the flow of traffic feeding and leaving the city in endless cycle. And to the south, outside the pair of wooden gates, corpses dangle from the gallows.

Andrew leans close. "Welcome to Boston."

seven

THE DEAD MEN HOLD MY GAZE AS WE PASS BY THE GALLOWS.

Crows rest upon the scaffold, cawing at one another and all those like me who must first travel around them. They scatter when a pack of boys run up the platform steps. Grabbing hold of the dead men's arms, the boys laugh and spin the corpses round.

Though an armed guard chases the boys off, the taut ropes continue their groan, swaying with new life.

Beside the gallows, a pair of upright and hinged boards hold another man—forced to stand, his head and hands slipped through the wooden holes in the boards. Whip-stroked rags hang from his person, tattered and bloodied, his face wan and withered.

"Andrew," I say. "What is this manner of torture?"

"The stretch-neck some call it. Others the pillory." Andrew grimaces as we pass. "Its cousin is the stocks, but that be a lesser punishment, to my mind. Those given over to stocks at least may sit and bow their head. The pillory affords the condemned no mercy."

The prisoner's sunken eyes follow me as we approach the pair of gates.

Those who walk enter through one gate in front of a watchful line of soldiers, whilst all in wagons, carriages, or those leading livestock enter through the other.

My shoulders twitch when we pass beneath the gate, my

mind warning I leave all that I know behind. Indeed, even the air differs—filled with the blended stench of waste and sickness alongside the sweeter scent of sea and foam.

Andrew tosses the reins into my lap then leaps from the wagon. He takes one of the horse bridles in hand, leading the team around a carriage, its wheel shattered and cabin tipped in the snow. Clear of the traffic, Andrew climbs back into the wagon bench with me and takes the reins anew.

I give them over gladly, my eyes wandering over all the sights before me. High to the north, a symbol from my youth stands tall—a wooden cross, perched high atop a steeple. To the west, three hills tower over the cityscape, one of them bearing what seems a tall iron finger.

"Andrew," I say. "What is that?"

"Beacon Hill," he says. "Light a torch atop its peak and all will see it for miles. Soldiers train and cattle graze to its southern slopes."

"And the northern?"

Andrew blushes. "I know only what I have heard." He glances back into the wagon, lowering his tone for me alone to hear. "But others in the taverns oft name it Mount Whoredom."

I recoil at Andrew's eager tone as he drives the horses onward.

"Think poorly of whores, do you?" he asks.

"You do not?"

"Not at all," he says. "They are people as you and I, no better or worse than most."

I fold my arms across my chest. "No doubt your intended should enjoy learning as much. Perhaps I should tell her mother and spare you all the trouble."

"Betty is a prayerful woman, aye," says Andrew, checking over his shoulder once more as if expectant to find her lurking. "And, as most I have met, more like to cast judgment on the whores, wretches, and drunks of this world rather than speak with them."

"Is that how you came to understand whores?" I ask. "By speaking with them?"

Andrew grins. "There were many a night I had talk alone from them. Most scorn such folk, believing them only woeful sinners." He glances on me. "Those same folk would name you and Ciquenackqua savages."

"Whores are not the same as we," I say. "They choose their lot."

"Do they?" Andrew asks. "What person should sell their flesh to strangers if afforded any other choice? Bishop sold his life for a time into slavery that he and his wife might come to these colonies. Would he have done so if not desperate for new life?"

"He did not sell his body as whores do," I say. "Only traded his life in service for a time."

Andrew tugs on the reins, driving the horses east toward the stretching ocean and largest of ships bobbing in the harbor.

"Aye," he says. "Sometimes our flesh is all we have to offer in this world."

I glance over my shoulder, back into the wagon. "The wise find more to offer than that."

"Speak wisdom to me then," says Andrew. "What did you bring in offer to aid us to achieve our ends?"

I keep my quiet, focusing on the ships sailing out of the harbor. Sailors work at their nets, their songs echoing across the water. Their tune sings to my soul, though not their bawdy verse.

"Keep your secrets then," says Andrew. "But I trust mine to you."

"You have plans of your own then?" I ask.

Andrew's cheeks tighten. "I have little doubt we should find the Reverend Mather, but there were others used in his plots that may yet abide also. This city is not so unlike the wilderness, Rebecca. One may be killed by a pack of wolves, or else a single bear. Aye, and both the city and the wild hoard secrets easily found if one knows where to look."

"And you do?"

Andrew nods. "The rich and powerful oft believe they keep their plots well hid, but sit in a tavern long enough, speak with those others deride at, and you learn of their whispered words quick enough. Whatever secrets Cotton may keep, those in Mount Whoredom will know."

I shrug. "Perhaps," I say. "Or else they may be in league with Cotton. Mercy claimed herself a whore and kept many among her company. Who is to say those same folk you name friendly will not betray you?"

"Then at least you will have tracks to follow." Andrew pouts. "We have none now."

The wagon batters us as its wheels leave the muddied road for sturdier fare—cobbled stone that sets us to rising and falling with its unevenness. The road leads away from the relative quiet of orchards and farms, emptying into a loud market.

Noise pervades everywhere—children screaming, merchants shouting out their wares, dogs barking up unseen alleys. Signs creak from rusted hinges against the salt-blasted wood and brick-sided buildings. Men load and unload cargo whilst beggars approach any who meet their eye.

I long for the quiet, peaceful ways of my people, though my eyes and ears continue to seek out each new onslaught to my senses. Memories of the life before stir in my mind, riding in a similar wagon with Simon Campbell and Sarah.

Some natives walk the streets also, dressed in white men's clothes.

I tug at the dress Betty forced me wear, wishing I might rend it off in favor of my furred skins, and I wonder if Ciquenackqua looks on me in the shameful way.

Andrew drives us into the crowd's midst, turning north.

Ahead, a wooden dock stretches near half a mile off the land and into the ocean, where even the largest of ships bob off its sides in deeper waters. The ships tug at their bindings, ropes thicker than any man.

I wonder what it must be like to walk a gangway, step aboard one, and sail across the deep waters to Bishop's homeland.

"The Long Wharf," says Andrew, noting my stare. "Impressive, no?"

I say naught, drowning in the constant movement and noise of the seaside market.

Andrew turns west against again, down a crooked and shadowed alley. He leans close, pulling back the leather flap to view our other companions. "We have arrived, my friends."

"Where?" Betty asks, peeking her head through to take in our new surroundings.

"An inn of ill repute," Andrew says, glancing at me. "So ill the owner dare not trouble naming it at all, in fact."

A squat and square home stands not ten yards from our wagon, crafted half of red brick and half unpainted, wooden siding. Similar derelict buildings and homes occupy the whole alley. None hold glass in their windows and few curtains either. Their thatched roofs sag in disrepair. Not a few vagabonds lurk in darkened doorways and vanish around hidden corners when I do not shy my gaze from them.

"Fool," says Betty. "Who is to say the innkeep be no Mather songbird?"

Andrew laughs. "I assure you, the innkeep here be friendly to our cause. She should go unemployed elsewise."

"Where have you brought us, Andrew?" I ask.

Andrew waves his hand toward the squat structure before me. "Your brother's inn."

I give him a sideways look. "George owns an inn?"

"Aye." Andrew kicks at a pebble in the road. "Though it should have belonged to both he and I, had I not—"

"Drank and whored your keep away, I shouldn't wonder." Betty climbs out of the wagon.

Andrew paces under a broke and blackened sign. Hung askew above the door, it bears no name.

"But why would George not speak of this?" I ask. "Our entire trek, he said not a word of owning an inn."

Anger swells in me that George should have held such secrets from me. Still, the longer I stare on the inn, it be little wonder why. "How long has he owned this?"

"Many a year now," says Andrew.

"George has never been to Boston, to my knowledge."

"Aye," says Andrew. "He left the sale and arranging of it all to me."

Betty frowns. "And you squandered the opportunity."

"Would we be here now if I had?" Andrew asks. "I lost my share, aye, but I yet ensured the property given into safe hands to protect George. Had I not succeeded in placing such a trusted innkeep, we should be left to sleep in the wagon now."

"Andrew." I touch his arm to calm him. "What use would George have in such a place? And here, of all places?"

"For the same purpose we use it now," says Andrew. "It were not so many years ago his hate burned bright as yours does. I think he took the loss of your father worse even than Sarah did. Bishop tempered it with council and patient preaching. He wished us become men before we struck out to claim our own vengeance. Now, I think the old man meant only to delay us."

I grin at such plots, swearing Bishop would laugh to hear us speak of him now. How his eyes should twinkle that his cunning thwarted my brother to save him.

"Why wait?" Betty asks. "George is a man grown. Why did he not—"

"Hannah," I say.

Andrew nods. "George loved your father dear and oft spoke of the need to avenge him. But once Hannah came into his life..." Andrew shrugs. "In truth, I think he half expected to leave the wilderness some day and settle here once he knew you and Sarah both were established and happy."

"He should have been in the wilderness all his life then," I say, dwelling on my sister's misery and my equal love for the hunt and my people.

"Aye," says Andrew quietly.

Mary climbs out the back of the wagon. She gazes up to the windows of the neighboring homes. "I like standing here in the open near as much as riding in the wagon all this way. Might we go in and be warm at least?"

"Aye," I say. "Mary has the right of it."

"Wait here." Andrew bounds into the wagon and emerges again a moment later, bearing the crate of our furred robes out the back. He enters the inn with the crate in hand, disappearing from sight.

The wagon jostles and Ciquenackqua rounds the side of it. His head acts on a swivel, taking in our new surroundings, His knuckles whiten, clenched round his war hammer.

"*Brother,*" I say in our native tongue.

His gaze snaps to mine, whether alert or half-afraid I cannot tell.

"*Come,*" I say. "*We have further plans to make.*"

Mary approaches me quick. "You would do well to cease speaking in such tongues," she whispers, motioning upward. "These walls have ears."

"Who here should speak our language?" I ask.

"More than you should suppose," she says. "And those that do not will be more apt to inquire on you and from where you come."

Mary points to fluttering curtains above us.

A woman vanishes from a window, quick as shadow.

The inn door opens and Andrew leaves the entry. "Come inside," he says, climbing into the wagon seat. "Faith keeps the inn here. She waits in the parlor and will see you well attended whilst I am gone."

I hesitate. "And where do you go?"

"You wished to learn more of Cotton," he says. "I am eager to please."

"Then take me with you," I say, reaching for the wagon.

Andrew halts me with a touch of his hand. "Women are not welcome among the places I mean to visit." His eyes gaze into mine. "Especially those as fair in face as you."

I pull my hand from the wagon. "Why must you go before we are settled?"

Andrew watches Betty enter the inn after Mary Warren. His chin dips.

"Forget her taunts," I say. "Andrew—"

"My blessing and my curse is I forget nothing." Andrew straightens. "I shall return before nightfall."

He slaps the reins, leaving me watch him drive away, headed further north.

Ciquenackqua tugs at my arm. "*Come,*" he says. "*You need not worry on him for now.*"

His easy tone sets me to stir.

The door yawns open with little light escaping outside the darkened entry. Though tight quartered, the comforting scent of smoke and hot food greets me once setting foot inside.

I follow the winding, dim hall. Around the corner, a fire blazes in a black-stained hearth. Betty warms her hands and scarcely bothers meet my gaze before resuming her stare of the flames.

Mary sits to table nearest a wall lined with barrels of varied sizes. Earthenware jars stock the shelves above them and dried meats dangle from hooks nailed in the rafters.

A dark-skinned woman, lean and strong, with kempt, braided hair, approaches from around the corner, setting a plate of sausage, bread, and cheese in front of Mary. She takes a towel from her dress, cleaning her hands with it as she looks on Ciquenackqua and I with fierce grey eyes.

"You are Faith?" I ask.

"Aye," she says. "And you my honored guests, or so Mister Andrew says."

"We are," I say. "Or so he tells me."

Faith turns her attention on Ciquenackqua, studying him close. "He your slave?"

Ciquenackqua stirs beside me.

I halt him before he can make for her.

Faith does not waver.

"No," I say. "Why should he be?"

Faith blinks. "The pair of you hungry?"

"Aye, famished," I say. "Though we would not trouble you."

"No trouble," says Faith. "Don't want none, don't seek none. May I say the same for all of you?"

Her tone crackles with the same heat as the popping logs in the fire.

"Our business is our own," I say, "though Andrew named you worthy of trust."

"Wouldn't have no business at all, if it weren't for Mister Andrew, now would I?" Faith asks. "You can keep yours to your own self. I pray only you allow me keep mine."

I nod. "You have my word."

Faith chews on my promise for a time then leaves behind the counter.

I sit to table with Ciquenackqua and Mary, my stomach growling at the steaming food heaped on her plate.

Faith returns with the same fare for Ciquenackqua and I. She sets the plates before us then brings a pitcher and cups of dirtied and dented metal.

"I've a need to launder the sheets yet," she says. "Weren't supposing Mister Andrew would drop in so soon and with guests too. Said he wouldn't be back till spring, last I saw of him 'fore today."

"Pray," says Betty, stirring from her position. "Did he ever keep a young woman in his company when he stayed here?"

Faith draws the pitcher close to her chest. "No, ma'am. Mister Andrew, he never once slept here. Not a night in his life."

"Why should he not?" I ask.

"Can't say," Faith says. "But he a good man, Mister Andrew. Never met one better in all my days. Took me in off the streets and gave me new life. Even my name."

"You had no name before?" I ask.

"Only one some master gave," she says. "Mister Andrew found me begging in the streets and offered me work. When he asked on my story, I told him faith set me free. Then when I begged him grant me a new name later on, why, Faith is what I got."

"A goodly name," says Mary, stirring for the first time since we arrived. "All should be so fortunate to receive such kindness from their master."

"Aye," says Faith. "But he is no master to me."

"I beg pardon then," says Mary.

"No need," says Faith, her gaze frequenting Ciquenackqua's face. "Few of my color ever taste such a life as mine and I mean to repay the debt I owe. Now, should none of you need anything further, I ought to turn to laundering them sheets."

She leaves our company in humble silence.

I devour the meal she offered. My stomach near bursting, I rise from the table and wander through the inn. Barren walls welcome me at every turn with little findings of note anywhere.

Despite myself, I cannot help but leave out the inn and stand upon the stoop, watching the ships, listening to gulls cry. My soul begs me venture out of the alley and stand upon the dock that I might stare on the ocean for as long as I am able. Still, my head and my promise to George urges me trust in Andrew and keep to the inn's safety.

Only when the sky darkens do I return inside. I find the

others much as I left them—Betty staring into the fire, Mary threading a needle through a dress from the crate Andrew left us.

My cheeks pull in a wan smile at the crackling of logs and the firelight playing across Ciquenackqua's face as he sharpens his father's war hammer. Lone reminders of home in unfamiliar lands and those soothing to my soul.

The furred robes inside the crates call to me and bid me take on the smells of the wild rather than the dress that reeks of Betty's house. Instead, I reach for a shawl to match the one she wears, wrapping it about my shoulders. I bask in its odor, forcing myself pretend at her guise. Then I fill my mind with thoughts of Sarah, and keep careful watch of both Betty and Mary in the hopes I might glean their humble ways and adopt them for my own.

Faith returns after the sun has set with an even larger supper—potted meat and potatoes, beans, and corn pudding. She pleases me further still when accepting my invitation to sit and eat with us, regaling us for a time with stories of her homeland, the West Indies.

The looming shadow of Andrew's whereabouts revisits us no sooner than the meal ends and all the stories cease.

While the others retire to bed, I return to the stoop in wait of Andrew.

Though stars blanket the night sky and the moon nearly full, I take little comfort in their light. The neighboring brick walls remind me I am a stranger in foreign lands, as do the lamps and naked candles lit in windows throughout the alley.

Before long, the night's cold and my thin dress force me abandon the stoop.

I venture into the inn and take up a new post by the dwindling fire. There I wait, long after its embers fade to a dim glow. My back turns sore from the rigid chair and sleep threatens to overtake me.

Andrew never returns.

-eight-

FAITH PLACES A BOWL OF STEAMING PORRIDGE BEFORE ME.

I scarcely look on it.

The clanking of a spoon against a bowl side learns me Betty shares not half my concern for Andrew.

"Where is Ciquenackqua?" I ask Mary.

"He keeps watch of the alley from an upstairs window," she says, dipping a spoon into her bowl. "I told him it all for naught should any wish us harm, but he will not stir."

"And do you suppose those folk will come?" I ask. "Those seeking harm upon us?"

Betty rises from the table in a huffed manner. "Talk of such plans all you wish," she says. "They matter little now. Andrew took the wagon and with it any hidden escape we might make."

"Then it seems we must make other plans," I say.

Mary looks up from her bowl. "You would abandon him so easily?"

"He swore to return before nightfall," I say. "It is a new day and still he has not returned."

"Patience," says Mary, returning to her food. "There may be a hundred things that keep him. Drunkenness be my first thought."

"Aye," I say. "Another might be our enemies have found him out. If he is captured, I would not wait for them to break him and learn of us also."

Betty laughs. "You mean to rescue him if he is captured?"

My gaze narrows. "If I am able to find him, aye."

"And how will you?" Mary asks. "You know nothing of this city, and have said well that I may not show my face for fear of similar capture."

I look on Betty.

"No," she says, turning to the fire. "I should sooner search out my wagon and horses rather than look for him."

"I do not mean for you to search him out alone," I say. "Perhaps your shield will aid us. You have said it has protected you these many years. No doubt someone of such power and influence should prove capable of learning the whereabouts of a captured man."

Mary rises also. "Rebecca, let you rethink this, I beg you. Have you forgotten what we spoke of not two nights past?"

"No," I say. "I have thought long on the promise I made George to trust in Betty's goodness."

"Then your trust is misplaced," says Mary. "Let you rather wait here awhile longer for Andrew."

"Have you ever witnessed fear take hold of an animal, Mary? Fear so great it bids them hold their position even when a hunter knows its prey should flee?" I ask.

"We are not in the wild now." Mary wrings her hands.

"We are. This is but a foreign hunting ground and one with larger game. I will not sit idly by in fear and wonder."

"Nor did Andrew," says Mary, pacing the floor. "Perhaps had he thought to stay awhile, we might all have discussed our plans plainly and seen them through as one."

Ire rages in me at her belittling tone. "You do not—"

The stairs thunder as Ciquenackqua runs down them, catching himself in the door.

My hands fly to my daggers at the sight of him. "What is it?"

"Andrew," he says.

A door slams against the shared wall separating us from the entry. Andrew stumbles into view a moment later, his hair and dress disheveled, his body reeking of smoke and alcohol.

"Where have you been?" I growl.

"Cease your shrieking, Rebecca," he says, rubbing his temples as he wanders past me and sits hard to table. "I have some bit of note for you."

I snort at the smell of him. "You are drunk."

"Not as of now, which is half my trouble." He glances around the room. "Where is Faith? Mary, find her, I beg you. I have need of food and ale if I am to see straight once more."

Mary grants his request easily enough, leaving out of the room to fetch Faith.

"Where have you been, Andrew?" I ask.

"Searching for all you desire," he says. "Is that not deserving of some little thanks?"

"We half thought you taken or worse," I say. "You swore to return by nightfall."

Andrew rubs his face, yawns. "Aye, but let you ask yourself if you would rather I had honored that oath, or else bring you the news I learned last eve? The creatures of shadow oft loosen their tongues the longer night wears on."

Betty crosses her arms. "And you wonder why both my husband and I deem you unfit to wed our daughter."

"Susannah sees me as no one else does." Andrew's eyes blaze.

"I see you plain enough," says Betty.

I sit opposite Andrew, drawing his attention lest he loose his anger on her. "What have you learned?"

Andrew fumes as he turns from Betty. "Cotton lives to the north end of Boston, near the wharves around Fleet and Ship streets." He clears his throat. "The commoners say he lay sick and dying, aye, and claim he has not left his home in three weeks now."

My lip curls at the thought of Cotton dying from anything other than my blade, even if it were a slow death of old age and pain.

"And what do those that required you drink until the dawn say of such rumors?" I ask.

"The Reverend plays at death." Andrew grins. "Tired of a goodly front, he desires to see his remaining time spent on matters of far more import than the saving of earthly souls."

"News you say." Betty belittles him. "I call them stories and rumors such as wretches live to spread."

"In my experience, even the wildest of tales have grains of truth in them," says Andrew. "I admit that I, too, thought these stories, such as they are, on the right side of mockery." He glances at me. "Then I visited his home."

"You did so without me?" I ask.

"Aye," says Andrew. "For fear my claims would go unfounded by a certain person among us."

Betty *humpfs*.

"But what I found there rang of truth," Andrew continues. "More than a few cloaked strangers visited the Reverend's home in the night. Aye, and none left either that I saw."

I sit back, thinking on his words as Faith brings food and drink for him.

Andrew gulps his first cup of cider then takes down half a second cup before turning on his eggs. "None that I spoke with, or else listened on, could speak to what the good Reverend works at, but all agreed they have not seen him." He drains the remainder of his cup. "I suppose we must find a way inside if you are to claim your vengeance."

"Perhaps," I say, mulling on what I next intend.

"Rebecca," says Mary, her voice meek and quiet as she makes herself known to me. "Cotton is an old man now. Believe what you will of Andrew's tales, but it may be the truth of these are sickness and age do indeed beckon Cotton to death's door. Perhaps all you need do is wait to attain your vengeance."

"I am done with waiting." I say, rising from the table.

Andrew sets his fork down. "You are displeased with me."

"No," I say. "I only wish to consider all my options before acting."

"A wise plan," he says. "Why not speak of your intent aloud for all us here? I have shared my news with you, why will you not show me the same courtesy unless you think I should disapprove?"

"Aye, you might," I say, making to leave.

Andrew catches me by the arm. "I promised George to keep safe watch of you."

"And so you have," I say, pushing his arm away. "But Betty promised to take me alone to meet her shield."

Mary steps closer. "Perhaps you should ask yourself why it must be you alone."

"The answer is plain," says Betty. "I do not trust the lot of you."

"Then why Rebecca?" Ciquenackqua asks.

"Mayhap I see promise in her," says Betty.

Andrew looks on me with concern. "Do not do this. I beg you."

"I trusted you to return," I say. "Trust me to do the same now."

"It is not you we doubt," says Mary.

I ignore their concerns, striding toward the hearth and Betty. "Will you lead me to your shield?"

Her eyes narrow in response, but she makes to leave.

"*Red Banshee.*" Ciquenackqua calls, halting both Betty and I. "*What would you have of me? Should I follow you and her?*"

"No," I say. "*Stay and keep watch of these others. Allow me to learn the lay of these lands before we risk your face in plain sight.*" I glance from him to Betty. "*But if she and I do not return together before nightfall, take the others and fly from these lands.*"

Ciquenackqua nods. "*I will see Susannah dead if she returns without you.*"

Betty's glare finds me, hearing her daughter's name.

I do not hesitate to meet it. "Lead on."

She storms out of the inn with me trailing behind her.

I match her quick and steady gait up the alley and around the corner, into the flood of Boston scents and sights. Betty turns from the docks and wharves, leading further into the heart of the city.

We pass young men who stink of perfume and wear the white hair of old folk, the poor and ragged begging for coin. A pack of even dirtier children work in tandem to distract the noblemen, whilst another of their gang cuts the purse from the rich man's belt.

More carriages and wagons press on through the crowds, their steeds adding to the manure already littering the streets. One wagon near runs me over, forcing me to leap from its path.

Still Betty presses on and I in tow with her.

The crowds thin as we press further inland. The homes grow grander with greater spacing between them. Those we pass upon the road dress richer and with more layers on their person. Unlike the dirtied rags of the poor or furred skins worn by traders I witnessed earlier, now both men and women alike wear and carry finery as I have never seen before—ruffled shirts, silver-tipped canes, and gold buttons.

We walk down a quieter road, one with barren trees lining its streets. I have no doubt they should be beautiful in season, but now their limbs stand barren. With no one near us, I take Betty by the arm, and then duck into an alley between two homes.

"What are you doing?" she demands of me.

"Tell me more of this shield," I say.

"I did not promise to tell you anything," says Betty, her cheeks flushing. "Only that I should lead you there."

I step forward. "And you think I trust you not to lead me into a trap?"

"You, trust?" Betty scoffs. "No. You do no such thing."

"I do for those who have earned it," I say. "And you have not yet."

"How can you speak so? Did my daughter not eat of the bowl you accused me of poisoning?"

"You spoke true then," I say. "But you yet keep secrets from me and my companions."

"Aye, I would not risk my protector's safety to strangers who threaten my family."

"And I admire your loyalty," I say. "If you had given up your secret so easy, I should not think to trust you with my own plots now."

Her expression bids me believe she expects a lie. I think of my *manitous,* and the masks it would teach me—trickery and deception, cunning and resourcefulness—all traits I must embody now to win my prize.

"I have no need of your shield, Betty," I say, leaning closer to her. "I am no fool to believe that your Judge Sewall will offer me the same protections he has given you all these many years."

Her eyes widen at my naming him. "How do you—Mary..." she says, affronted. "But if you knew, then why force me to accompany you? I have naught else to offer."

"You have much and more," I say. "Mercy Lewis made many threats when she took both Mary and I captive, but I well remember one threat of note—that she should have killed Mary then and there, but it would not serve to rob the *others* of their vengeance." I study Betty's face. "How many of your Salem sisters yet remain?"

"I—I know not," she says. "I have not kept in contact—"

I step forward, backing Betty against the brick wall as her eyes wander for an answer. "Andrew named Mercy as Susannah's aunt. Why should your daughter call Mercy that if you have such little contact with your former allies?"

"Please, I—"

"How many?" I ask.

Betty hesitates. "I-if Mercy is dead, then I know of only one other who yet serves Reverend Mather."

"Her name," I demand.

"E-Elisabeth Hubbard."

"And where does she reside?" I ask. "Here in Boston, mayhap?"

"Please," she says. "Do not force me—"

"Forget your Judge Sewall," I say. "I would meet her instead."

"But why?" Betty shakes in my grasp. "Why would you reveal yourself?"

"Who am I?"

Betty looks on me as one confused.

I grin. "I am a stranger to these parts. A face among the crowd…and one forgotten as easily."

"Y-you do not know Elisabeth," says Betty. "There be no telling what she might do if guessing your truth."

"Do you suppose I came all this way thinking of how I might return?" I shake my head. "I care little for my own life, but vengeance aplenty."

Betty wraps her shawl tighter. "An easy claim when you yet have choices before you."

"I have made my choice."

"Aye," says Betty. "And I would counsel you rethink it whilst you still can."

I snort. "Do you think I have not long thought on such matters during my trek? Even if Elisabeth were to guess my intent, she would not kill me."

"How can you speak so?"

"For all her blood lust, Mercy Lewis spared Mary and I several times over. So, too, could Hecate have taken mine and my sister's life when were girls, yet she did not either. Why?"

"I know not," says Betty. "How could I?"

"Someone does," I say, releasing my hold of her. "Mayhap Elisabeth will have the answer to why Cotton Mather has so long sought out my family."

Betty rubs her arm, shivering as we stand in the snow. "Even if Elisabeth knows, she would not tell you."

"She may yet," I say. "No doubt she will be thankful for my gift."

Betty's face speaks plain she has no idea to the gift of which I speak.

"Take me to Elisabeth Hubbard," I whisper. "And I will give her Mary Warren."

-nine-

"GIVE HER OVER?" BETTY SAYS. "YOU SPEAK OF MARY LIKE SHE is a beast of the field."

"I value a beast all the higher," I say. "They, at least, sustain others with the milk of their udders and meat off their bones. Even their hides give warmth. What has Mary Warren provided to any in this life, but misery? Think you I dragged Mary all this way for her good company?"

Betty's lip quavers in answer.

I sneer. "For every step we traveled, I thought to send Mary out in plain sight once we arrived. Aye, learn what ill manner of creature the scent of her should flush out." I cast my gaze around the surrounding homes. "Today I learn the truth of it."

"I cannot do this," says Betty. "You would have me commit a grievous sin."

"And yet it was you who asked me to rid her of our company or else you would not share your secret shield," I say. "Would you rather I have killed her in your home and been done with her treachery?"

I keep careful watch of Betty's face for any hint she will step into the trap I have laid. Should she agree murder would be the best course, I will know her pretense as a good-hearted and forgiving Puritan woman for lies.

"I would rather have lived my life not knowing either of you." Betty casts her gaze to the floor, proving herself too smart a creature for such snares. "And I would not wish murder upon anyone. Punishment, aye, but murder?" She shakes her head. "Never."

"You think yourself above murder, Betty?"

"I am a sinner," she says. "As all others in this world, but I have enough ghosts to haunt my dreams. I would not add another to their company. Not even the soul of Mary Warren."

"To say such a thing, you must believe Elisabeth Hubbard will kill her then," I say.

"I know not what Elisabeth will do," says Betty. "Only that I do not believe Mary would come to this place if she did not place her faith in you. She has abandoned others all her life, yet she followed you here."

"Perhaps," I say. "But her abandonment led to the death of my sister-in-law and my father's. I care near as little for what faith she places in me as for your thoughts on sin."

Betty recoils. "Who are you to plan such lies and schemes as these?"

The ugliness in her tone stokes my unease of being in her company, yet the fire in me would have her understand our unease should be of equal measure.

I stand straighter, looking down on her. "I am Red Banshee, and I have a song for those who wronged my family. Would you prefer I sing it for you?"

Betty glances out into the street as if hopeful someone will chance upon us. "Mary will give you and the others up once she is taken, the same as she turns on everyone."

"Can one speak without a tongue?" I ask.

Betty gasps. "You would not..."

"There are few things I would not do," I say. "Lead me to your Salem sister now or—"

"I am not one of them." Betty's tone rises. "Have not been since the day my father sent me away, as I have told you."

"And yet you know the way to Elisabeth's home." I reach for Betty's face, feel her flinch as I caress her cheek. "You claim a godly life now. Kept safe by your protector all these many years, as I were kept safe for a time by mine."

My thoughts turn to Father, the memory of Mary Warren giving our presence away and the sight of him beaten and dragged away for his sacrifice to save me. The Black Pilgrim dead and gone on her account.

"And then my shield were taken from me." I hiss in Betty's ear. "Along with all else I held dear in this world, save my brother's life."

I reach into my robes and unsheathe the bone-handled dagger I took from Mercy Lewis, the same dagger that took the lives of my sister, Sarah, and Bishop. I bury its tip in the wall beside Betty's ear.

"Look upon the hilt," I motion to the dangling red and black ribbons. "Do these strike a chord in you?"

She trembles in my grip.

"Aye, of course not," I say, my tone dripping with disdain. "Allow me share with you what I have learned—"

"Pl-please. I know what they mean. M-Mercy told me the same day she delivered a similar dagger into mine own hands." Betty sniffles. "Aye, the morning after Ann Putnam confessed her sins and begged public pardon for her part in Salem. 'The ribbons are a warning,' she said, 'of the blade you will find in Susannah's chest if committing an act of likewise contrition.'"

I pull away. "But you and Mercy were—"

"I am *not* one of them," says Betty. "Why do you believe

I wept when you told me of Mercy's death? Your vengeance would free me of their threats." Betty's voice pains with truth at the last, one I find difficult to now allow sway me. "Aye, and Susannah too. Only do not force this upon me, I beg you. Let us go instead to Judge Sewall—"

"After, perhaps," I say. "For now, I would look into the eyes of an enemy."

"But Elisabeth...she..." Betty shudders. "You do not know what she is capable of."

"She can be no worse than Mercy."

"Mercy were a dagger in the dark, aye," says Betty. "I never questioned she should make good on her threats, as I doubt you would make good on yours, but Mercy, at least, would grant a quick death."

"No, she would not," I say, my thoughts turning to the night Mercy took my sister's life. The blade pressed against Sarah's forehead, her lifeless body in the dirt, and the bone-hilted dagger that nailed her scalp to the striking pole.

"Please." Betty wrings her hands. "Do not force this on me."

Her fear sets my jaw to clench. I touch my fingers to Betty's chin, bidding her look into my face that she might understand fierceness. "Lead on."

Though hesitant, Betty relents to my demands.

I follow her out of the alley, heading northwest. Gulls cry overhead, not a few of them swooping down to harass any patrons carrying bread from shops in the market.

After near a mile of treading the street maze of Boston, we reach the northern slopes Andrew spoke of upon our arrival. Seedier folk than any I have yet met in Boston loaf in the alleys. I feel the gazes of men wander up my bodice, not a one showing the decency to avert their hunger when I catch sight of them leering at me.

The fall of hammers upon anvils and the fiery sparks they birth upon the striking call me back to my true purpose.

We pass a smithy as he takes a still glowing bit of iron and douses it in a near bucket. The hiss and steam it gives bids me wish my own anger were cooled so easily, that I could do as Betty asked me, to forget my hate and return to wait out George's ailment before heading back to the wild and reshaping our lives.

Forgetting myself, I reach for the pouch once hung round my neck, only to recall I lent it to George for the same power.

"We are nearly there," says Betty, pausing to wake me from my trance. "Elisabeth lives but the next street over. Are...are you certain of this plan? We may yet turn back." Her eyes round in search of the area. "Aye, we should return from whence we came."

"Keep on," I say, though my heart races with each step taken, beating so hard I fear the whole of Boston will hear.

Betty leads me down a new alley, halting before we step out onto the road before us. "There," she says, pointing to a home near fallen in upon itself.

I nod. "Wait here."

She clutches at my dress. "What if you should not return? Your native friend mentioned my daughter's name. Why?"

"Let you wait here for me, or else learn firsthand what I told him in another time and place," I say. "Though I doubt you should find it agreeable."

"Aye." Betty grimaces. "I will wait."

I cross the street, pausing at the steps of Elisabeth Hubbard's home. Stained lace hangs in the windows, their adornment matching the darkened panes reflecting the greys of winter. I climb the stone steps and knock upon the door. Then I wait, shuddering with cold and the unknown to come, recalling my *manitous* and the masks I must don.

The door creaks open, answered by a waifish woman, her pale cheeks scarred and picked at. Indeed, her sickly frame and thin, bedraggled yellow hair first bid me think of her as weak. Her gaze warns I wrong her with such assumptions.

"Who calls?" she asks, her voice deep and throaty.

"Are you the keeper of this home?" I ask. "Miss Elisabeth Hubbard?"

"Who are you?" The waif scratches at a mole on her neck. "Miss Elisabeth hadn't gone by Hubbard in ages. Been a Bennett nigh on twenty years now, in keeping with her late husband's surname."

"I care little for what her name is now, only that I would see her." I say. "Pray, let you tell your mistress I bring her news of Mercy Lewis."

"Don't know no Mercy Lewis." The waif scratches her shoulder. "And Miss Elisabeth don't take strange callers."

"She would do well to suffer me," I say. "I bring her a gift of great import."

The waif at the door looks down her crooked nose at me, maneuvering to look around me. "Don't see no gift."

"Nor will you," I say. "It is for her alone."

My mind warns I should do as Betty taught and not meet the waif's stare. Despite her teachings, I cannot bring myself to look away.

"What good could you want with Miss Elisabeth?" she asks.

"That is for she and I to discuss."

The waif snorts. "Won't speak with her at all less'n I let you in, now will you? Don't suppose Miss Elisabeth'd mind if I let you freeze out here in the snow. You've a bit of mischief to you, I expect. Look the right side of trouble, you do."

"And you seem a dog to my eyes," I say, moving up the steps.

The waif steps back into the darkened home, but she does not flee. Instead, she takes up her former position in the door, reclaiming herself from the cravenness I worked on her.

"Go," I say. "Run and fetch your mistress. Tell her a follower of Mercy Lewis visits her now. Aye, and brought one of her Salem sisters with me."

The waif's eyes flash at my mention of Salem, setting her to stir from the door faster than if I threatened her life.

"Come in, come in," she says, bowing out of the entryway, opening the door wide for me to enter. "Meant no offense, truly I didn't."

I step past her and into the blessed heat emanating throughout the home. As the waif closes the door behind me, the hunter in me warns I have no other means of escape. I feel the walls close and my heart flutters with panic, the need for open air and sky.

"Might I wait by your fire?" I ask. "The winter cold has sapped my spirit."

"As you like," says the waif, ushering us enter. "There's a hearth in the parlor there round the corner. Mind you take some warmth of it whilst I speak with Miss Elisabeth."

She leads me into the next room where a roaring fire crackles beneath an open stone hearth. Despite the ruin outside the home, inside is another matter. The furniture gleams of polished mahogany, unlike the dull tones in Betty's house. So too does Elisabeth's sitting room have more space than even Betty's kitchen.

The waif fumbles at a curtsy then turns and makes her leave. Though she cannot weigh more than a hundred pounds, the wood floor creaks beneath her. She scurries into the next room and out of sight. A moment later, she thuds up the stairwell.

I take a deep breath then approach the hearth. A pair of unlit tallow candles stands to either side of a lone wooden cross atop the mantle. I turn my gaze instead on the fire, extending my hands, allowing its heat warm not only the numbness in them, but my soul also.

The parlor doors squeak open.

I break my stare of the flames, turning to face my enemy, half expecting a demon in my midst.

Instead, a woman well on fifty years old trains her focus upon me. Were it not for the sharpness lurking in her eyes, her dress and stern face would lead me believe her a Puritan woman as any other.

"You are Elisabeth Hubbard?" I ask, the hairs on my neck raising.

"Who are you?" she demands. "And what business have you approaching me in my home?"

I cast my gaze to the floor, in keeping with Betty's teachings. "If it please you, I am but a humble servant of Mercy Lewis."

"An odd notion, that," says Elisabeth. "Mercy has ever been anything but humble. Strange that she should keep such followers in her company. Would you prefer to speak plain, or continue your lies?"

Her tone bids me realize I cannot wear the goodly face of my sister, nor even allow Elisabeth see my hate plain. I must don not only a mask now, but take up the lying tongue of Mercy Lewis.

I glance up, meeting Elisabeth's stare in kind. "Aye, I am not humble."

"Clearly, else you should not have bothered approach me," Elisabeth says. "But you are here now. Tell me, why should Mercy not come herself?"

"She could not. Mercy Lewis is dead."

"How?" Her left eyebrow cocks.

"The savages." I steel my voice to spit the lie. "Betrayed her at the last when things turned bleak."

"Indeed," she says. "I cannot claim surprise at such tidings. It were always the darkest of tasks Mercy sought most. Still, it pains me that she has gone from this world." Elisabeth purses her lips. "And how is it Mercy came to die, but you managed a safe return?"

"The savages crave white flesh," I say, thinking back on Mercy's lies and her mention of wooing Two Ravens. "And they have never found a better lover than I."

"So, you are both liar and harlot." Elisabeth quips.

"I am whatever I need be to survive," I say. "I should have thought you happy to see me."

"A fool also then," says Elisabeth. "I have never met you before, not even in Mercy's company. I know naught even of your name, girl."

A memory of the days Sarah spent lecturing me of her god and her bible rise in my mind. For all the stories she told of humble, reverent women, one sticks in my memory more than any other, that of a righteous judge and warrior.

"Call me Deborah," I say.

"As if we are old friends?" Elisabeth's thin lips part in a cruel smile. She chuckles as she swings close the parlor doors, then strides to sit in one of the polished benches, clasping her hands in her lap. "But we are not friends, Deborah…not yet, at least."

She opens a drawer from the table before her, removing a vial filled with purplish-black powder. Uncorking its top, she snows the dusky contents upon the table.

"Here," Elisabeth says, drawing her hand over the mound of powder. "A gift for your safe return from savage lands."

I flinch.

"Why are you troubled?" she asks. "No doubt you have been long in your travels. I know all too well the pains that come with the absence of Devil's powder. Do you not ache for it now?"

"I do," I say. "But my time upon the road sucked the torturous need from my body. I have little desire to allow it hold sway over me again so soon."

Elisabeth clucks her tongue. "Would that I were as strong as you."

She leans towards the table, delving her nose full into the powder, snorting near the lot. She shudders and moans as she draws away, her eyes wide with greed. Watching me, she takes a bit of cloth from the sleeve of her dress and wipes clean the lingering traces of powder upon her nose.

"My servant mentioned you bring me a gift," she says.

"I do indeed," I say. "Mercy mentioned several times over how pleased her Salem sisters—"

Elisabeth cackles, bending low to snort the remaining powder. "By my count, you look upon the last of us."

"And what of Mary Warren?" I ask, cutting her mocking tone short. "Would it not please you to know she yet lives?"

Elisabeth leans forward, beaming. "Indeed it would. Pray, where is Mary now?"

"Kept safe at a place of my choosing," I say. "And will remain so until I receive all that I desire."

"A mountain of Devil's powder?" Elisabeth laughs, shrill and hysteric. "That you may never feel pained by the loss of it again?"

"To take Mercy's place in your coven"—I step closer—"and become a Salem sister."

Elisabeth straightens. "Why should you seek such an honor?"

Her tone warns me choose my next words carefully.

"Mercy spoke highly on the bonds of your sisterhood," I say. "One to shape the world and leave a righteous legacy. Is it wrong of me to desire welcome among your company, that I might leave my mark on the whole of history also?"

"Only those who triumphed in Salem may join that sisterhood." Elisabeth folds her hands in her lap. "But we may yet find a place for you among our coven, should you prove your worth."

"Does my gift not prove it?"

"It should suffice," says Elisabeth, scratching at her face. "But I am troubled. With Mercy gone, why should you bring Mary all this way?"

"In keeping my oath to Mercy," I say. "And a show of my good faith to you."

"A show, aye," Elisabeth scowls as she eases back into her seat, her gaze never leaving mine. "Perhaps there be the truth of it. No doubt you believe such a gift will gain my trust."

"Mary is all I have in offering." I open my hands to her. "Let you think of my intentions as you will."

"I am yet uncertain as to your intent," says Elisabeth. "But I think you bring me more than Mary Warren alone, girl."

My pulse quickens. "What else could I have?"

"Much and more." Elisabeth studies me. "I cannot say whether you be fool or no, but you have my intrigue." She looks on the flames, smiling. "And I should very much like to meet with Mary Warren again."

Her voice trails as one lost in a memory and, for a moment, I fear the snorting of Devil's powder has forced her forget my presence. Then she chuckles in a way I like not at all, her eyes finding me once more.

"Let you deliver Mary to me this night—"

"No," I say. "I did not suffer her presence to give up my prize that you alone might receive the praise."

"Then why come at all if you will not share the glory?"

"Mercy oft told us followers only the Reverend Mather could truly welcome us into your order." I meet her stare. "I will give Mary Warren to him alone, that he might deem me worthy."

"Mercy told you much." Elisabeth scowls. "Alas, death treads closer to the Reverend Mather with each passing day. We cannot trouble him with such trifling matters as these. Let you bring her to me instead, and I shall—"

"*No*," I say, noting scorn draw across her face at my rudeness. "You think me a fool? I will give her over to him or else slit her throat and be done with it."

"As you will," says Elisabeth. "We should only want her to see the deed done ourselves."

"Very well then." I walk for the parlor doors.

"Wait." Elisabeth calls as I touch the ringed, metal handles.

I halt, turning back toward her.

She rises from her bench, approaching me slow, scratching at her neckline. "Why do you desire so keenly to meet with the Reverend Mather?"

"Mercy spoke of him as a great man," I say.

"A man? No." Elisabeth treads closer to me, transfixing me with her gaze. "Words alone cannot describe what he is. Father, reverend, sage—powerful titles in this world, but they mean naught to those who walk the boundary between this realm and the next."

Her reverent tone turns my blood cold.

"He is the Devil's Warlock. The keeper of all knowledge in the Invisible World, bending its secrets to his whims and wishes." Elisabeth closes her eyes, shuddering. "You will never in this life, or the next, meet such a being as he."

"As you say."

"You doubt me?" Elisabeth asks.

"I doubt all that I have not witnessed."

"Then we will help you see," Elisabeth says, her bloodshot eyes crazed as they train on me. "Tomorrow eve, we meet to dance and make sacrifice beneath our Mother Moon. Bring me Mary Warren before the night falls, prove your worth, and together we will journey to the gathering circle."

"I will bring her," I say. "And deliver her only to him."

Elisabeth steps closer, placing her arms about my shoulders. "This life is but circles within circles, girl. Aye, with gatekeepers at the entrance of each." Her eyes flame in a way I like not at all. "Deliver Mary Warren and I grant you passage into the next realm wherein the Devil's Warlock awaits you. Perhaps he will reveal your true purpose in this life. Aye, the same as he once revealed mine."

I nod. "Until tomorrow then."

Elisabeth grins and claps her hands.

The parlor doors swing open with the waif behind them. Before I can speak a word, the waif takes me by the arm and near trots me out of the room. She leads me toward the entryway, opening the front door. The waif bows her head, revealing bald patches I had not previously noticed upon her scalp where her locks have been picked clean.

Her shoulders twitch as I pass.

My mind warns she did not do so of her own choosing.

The door closes the moment I stand upon the stoop, the knob near striking me in the back. I waste little time leaving off to distance myself from the home.

Betty sighs at the sight of me when I round the corner. "Truly I had not thought to see you again," she says as I stalk past her up the alley. "What did Elisabeth say?"

"Many things." I say. "As did I."

"And how many of those do you suppose were true?" Betty asks.

"One of mine, at least." I say, thinking on my promise to deliver Mary Warren. "Come. We need return to the others."

Betty leads at a spry pace, each turn and step taken with deliberation.

Despite her confident direction, unease settles within me. Tingles run down my spine as if unseen eyes linger upon my back, their phantom gaze watchful from the window of every shop and home we pass.

I run ahead of her, forcing her to halt, when she attempts to lead me south, rather than east to the inn.

"Where are you taking me?" I ask.

"To Judge Sewall's," she says.

"No," I say. "I have no need to meet him now."

"I made a promise to you in my home," says Betty. "I will see it kept."

"Consider it honored," I say. "There is no need for you to

venture further. Not when we should return to the others and lay further plans."

"Aye, you should." Betty attempts to push past me.

I do not relent.

"You have forced this recklessness upon me," says Betty. "Please allow me this small kindness, I beg you. I would know my daughter will be kept safe no matter the outcome of your fool plot with Elisabeth."

"Susannah will be safe," I say. "I made no mention of you or her."

"For now." Betty's jaw quivers. "I will see it remain so."

Again she moves to pass me.

Again I halt her. "We need rejoin—"

"Will you draw your blade and strike me down, here upon the road?" Betty glances up at the surrounding homes and their windows. "Or will I first scream so loud that others might hear and hurry to my aid?"

Her meek mask dropping, I recognize the farce in my attempts at donning such guises.

"You are but a girl, and I a woman grown," she says, her face livid. "Aye, and one well versed in this game you play at."

I rise to her scolding.

Betty studies me up and down. "What should some guard, or soldier, find if I bid them search you now?"

My hands fly to the hidden hilts of my blades. "You would not…"

"Won't I?" Betty asks. "You do not know, nor trust, me well. How can you say what I will or will not do both when and at my choosing? You have only how you respond to alter the minds of those who should come to aid me."

I stumble for words at the new woman standing before me.

Betty pulls me into a near alley, her gaze cautious for any who might chance near us. "Should I call out, it would be the goodliest of men to heed my plea, those seeking righteous defense of the weak. And how should I respond in kind?"

"You—"

"I would be grateful, no?" Betty asks. "Aye, to hear the reverends preach, one might think I should bow before every whim and wish of such men, for what are we women to them but servants?"

My lip curls at such a thought. "I am no servant."

"Then you are truly a fool," says Betty. "For all the nonsense our reverends preach, there be plenty wisdom in the good book for those who know where to find it. To kneel before the master—"

Betty steps close enough to embrace me. Instead, she touches the hilt of my father's dagger, digging it into my side.

"Means you draw near him."

A horse-drawn carriage approaches us.

Betty steps away as quick, donning her pious mask again in humble bow.

I grin the moment she looks up. "You are more than I first thought you, Betty Barron."

"Aye," she says. "And you are the same as I first thought you. Prove me wrong now and allow us visit my true friend."

"No," I say. "You did not wish me involve him, and so I will not now. Lead me back to the others. There is much to discuss and you will need your rest. You and Andrew have a long ride come the morrow."

"What say you?" she asks.

"You have done all I required, Betty," I say. "Now I would ask one final favor before you go."

"If it means you will release me—"

"I will," I say. "If you aid me convince the others we met with your Judge Sewall."

Her face pinches in question. "Why?"

"That matters not," I say. "Only that they believe it. Aid me sway them and I send you on your way home tomorrow."

"And I am trust you in this?" she asks. "You, who I have seen now lie to both friends and enemies alike."

I shift on my heels. "Ciquenackqua knows of my true intent. Andrew and Mary do not," I say. "They *cannot*."

"Why not Andrew?" she asks.

I sigh. "However you might think him, he is a man of good intent. In my heart, I know he should disapprove of the acts I would commit in the name of vengeance."

"Such thoughts should sway you against them then," says Betty, the corners of her eyes wrinkling.

"They will not," I say. "And I will not suffer his disagreement with the actions I take. There be no way for me to know how events should fare tomorrow night, but I will not force you or Andrew to play a further part in them."

"He will not leave you," says Betty.

"He will," I say. "For the love he bears your daughter."

"Then you are even more foolish than first I thought." Betty huffs. "I have seen the way he looks on you. However you might ignore him, Andrew Martin loves you more than anything in this world."

"All the more reason for me to send him away," I say. "I would offer him naught but further heartache."

"There be one of the first truths you have uttered in a long while, I think," says Betty.

I shake my head. "I speak truth now—aid me again and let us say we mean to meet with Sewall again tomorrow. Then your part is finished in this."

"So you say." Betty sighs. "My part in Salem ended long ago, yet here I stand, caught still between the forces of this world and the invisible one."

"By tomorrow eve, one of them at least will cease its pull on you."

"Perhaps," says Betty, her tone doubtful. She turns on her heel with little delay and leads onward at a brisker pace than ever she has previously led me.

I take in the sights, searching for any buildings of note to mark my surroundings in the event I should become lost. Still, Betty leads at a frantic pace, turning up alleys and rounding corners so that I cannot discern my bearings.

We reach an open market, bustling with commoners and rich alike. As we wander through their midst, I catch sight of another pillory, built before the gallows in twin to those outside the Neck gates.

Dirtied and half-dressed children play below the platform. One by one, they rush the pillory, laughing as they strike at the board.

Or so I first believe.

Only when they pause to talk among themselves do I learn it be no board they strike at, but a man—forced to stand, his head and wrists inserted through the holes to secure him from escape.

The letter *R* stands out against each of his cheeks, the raised skin and discolored scars marking both as recently branded.

His crudely shorn head and the accompanying scabs adorning it speak to an untrained barber's hand or else one who cared not for the work and sharpness of their blade. Nails pin the imprisoned man's ears to the wooden beam, forcing him look upon the crowd, uncaring that a purplish-black bruise near closes his right eye full up. Yet for all the scars and bruises, hate lives in his one good eye.

I witness it extinguished the moment he looks on me.

My hand flies to Betty, willing her keep me from falling.

"What is it?" she asks. "What troubles you?"

My chest draws tight, my stomach churning, knees weak. I glance at the imprisoned man once more. My hand flies to stave the anguished cry threatening to escape my lips.

Betty follows my stare to the prisoner. "Do you know him?"

My body shudders in reply.

"Who is he?" she asks.

"F-Father."

ten

I SNAP FROM MY TRANSFIX WHEN ONE OF THE BOYS THROW HORSE manure at Father. Some in the crowd roar when it strikes him in the face.

Father keeps his silence, though the crowd encourages the children.

A few shake their heads and keep on about their business.

Not one voices disapproval.

I abandon Betty, pushing through the crowd to reach Father's side, catching the arm of another boy preparing a second attack. I shove him away and smack at those within reach, near begging any of the others test me.

The children scatter, disappearing into the crowd or else down unseen alleys.

I wheel on their elders, finding the faces of those who jeered not a moment ago now also vanished from my sight or else turning their attention elsewhere. My blood rages as I scan the crowd, willing anyone speak out with ill intent.

Betty alone dares approach me. "Let you quit this now, I beg you," she says, her voice pleading. "Or else they see fit for you to join this man."

"R-Rebecca..."

The mere call of his voice douses the fire in me. Though rasped and full of sickness, he yet stands tall in the pillory, neither his spirit nor body broken by his bonds, his face dirtied by the elements and the excrement thrown upon him by the crowd.

I cannot bring myself to answer to his call. A mixture of grief for his current state and elation he yet lives washes over me as I approach him, falling to my knees that he might look me full in the face.

His jaw clenches, his strength opposing the weakness streaming down my cheeks.

"How did it come to this?" I ask, tracking my fingers over the *R*'s branded upon his cheeks. "What have they done to you?"

His mournful stare tells me my questions matter not.

"W-water." He coughs.

I hurry to a drift of clean snow by the scaffolding and fetch up a handful. Cupping it to Father's cracked and bloodied lips, I feed the snow into his mouth.

Betty clutches at my shoulder. "We should be gone from here," she hisses.

Father coughs again. The whole of it wracks his body, forcing his wrists and neck to pull at the wooden bonds encasing him, the nails in his ears tearing at his skin.

"More," he says.

I give over several handfuls until he is sated, or else need not ask again. Wetting the sleeve of my dress with snow, I clean the excrement and dirt from his face, then the fresh blood off his ears. Each bit I wipe away revealing more of the man who taught me all the good in life.

Dried blood clings to the deeper wounds that have worn the flesh from Father's wrists.

I move to clean them also.

Father halts me with a tender touch, despite the roughness of his hand, and guides my face to look on him. "George?" he asks.

"He and Andrew live," I say. "Creek Jumper also. Ciquenackqua said you saved them both."

"Hannah?" Father wets his lips, his good eye trained on me. "B-Bishop?"

A new wave of tears takes hold of me. I shake my head and cast my gaze to the ground that he might not see me cry.

Father's hand opens to me, grazing my cheeks, wiping the wetness from them.

I lean my face full into his palm, craving the safety of his touch, feeling him respond. What little endurance remains in me vanishes the moment his fingers tremble.

"Oh, Father." I cry, kissing his hand. "I thought you gone from this world with all the rest."

Father blinks back the glazing in his eyes, the Black Pilgrim's stoic nature claiming hold of him. And though it be his body bruised and beaten, and he the one subjected to the elements and scorn of any who chance by, in his stare I yet find vim.

"Fly," Father says, holding my attention, his voice hardly above a whisper. "Leave me."

"I will not," I say through gritted teeth. "The others are here too. We will—"

Father clutches the back of my hair, pulling it tight. "*Fly*."

He releases his hold of me at the approach of fast-moving footsteps.

I stumble backward, tripping over my dress, falling upon the cobbled road.

"My humble apologies." A sharp dressed young soldier stands before me, lean and sturdy. He appears near enough my own age, yet he wears the white hair of an old man. His eyes search my person as he kneels and offers his hand toward me. "Are you all right? I did not mean to fright you."

"Aye," I say, standing of my own merit. "Many thanks for your concern."

He averts his lingering gaze when I do not shy away. "That were a most charitable and Christian act you showed this man." He gestures toward Father. "One I have scarce seen among other folk who pretend at such piety. Do you know him, perchance?"

I glance at Father, hesitant on what to say.

Betty steps to my side. "If it please, sir, my niece meant no offense. She has ever held a soft place in her heart for beggars and thieves, Mister..."

He blushes. "It seems I must beg your forgiveness once again," he says. "Isaac is my name. And there be no offense to my eyes. No doubt the Lord wishes more in this city gifted such mercy toward sinners and the poor in spirit."

"Aye, no doubt," says Betty.

"Pray, what is this man's charge?" I ask Isaac.

"*Niece*," Betty scolds. "Let you not inquire further of this good man."

"It is of little consequence," says Isaac. "I, too, were curious of his crimes when first I saw him delivered to this ghastly device."

"What are his crimes?" I ask, willing my voice not break.

Isaac pulls at his collar. "I know only what I have heard, and those black sins that should not be spoke aloud in the presence of such goodly women as you and your aunt."

"I would still hear them," I say. "Sir."

Isaac blinks. "As you wish," he says, casting his gaze on Father. "I have heard my fellows name him Black Pilgrim, in keeping with the name given him by the savages. They claim he hath no loyalty to the crown or any manner of person in these parts. Indeed, it has been said he forsakes God's tender mercy, for he will not beg forgiveness nor confess his transgressions."

"And so you deem him criminal for it?" I ask.

"I am no judge, only another poor sinner as all men are," says Isaac, motioning toward the market's crowd. "This man's pride alone keeps him here. Surely you, a goodly woman, believe this?"

"Forgive her youthful spirit, sir," says Betty before I speak further. "I assure you she is over zealous in her want to keep our Lord's commandments."

"Indeed." Isaac brightens. "It were her fervor for such work that first drew my attention. Have I seen either of you at church?"

"Not any here," says Betty. "We hail from Andover and have come only to visit for a time."

"Ah," he says. "I might have thought as much. My men oft say I have a gift for faces and I could not recall witnessing either of yours before. Perchance you both should be here come the Lord's Day, I should welcome you to attend at the Old North with me."

"Many thanks," says Betty. "But we should be gone from Boston before then."

"Shame," says Isaac. "I should have liked to introduce your niece to my good friend, the Reverend Mather."

I stir at the name, my pulse quickening. "Cotton?"

"Oh no. His son, Samuel," says Isaac. "He and others have recently taken over his father's pulpit. No doubt my good friend would enjoy learning of such charitable acts as you have shown."

"You know him well then?" I ask.

"Aye, Sammy and I attended at Harvard together," says Isaac. "And his father, Cotton, showed me much favor also. A goodly family of high esteem, the Mathers. I warrant you will find none greater in this city."

His tone bids me think of a warbling turkey, his eagerness for compliment snatching any response from my tongue.

"Isaac is a learned man, niece," says Betty quickly. "Forgive us, sir, for keeping you from your work."

"There be no need for forgiveness, I assure you," says Isaac, turning his attention to me. "Your act was a welcome respite. One I should be fortunate to encounter again."

Betty stirs at my silence. "We thank you for your kindness, sir. If indeed our business should keep us, you may look for us in attendance at church."

Isaac beams. "Very well," he says. "I shall hope to see you then, Miss..."

"Deborah, sir," I say, failing at a curtsy. "Deborah Martin."

"A fierce and wise name, for an equally lovely young woman," he says. "I bid the both of you good day then."

"Good day." Betty curtsies.

Isaac continues into the crowd and though I should quit my watch of him, I cannot bring myself to do so. Not even when he glances back.

"That were a foolish thing you did," says Betty, drawing my attention. "Deborah Martin."

"What?" I ask.

Betty leans close. "None here know your name or face, but there yet be those who may know mine. Let your good Aunt Betty do the speaking should next someone require it. Elsewise, let you bow your head and keep silent. That were a very forward man, just now." Betty grimaces. "One we should do well to steer clear of."

"I think otherwise," I say. "He claims ties to the Mathers. I deem that a friend worth having."

"I deem my head worth having," says Betty. "And it warns we should leave from here now, else you would share this man's fate, whoever he may be."

I ignore her concerns, my gaze locking on Father. My heart urges me not abandon him, though knowing I can do naught for him given the time of day and bustling square. Nor do I trust Betty to rejoin my companions.

"Go," he says.

I kneel beside him. "Aye, I will fly from here for now. But I shall return to free you."

He grimaces. "Rebecca—"

"Warn me all you will," I whisper to him. "But hear me now, Father. Freedom and the hunting grounds wait for us, George and Creek Jumper and many others among our people also. You and I will leave this place together before the end."

"Rebecca," he says.

I pull away, staring into his good eye. "Aye, Father?"

"*Fly...*"

"For now." I rise and stride away, fearful looking back on him will turn me craven.

Betty falls in beside me. She takes me light by the arm, guiding me down the rat's nest of alleys. After a time, she pulls me aside in a corner where none may see.

"Let you hide those now," she says of my tears.

"I-I cannot," I say. "He were dead and gone to my mind not an hour ago. Now I see him living, his pain made a show for all to see and mock. How should I quit my sorrow at witnessing him so—"

"You think he is the first to be given over for mockery and shame?" Betty asks. "Those pillories and stocks, aye, even the gallows he stands near, they were not crafted special for him. These are dark times, girl, and it has ever been the way of pain for those who will not bow nor break for the pleasure of powerful men."

I glance back in the pillory's direction. "He has committed no trespass."

"He has," says Betty. "Silence is his trespass. Not against God, but man. It is the same for all who hold to their own way rather than seek haven among the many. So it has been for all of time. So it will be long after you and I are dead and gone."

I lean against the alley's cold brick wall, my head pounding with anger and sorrow.

A winter wind shrieks past us, chilling me deep, reflecting the name given me by my native brothers.

"I am Red Banshee." I say to the wind. "And I will see him freed."

"Perhaps," says Betty. "But it will not be this day. Come." She tugs at my wrist. "The others await."

I allow her lead, and stumble after, uncaring of where she takes me. My thoughts dwell only on Father, my hands trembling with what I will visit upon those who wronged him.

By the time we near the inn, the sun dips behind us, casting our long shadows up the alley. Each step we take fills me with thoughts of freeing Father of his confines, seeing him back to the inn, warmed and fed. I wonder how he came to be in Boston and what roads or paths he traveled.

Still, my head warns my questions matter little. All I need concern myself with is his safe release. The mere thought of being in his presence, sharing fire and stories with him, soothes my spirit.

Such thoughts vanish when Betty halts, her left arm shooting across my chest to stop me also.

I glance up the alley toward the inn.

The door hangs askew from a single hinge. Blood darkens the stoop.

I rush forward without thinking.

"Rebecca, wait!" Betty calls.

I dash up the alley and leap through the threshold, pausing only to hike my dress. I draw both my father's dagger and the bone-handled blade I took from Mercy Lewis.

A blood trail leads up the hall.

I pause at the scuffling noise from the adjoining room. Pressing my back flat against the wall, I inch toward the parlor entrance, my heart thundering against my chest. Both daggers slip in my grip, my hands turned cold and clammy. I force my fingers close tight round their hilts, near drawing blood in my palms.

Pained moans wait for me around the corner.

I pause near the doorway, glancing up the stairs for any hint someone lay in wait, finding no one.

I am a Miamiak. I breathe deep. *We do not fear.*

The moans continue.

Leaning around the corner, I peek into the parlor room.

Blood pools upon the floor, chairs lay splintered, tables overturned and broken. The fire burns bright in the hearth, illuminating the woman who stands before its flames.

Her arms stretch across the mantle beam, held in place by the bone-handled daggers driven through her wrists in a mocking show of the wooden cross hung upon the wall.

My gaze homes on their dangling ribbons, red and black, and their gleamed hue in the firelight.

Faith shudders, glancing on a third dagger plunged in her chest. A rasped and labored breath escapes her lips. She weakly lifts her head, eyes glazed and wet. "F-forgive me, Miss R-Rebec...ca."

I sheathe my blades, rushing toward her.

She cries out, wincing, as I touch my hand to the bone-hilted dagger in her wrist.

I stare on her wounds, knowing any attempt to remove them will be for naught.

"Th-they c-came of a sudden," she says. "D-demons in human flesh."

"Faith," I say, touching her face. "Where are the others?"

"G-gone," she says. "Mister Andrew...gave himself o-over when they threatened M-Miss Mary. T-took both in chains, last I saw."

Her eyes roll back and her chin dips toward her chest.

"Faith," I cry, placing my hands to her cheeks, holding her head up. "Faith!"

Her head snaps back, her gaze blinking back to life. "He a good man, M-Mister Andrew."

"Where-" I struggle for the words, my chest drawing tight. "Where is Ciquenackqua?"

"So strong..." Faith's voice falls to a whisper, her head lolling in my hands. "How were they...s-so strong?"

"What of Ciquenackqua?"

Her eyelids droop closed.

"*Faith.*"

"Aye, f-faith set me free," she says quietly. "F-faith is...a-all I got..."

I catch her body from sagging as she breathes her last breath. Her head rolls against mine.

Betty gasps in the entry, her face pale, hand clapped over her mouth.

Gently, I release my hold of Faith and back away, careful to ensure the daggers will hold her weight.

Betty approaches, clutches at my hand. "What beasts should commit such evil as this?"

"Not beasts," I say, my thoughts turning to the stories Bishop oft told me of their existence in the Old World, his tracking of them across the ocean and throughout the colonies. A hunt I mean to finish. "Bitches from the depths of hell."

Betty gasps at my swearing, though I do not take it back. "We must take her down from here," she says.

"No."

"How can you speak so?" she asks. "Let us at least grant her some small dignity."

"Take her down and you make her but a nameless corpse among the many," I say, thinking back to the dead men swaying near the Boston Neck. "Leave her and allow any who enter in see what the scourge of this city made of her."

"None will see her," says Betty. "None but the thieves and vagabonds who come in the night to steal that which others have not took already. I doubt most should even learn her name. If she were a man, perhaps, but a woman, aye, and dark of skin also?"

"Aye," I say, taking in her meaning. "She will go unknown with all the rest. Her name lost to this world the moment we abandon her."

Betty looks on me. "Allow us show her some little courtesy, I beg you."

I stare on Faith, burning the image of her waylaid in my mind. "She wears her faith even now." I point to the wooden cross on the wall. "Think you they hung her this way for any other reason? She stays as they left her."

I leave Betty, drawing my own blades again, moving out into the hall and up the stairwell, quick and quiet. Sneaking into each room, I find them all the same—beds overturned, clothes and sheets torn and tossed.

My bow lay snapped in pieces upon the floor, my quiver and all the arrowheads taken also. Mary's cloak, worn and thread-bare, lay strewn across a broken chair. I don it over my dress then leave out of the room, hurrying down the steps.

Betty waits for me at the bottom. "What do you intend?" she asks.

"Much and more that I would not force you witness," I say. "I know not how they learned of our presence here, but I will discover the truth of it."

"Does it matter now?" she asks. "Say they followed Andrew, or else listened on conversation in the alley. Spies mayhap, saw us on the road. There be any number of manner for Cotton Mather to learn of your presence here."

I move to pass her.

Betty clutches at me. "Rebecca, this is folly. *You are out-matched*," she says. "Look you only throughout this inn if you would see the truth of my words. Whoever worked such evil on Faith will surely do the same to the others. Aye, and you also if you persist."

"They are why I must persist," I say, fury flowing in my veins. "All who came this far did so only on account of me. I shame them all if I fly now."

"It is no shame to desire life," says Betty. "Come with me. My wagon and horses are gone with the others, but my friend, the good Judge Sewall, will help us flee if we reach him in time."

I shake my head. "You have done all that I required of you, Betty. Now I beg you do only one thing more."

"What?"

"Do not sway me from this." I fix my gaze on her. "Leave this cursed place. Fly back to your home and live the life you so desire with your good daughter. It seems I must first witness death and ruin claim all that I hold dear before it finds me. I have no desire you should join me in learning what awaits at the end of this path."

"Do not do this," she says. "I, too, thought my life ending once. Then the true and merciful love of God were shown me. It may be He yet wishes to shine His light upon you also."

"Your god should never look favorably upon me," I say. "My sister oft read of his book to me many a night when I were young. He would have me turn the other cheek, even now, but I will not. Now go." I lead her down the hall. "And leave me to my work."

Betty hesitates upon the threshold. "You are certain in your want of this?"

I nod.

"I will not condone the actions you take," she says. "But I will pray God for your safe-keeping. Aye, and that you may give yourself to His love rather than allow your hate consume you."

"Hate consumed me many months ago," I say. "I have only its embers now."

"Be that as it may," she says. "I will pray for you."

"Save your prayers." I leave her in the doorway. "I have no need of them."

I hurry up the alley, glancing back when nearing its end.

Betty has vanished from sight, whether back inside the inn or else gone to seek out her Judge Sewall I know not.

My mind warns me not tarry.

I hurry on toward the fading sun, back the way she and I came, bound for the pillory. Always, I keep my gaze upon the three hilltops and the steel finger perched highest of all. Each step taken bids me hurry faster, my strides turning longer. I force myself not to run and fright others yet upon the road.

I am not long to reach the market square.

Though the last light of day wanes, some merchants yet conduct their trade. Most have gone and those who filled the square with them.

So, too, do I find the pillory stands empty.

I run to the hinged boards where Father stood not hours ago. His blood stains the beams and surrounding snow, the blood trail leading off a ways before all is lost to the tracks of the many who since wandered over top it.

Falling to my knees, my heart lay heavy in knowing I am now well and truly alone.

eleven

"MOVE ALONG, WENCH!" A MAN SHOUTS AT ME FROM ATOP HIS wagon perch.

I roll aside lest his team of horses and wagon run me over.

The driver swears at me and slaps the reins anew. His wagon creaks by, leading behind it a gaggle of slaves—native and black—all bound together as one. Their heads bowed, they trot to keep up, the clanking rankle of their chains a bitter song to pace them.

I rise from the snow and muck wetting my knees, giving thanks I am not chained as they are, that I may go both where and when I like at my choosing and commit such acts as I wish.

Glancing up at the twilit sky, I muse on Father's teachings and what he might do were our situations reversed. Thoughts of how he and the others were taken plague me. So, too, do I wonder where they might be and if any have shared the same fate as Faith.

My heart bids me search for them. My mind warns it would be folly with the city so large and I a lone stranger in it. I am feared of inquiring on anyone, believing questions should only draw further attention to me, especially at this late hour.

Night strengthens its hold on the city as I stir from the square, headed west toward the lone house whose owner I know.

With daylight banished, the underbelly of Boston wakes to play. I stalk past drunken men who clutch and whistle at near anything that passes them.

My anger hopes they taunt me in such a way.

None do.

Whores walk the streets in pairs, each taking their turn at revealing flesh to the moonlight and cold. Not a few of them twitch and tremble, though I gather not from cold alone. They scratch at their shoulders and cheeks, the need for Devil's powder living in them.

For all my fear that one will stop and note my face, the whores care little for me, their sights set on more prized game than me. The sober men leave me walk with little regard, their notice given over to easier prey.

I am not so fortunate to avoid the packs of street urchins lurking in darkened alleys.

A few lunge at me. They scurry back quick enough when I flash my blade.

I feel their eyes follow me long after they vanish from sight.

I reach Elisabeth Hubbard's street within an hour and hide in the alley across from her home. Settling in shadow, I press my back into a bricked corner so none might surprise me from behind.

For several hours I keep watch of Elisabeth's home, waiting for any hint of light inside, to witness someone leaving or else venturing in.

The elements wear away my resolve. Brutal, biting cold forces me take shelter inside my robes, drawing it over my face and head. My eyes weigh heavy, bidding me sleep.

I draw my blade an inch from its sheathe and slice my thumb upon it, using the pain to wake me alert. Yet even its throb cannot stave off the cold sleep beckoning me accept its dark and peaceful gift.

I raise my head from the fur's warmth, my lungs shuddering as they breathe in even colder air.

Neighboring chimneys sputter smoke. Elisabeth Hubbard's remains barren.

I stand, my muscles aching with stiffness, and rub the soreness from my legs. Then I will myself onward, using the alleys to maneuver round the back of Elisabeth's home. With the night as my ally, I skulk toward a low window, trying my hand to open it, finding it locked or else froze shut.

Stifling my cough, I draw my dagger and shatter one of the windowpanes with its hilt.

The glass tinkles as it falls.

I scan the area for any who might have heard.

No one comes, nor do I hear any signal someone means to seek me out.

I reach my hand through the newly made hole and fumble at the latch, opening the window slow, careful for it not to groan or shriek at too quick a movement. I slip inside the home and lower the window closed.

My heart beats quickly as I stand in the pitch of dark. My mind sports Elisabeth and her coven may hide inches away and I should not see them until they desire it.

With night robbing my sight and the house deathly quiet, the scent of smoke guides me. Crouched low, I feel along the wall with one hand, my dagger drawn in the other. I slink toward the scent, my ears perked for the slightest sound I am discovered.

Though slow, I feel my way around and note my eyes adjusting to the dark.

A flight of stairs stands before me, the same that thundered under the waif's small weight.

I abandon them, moving to the parlor.

The smallest of embers yet glow in the hearth.

My shoulders tremble at the notion of stoking the flames anew and giving away my presence. I approach the hearth warily, kneeling beside it, extending my hands to scoop up any offered heat.

The embers grant me little in return, most more cool than warm.

The skills Father taught me in the wild bid me understand this fire cannot have been fed since I left Elisabeth's company yesterday afternoon.

My mind churns with the thought.

With the weather turned frigid, how can it be they have not fanned the flames? I wonder. *Why should they allow the fire wane without they had not thought to be here?*

I wrestle with the notion I am alone—both Elisabeth and her waif gone for the night.

But to where?

I am not lost to the notion Elisabeth may have lied of the gathering's time and place, or mayhap there were no gathering at all. Still, I will myself away from such thoughts, fearing what I should do if the truth of my situation lay in the answer.

Fear and doubt eat at my insides. That I have broken my oath to George by distrusting those in my company, and forgotten Father's teachings to lay in wait rather than give myself over to action.

I forbid myself to sulk in the event I am wrong—that Elisabeth or her waif yet reside upstairs. Instead, I sheathe my blade and take up several coals in hand, sucking the heat from them whilst plots and plans dance in my head.

My blood warming, I think more on Father and how I should emulate his quiet and patient ways. I scoot my back against the wall, pressing along its side until reaching the safety of a corner.

All night I wait, not stirring until the coming dawn lightens the room.

I set the cold embers aside and draw both my blades, making for the stairwell. Their steps do not thunder beneath my feet and squeak but a little.

My spirit grows bolder with each step taken, my breath calm as I ascend.

I reach the landing and find several closed doors.

The first, to my left, hangs open. It holds naught inside but a barren, wood floor covered with thick dust.

I step closer to the second door, nudging it open.

The door squeals on its hinges.

I tense in wait, my gaze darting to the slowly opening door and to the yet closed door down the hall.

No one comes.

I cross the threshold into a room of meager fare. A quilt adorns the bed and an ewer sits upon the dresser beside a mound of Devil's powder. What lay beyond the powder intrigues me more—a black candle, burned near to a nub, all its wax dry, pooled around it like a bed sheet folded upon itself in swirled waves. Behind the candle, a hand-drawn portrait of a face calls a memory in me from the life before.

Though the portrait depicts him young as I, there be no mistaking the face of a man who once wore many masks. Mercy and her brood named him Simon Campbell, whilst I think of him only as Paul Kelly.

I approach the dresser, taking up the portrait in hand.

The drawn, stern eyes threaten me submit and the life before bids me recall in equal measure the voice in which he cowed George and Sarah with. Other memories take hold also—how his laughter set my spirit to soar, the power in his embrace.

A moan from the adjoining room yanks me from such musings.

I tuck the portrait into my pocket and creep toward the door, peeking around the corner.

The moan comes again.

I slip out of the room and onto the landing, stealing toward the closed door at the hall's end. My breath sets me to panic as I reach for the handle.

It turns easy enough.

I press my back against the wall then open the door, its sharp-squealed hinges paining my ears. My body strains in wait of a war cry, a witch scream, anything.

Only silence waits.

Peeking into the room, my gasp ruins the quiet.

Putrid stench punches me hard in the nose, forcing me step back.

Iron cages line either side of the room, their bars running from floor to ceiling. A small wooden alley exists down the middle—a safe haven from the reach of those in cages.

I traipse inside the room, snorting the stench away with each step.

Rotted bodies lay inside several cells, their frames withered near to the bone, skin black and covered with sores and scars. Buckets stand full to the brim with foulness, pushed to the furthest edges of the cage as if the captives wished to distance themselves from the odor even in death.

My throat chokes on it and I turn to flee the room.

A raggedy, pale hand shoots from between the bars of a cage.

I fall back against the opposite cages, the hand waving in search of me.

"M-Mercy..." the woman pleads, her hand shaking more than her voice. "Mercy, please!"

Wispy white hair hangs off her scalp in patchwork fashion. Her vacant eyes search the room, as if she does not see me, but gathers someone is near. She looks a living corpse to my eyes, the same pox upon the other dead covering her skin as well.

"Mercy," she says. "Mercy...please, mercy."

"Mercy Lewis?" I ask.

"Pl-please..." the woman says. "Mercy, p-please."

"Mercy is dead," I say.

The woman continues her same plea, over and over, until I gather she knows naught of anything else in this world. She vacates the bars, falling into the corner, whimpering as she tucks her knees to her chest and rocks back and forth. "Mercy... Mercy..."

Pity bids me call out to her and end her suffering.

My mind warns doing so would leave evidence of my intrusion should Elisabeth or her waif return. I give the cell a wide berth, moving to leave the room.

A strong hand catches my hair and jerks me back against the bars.

"The Devil waits for us," a man hisses in my ear.

Fear hardens me. I lunge away, leaving a handful of my hair in his grip, and wheel about to his scorned laughter.

"His servants come soon." His eyes mad and teeth rotted black, he pushes his face full between the bars. "To coat me with sin in matching the dark of my soul. Come," he reaches his hand out the bars. "Come give yourself over also."

"Mercy!" the woman takes up her cry again. "Mercy, pl-please!"

I run from the room, her pleas and his laughter ringing in my ears as I slam the door closed behind me. I waste little time in flying down the steps and then fleeing out the window I sneaked through.

I hasten down the alley, their voices rampant in my mind.

I reach for the hilt of Father's dagger, my fingers trembling upon it, my breath rapid.

You are outmatched. Betty's words linger in my memory, as does Father's insistence that I flee, both their warnings resonating clear. No small part of me desires to flee south and inquire where to find her Judge Sewall. Aye, and beg his humble aid that he might see me safely away from this cursed city.

Fear swells within me, forcing me imagine Father and my other companions accosted and given to the horrors Elisabeth Hubbard visits upon those kept hidden inside her home.

My nails draw blood in my palm, wetting the hilt of Father's dagger. I will myself to strike fear from my heart, revisit the home, and give the mad woman the mercy she begged of me rather than leave her to suffer.

Then I witness the waif.

Strolling up the street, yawning as she comes, she enters the house with little regard that I watch her.

I ease back into the alley, questioning whether I should approach or no. The fear I felt gives over to hate, bidding me unleash a frenzy upon her.

Thoughts of Father caution elsewise, urging me lie in patient wait for Elisabeth to arrive or else allow the waif lead me to her.

I settle into the corner, my gaze leveled on the doorway, waiting.

The day passes with neither the waif leaving, nor Elisabeth returning. The door does not open until the sun fades and only then do I witness the waif again.

She locks the door, a scarlet, hooded garment tucked under her arm.

I follow her west.

She abandons the last piece of road and scurries across an open field toward the ocean.

The field provides me little cover, forcing me wait until she disappears opposite the hill before continuing my pursuit.

Even then, I keep my distance, careful not to give her any sight of me. I fall to my belly at the hillcrest, crawling toward the top and peeking over.

Fog crawls across the water, creeping onto land, near blinding my sight of the waif.

She hurries toward the rocky beach, pushing one of several small boats into the water. She leaps inside then takes up its oars, rowing out to sea.

The fog swallows her and the boat whole.

I count to twenty then rush down the hill, hauling one of the other boats toward the water. Unlike the waif, I am well practiced and avoid wading into the ocean. I shove off the land and leap inside the boat at the last, my weight carrying the boat into deeper water. The pair of oars feels foreign in my hands, the canoe I oft shared with Father requiring me use but one oar and allow him the steering.

I fit the oars into the metal rings and tug at them, testing their movement. Then I dip my oars deep and pull hard at them, remembering the words of my Father and our people—the water rewards skill, not panic.

Slowly, the shoreline fades, the fog enveloping me from its sight.

The gentler waves soon give way to others that buck beneath me. They raise me up and down, setting my stomach to lurch. Water crashes around me, soaking my robes.

My muscles ache and arms tire against the untiring power of the sea. The fog clouds my judgment, bidding me wonder if I have traveled a few feet off the coast or else a hundred leagues.

Still I row, hate fueling every muscle, every pull of the oars.

Mather. I imagine their groans saying. *Mather.*

I count the time with each row. My gaze wanders skyward in silent prayer. I long for a glimpse of the heavens that I might use the star bearings Father taught me.

The ancestors do not answer quick, yet they do lift the fog after a time.

At first, I believe the approaching shoreline that I left.

Then I witness a sight more pleasing than stars or sky.

Shadows darken the horizon, the tops of trees sway like skeletal fingers.

Deep in the forest, something glows—a rising fire, its flames pulsing to the tune of drums.

The gathering begins.

—twelve—

I CROUCH LOW IN MY BOAT, PEEKING OVER THE SIDE FOR ANY sight of those upon the shore.

Several other boats lay turned over fifty yards up the beach. There be no sign of their owners.

I slip over the side and dip into the water.

The cold lunges into my body, stabbing me, forcing me draw breath. My toes kick in search of a foothold, finding naught.

I sink up to my neck.

The weight of my robes tugs in threatened warning to carry me down to the ocean bottom.

I shed the robes and release my hold of the boat, then swim toward the shore with my hands and feet beneath the water to quiet my movement. I make for a plot of land further up the beach where there are no boats. The mucky bottom sucks at my feet as they touch down. I will myself on to more solid ground and soon collapse upon the snowy shore.

Move. A ghost of Father's voice urges me. *Move or die.*

The sight of fire deep inside the forest warms me.

Trembling, I rise from the beach and stumble toward the growing light. The movement feeds my soul. I plunge into the wooded depths.

The wilderness welcomes me.

Safe in its haven, I flit from tree to tree, steadily approaching the fire deeper inside the forest.

The drums beckon. Though their hypnotic beat plays not for me, I lose myself to their rhythm. Pipes take up the song also, the sharpness in their queer tone a reminder I hunt in foreign lands.

The forest rings with arrogance—voices laughing and calling to one another without regard their greater number means little to me. The lack of brush and bramble grants me clear sightlines through the forest.

I have little need of such gifts.

The woods are my home and the witches live only so long as I allow.

Even without the fire to guide me, I would find their trail easy enough to follow. Their tracks litter the snow alongside tree limbs broken by their carelessness. By the sound of them, several travel in groups.

My search for a lone witch does not take long. Her thrashing and cursing at the brambles draw my attention.

Like Elisabeth's waif, the witch keeps a scarlet robe tucked under her arm, almost as if she would not risk its purity despoiled by the woods and snow she struggles through.

I easily keep pace with her for a time to ensure she is well and truly alone.

She never once looks back as she stumbles on, unknowing I stalk her. The witch utters not even a surprised cry as I fall upon her, granting her a merciful and quick death.

I strip the dress she wears and shed my own wet clothes, trading mine for hers. Hers stink of unwashed filth and do little to warm me, though hers, at least, are dry. I tuck her body in the shadow of an old oak then don her scarlet hood to conceal my face.

The witch's blood staining my hand, the scattered glee and

laughter of her coven, they wake the hunter in me. All of my being wishes to fall upon the others and leave their bodies in the snow to fear the rest.

The thought of a greater prize bids me wait, for now.

I keep on toward their gathering, following their howls.

The bonfire grows brighter with every passing minute, thrice the height of any man. Indeed, it seems the witches set their torches to a home the flames burns so high.

I halt near the clearing and slink behind an elm, kneeling in patient wait, my mind and body turning to stone.

Around twenty exist near the flames, all of them dressed in the same scarlet robes. All shake and scratch at themselves. Some group together, conversing in hushed tones. A few sit alone, staring into the fire.

One walks among the others—Elisabeth Hubbard's waif.

My lip curls at the sight of her giving orders to several in the crowd.

They scatter at her words.

My gaze remains with her as she lights a torch from the great fire, then carries it to a pillared hill with two levels. She pauses at the first level, new fires sprouting to life as her torch kisses those previously unlit.

Gnarled and black-stained trees grow to either side of the stone steps, the tops of each sawed off, leaving little more than tall stumps.

The waif continues to the final level, gifting light to a trail of torches as she traipses up the wide and stone-carved steps. She walks a circle upon the hilltop, her torch granting flamed life to others staked around the hill, all creating a halo of light that flickers in tandem with the beating drums.

Their rhythm swells hate in me, my fingers quivering for action rather than merely watch the waif.

She kneels beside a stone table, gleaming black, at the circle's middle. Her flame kisses the kindling to either end, lighting the flames beneath two deep cauldrons.

The witches she spoke with appear out of the wilderness. They hurry up the steps after her, all of them with more wood to feed the cauldron fires.

My anger grows as each witch takes up a post and fans the flames.

The waif rises from the table, bearing a pair of wooden spoons near the size of oars to either cauldron and gifting them over.

The witches dip the spoons deep, slowly working their handles around the cauldron, the efforts requiring two witches each to move the spooned handles.

More witches dash through the wild around me, a few drawing so near they step within my grasp. I allow all pass by unharmed, waiting as I deem Father would.

The lot of them shake and shudder for need of Devil's powder as they run toward the fire, drawn to its power and the call of drums and flutes. I note none among them wear warm or rich garb, their bodies covered in dirt and grime.

Soon enough witches to fill a village ring the fire, dancing in tandem to the music. Native, white, black, brown—all colors of people under the heavens keep time to the rhythm.

My nose wrinkles at the inhuman scent of the teemed mass gathered round the flames, the heat sheening their unwashed skins with sweat, producing an inhuman odor liken to the rotted dead.

And throughout the dance, the waif stands atop the hill looking down on all.

I begin to think hunting the waif for naught when a deep, bellowing horn sounds, its call ringing over both drums and flutes, quieting both.

Like the whole of nature kneeling to the howl of an alpha wolf, those in the dancing circle turn silent in the horn's echo.

I awaken.

Several hooded, scarlet-robed figures lead out of the woodland dark. They raise ram horns to their lips. Hollowed and curved, the horns blow as one in sharp, shrieking bursts.

Behind them, a pair of hooded figures lead two horses—one a red mare, the other a black stallion. Elisabeth Hubbard sits upon the mare, garbed in a violet robe, her hair unbound, spilling over her shoulders.

My pulse quickens at the sight of her partner.

His robes bear the same hue as the stallion he rides upon. A bison bull's skull shields his face and head, its horns likes the ends of spears, tipped in blood.

A horde of hooded figures encircles Elisabeth and her partner—men for him, women for her.

Several in the dancing ring rush the riders, their hands outstretched, begging.

I question whether to join them, noting how near they draw to Elisabeth and her partner. A quick kill would send them to scatter, granting me an escape also.

But I do not seek their deaths alone.

I will have Cotton see me plain before the end and know my face.

The guardians shove the beggars away, keeping all from reaching either rider, whilst their fellows lead the horses to the stone steps.

Elisabeth and her partner dismount. They clasp hands and tread up the steps.

The horns sound again, this time to whistles and shouts from those in the dancing circle.

With their attentions turned, I slink out of hiding and slip among the gathering circle. I weave through the crowd, ever drawing closer to the steps. Each step shudders me that I will be found out and not accomplish my goal.

Still, I keep on, driving deeper among them.

A new train of hooded figures emerges from the woods. They lead three captives, bound and strung together, all of them garbed in white robes, their faces shielded by cloth sacks. Two walk tall, unrelenting as the witch crowd jeers at them with shrill voices. The third captive shrinks at every taunt, their head turning this way and that, searching out where the next blow should hail from.

My gut wrenches when the captives are led up the steps, their masters halting them at the first landing. I start forward.

Wait. A patient memory of my father whispers across my mind.

Elisabeth steps forward. "Sisters," she shouts to the crowd. "Brothers! Family all! Tonight we heed our Father's call."

Cacophony surrounds me.

Elisabeth grins. "Look you now on these three treacherous souls"—she points to the captives in white—"each a grievous sinner in the eyes of our Lord. Tonight, the Devil's Warlock reaps vengeance upon them!"

The witches clamor for more.

My fingers dance on the hilt of Father's dagger when the bone-masked man steps forward.

Wait...

"Our Master is not without mercy," says the Warlock, his voice booming deep. "Let the accused cry out for mercy, if they would claim such gifts as the Lord offers."

One of captives falls to their knees, trembling.

Though I cannot rightly hear their mumbled and whimpered voice, I take the captive for a woman.

"Prepare these others," says the Warlock. "And bring her to me."

The crowd stirs in eager whisper at the sight of the captive fetched off her knees and dragged up the stone steps. They separate the other two, leading them to the opposing trees, binding them to blackened trunks.

The guards allow the woman captive to fall before the feet of both the Warlock and Elisabeth.

The Warlock steps forward, removing her hood with a jerk.

The mad woman Elisabeth kept imprisoned in her home cringes to the crowd's jeers.

Relief spreads through me that the captive were not one of my companions. Then I think on the other two, tied to the trees.

My blood runs cold.

Andrew? I wonder, my sight turning from one captive to the next. *Ciquenackqua?*

"Confess." The Warlock pulls my attention as he wrangles the gag from the mad woman's mouth.

"Mercy..." she cries. "Mercy, please."

My soul weeps that it were not I to grant her desires before I left the home. Though I do naught to halt her fate, my fingers clench in silent rebuke.

"Confess," he commands her.

"M-Mercy…"

"Odd you should cry out for such." The Warlock draws close to her, his voice bellowing. "Did you not abandon your mistress of the same name?"

"Mercy, aye," says the woman.

Fury stirs in me at the name of my sister's killer. The mad woman's confession removing what guilt I felt for her.

"This sinner turned away from what our liege asked of her." The Warlock plays to the crowd. "Spurned her sisters and mistress when all needed her most, leaving them to the daggers of savages to save her own life." He points to the woman. "And she dared return to us, begging for the power to witness spirits again."

"Mercy…"

The Warlock ignores her pleas. "Our Lord demands obedience. Abandon the commands He entrusts you at your peril."

Near faster than my eye can follow, the Warlock unsheathes a bone-dagger and plunges it into the woman's chest. He removes it as quick and kicks her body hurtling down the steps.

My fingers tremble with desire of my bow, that I might fly arrows into his belly and watch him tumble down the steps to me.

The crowd roars approval.

"Only servants of the Christian god beg for mercy," Elisabeth shouts, descending the bloodied steps. "Fools that these fellows may be, they at least had sense to accept our Lord's judgment for their sins."

She approaches the captive on her right and removes his hood.

Despite the fervor with which he spoke to me, the other captive from her home trembles now in facing Elisabeth. His eyes searching for answer anywhere but in her face.

Did you serve Mercy Lewis too? I wonder on the captive.

"Confess," Elisabeth says.

"I-I am a blasphemer," he says. "My traitorous wife bid me lie on the spirits the Dark Lord has showed me. She asked me go to God and pray forgiveness."

"And did God show you favor?"

"No," says the man. "I f-felt naught but hunger."

"For his love?" Elisabeth asks.

"For powd—"

"To see spirits," she silences him.

Lies.

"You begged god's forgiveness and received no favor," says Elisabeth to her captive. "Ah, but spirits. Who here has not peered into the Invisible World as our Lord promised? Who among us does not wish to see them again?"

The crowd cheers.

Elisabeth grins. "Would you see spirits again?" she asks the captive. "Will you submit yourself to His judgment?"

"A-aye, mistress."

Elisabeth gazes up at the witches stirring the cauldron.

My throat runs dry as they ladle buckets inside then draw them out again, their wooden sides coated black.

The waif takes up both buckets by their handles, steam rising from them. She bears the buckets down the steps toward her mistress.

Elisabeth faces the crowd. "Will this man accept our Lord's judgment with a willing heart, or else cry out for mercy?"

I scarcely hear the crowd's answer, my heart thundering over them when Elisabeth receives a steaming bucket from the waif.

"Sinner," Elisabeth says to him. "You have blasphemed

against our Lord and so we commit you to the darkness now, that your skin may match your soul."

She upends her bucket over his head, coating him in black, oily pitch.

The crowd roars to the man's screams, crying for more as his shoulders pull at the bonds binding to the tree.

I bear the crowd in silent loathing as Elisabeth takes hold of the second bucket.

"Mercy," the man cries, the crazed whites of his eyes popping amid the black that coats his face. "Mercy!"

The crowd moans their disapproval.

"Listen to his cries." Elisabeth shouts above them. "Were he a true believer, our Lord protector should have safeguarded him against the pain."

I touch Father's dagger hilt, wondering if her Lord will safeguard her against the pain I will deal her.

As if reading my thoughts, Elisabeth wheels to the crowd, dipping her hand deep into the bucket.

Her display quiets the onlookers and gives me pause.

"Look you to me now!" She unveils her hand, showing it painted black and dripping. "My faith runs strong in our Lord. He frees me of pain and broke the shackles men would place on me. Only blasphemers cry out for the foreign god." She drops the bucket and looks to the waif. "Give the whelp his mercy."

The waif draws a bone-handled dagger, driving its tip through the man's chest before he can beg elsewise.

My anger matches the show Elisabeth makes for the crowd. She stalks to the third prisoner and yanks off his hood.

I thank the ancestors my pained cry goes unheard among the crowd.

His body and face broken, Father glares at Elisabeth with his lone good eye.

I start forward, pushing through the crowd, no longer caring if I go unseen or no. My hand flies to his dagger hilt and pulls to unsheathe it.

"Wait."

His voice halts me dead, the lone word spoke in the tongue of our people. His eye centers on me in silent rebuke. With a single word and glance, he bids me give up the crazed notion I might rescue him.

"A savage lover," Elisabeth says to the crowd. "Traitor to his own kind. Tell me, do you yet speak English, dog?"

I hesitate, wanting nothing more than to push my way up the steps and slay her.

Again, Father's stern gaze warns me against such actions.

"Confess," says Elisabeth.

My chest shudders when Father grins.

"Come, fair lass," he sings, his voice quiet and soft in repeating the lyrics Bishop oft sang us. "Just you and me."

Elisabeth steps back.

I grin at the sight of her so feared.

"We're bound for them colonies far o'er the sea..."

Father's voice sets the crowd to disquiet. A hush draws over them and not a few creep nearer to the outer fringes.

"Cease this," says Elisabeth. "And let you confess—"

"'Augh no,' she said, 'you stubborn ol' fool—'"

"Cease this!"

Father glares at Elisabeth. "'I've heard of those lands, and them savages cruel.'"

The witches look on one another and then to Elisabeth, rumored whispers stirring among them.

I stand wide-eyed, awestruck by Father's defiant show.

"So the Lord sent me a *bastard*," Father shouts, his voice carrying over Elisabeth's commands for buckets of pitch. "I came to name Priest."

The waif and cauldron servants bear their offerings to Elisabeth, near tripping over one another to reach their mistress.

"You have blasphemed against our Lord," says Elisabeth. "A grievous sin indeed—"

Father's song grows louder still, his voice gravelly and growling. "Ugly as sin, and a stubborn ol' beast."

Elisabeth bares her teeth. "And so we give you to the darkness now—"

"No," I say, my voice lost in Father's song.

"'Come lad,' said he. 'We'll hunt us some witches!'"

"That your skin may match your soul."

Blood streams down my wrist as I bite down to keep from screaming.

Elisabeth and the others move toward him, lifting their buckets.

Father never relents. "All o'er we went and by God, killed us them bitches!"

The buckets empty, their contents covering the whole of Father's face and body in steaming, black pitch.

Blood pools in my mouth as Father's body stiffens at the onslaught, pulling against his bonds. His head lolls back against the tree trunk, gasping for breath, snorting pitch clean of his nostrils.

"Do it." Elisabeth coos to him. "Beg me end your—"

Father raises his head and spits in her face. Then he chuckles. Several in the crowd flee the circle. More follow still when

Father opens his good eye, the lone bit of white among the dark. He turns his gaze on them, his chuckle turning to mad laughter.

"More," Elisabeth screams. "Bring me more!"

Only one heeds her, though he brings no bucket.

Father's finds me in the crowd, his gaze holding mine, as the Warlock thunders down the steps.

I step forward. *No...*

"*Wait.*" Father barks in our native tongue.

His voice halts me again, long enough for me to note there be no crossing the distance and reaching his side without Elisabeth or her minions learning I mean them harm.

My body quakes as I submit to Father's want.

The Warlock brings his dagger up for the killing stroke.

Father lifts his chin, accepting the blade, his gaze unwavering in the face of death.

My eyes shut to the tune of cheers.

-thirteen-

"Wait..." says Elisabeth.

My eyes flash open, finding her sidled between the two men.

The Warlock stays his hand. "What say you?"

Elisabeth dances her fingers across his dagger blade, pushing it away at the last. "I have long waited for such a test as this man offers," she says.

"Then you are a fool," says the Warlock. "This one will not bend nor break. I have seen enough to know."

Elisabeth fingers the hem of his cloak. "All men break. Give me time and I will learn where his true pain lies. Aye, and teach him the import of confession." She turns to the crowd. "Aye, the Lord will lead us to this man's breaking!"

The Warlock sheathes his dagger as the crowd sounds anew.

I release my breath, not realizing I held it back until now.

"Let the Great Rite begin!" Elisabeth cries.

The witches surge forward, near knocking me down, all of them pushing to reach the steps first.

I fall in with them, gazing up the landing as the Warlock and Elisabeth climb the steps and approach the stone table. When they turn back to face us, she holds a silver chalice, the size and weight of it requiring her use both hands to keep it aloft.

The drums sound anew, their rhythm slow and steady.

The witches around me chant as one. "*Hama shelabedi—hama shelabedi—hama shelabedi—hama shelabedi!*"

Elisabeth raises the offering toward the Warlock. "Mother, Mother, let these who would serve never tire!"

The drums quicken.

Tremors run up my spine, my ears filled with the chants of enemies surrounding me.

"Father, Father, hear my plea," cries the Warlock, lifting his bone-hilted dagger over top his head. "Let these who would call spirits, come unto thee!"

The Warlock lowers his blade, dipping it into the chalice.

The drums crescendo, pipes ringing in shrill whistles, all while the witches chant. *"Hama shelabedi—hama shelabedi—hama shelabedi—hama shelabedi!"*

"It is done," Elisabeth shouts, silencing one and all, lowering the chalice.

The waif appears from behind her. She kneels before Elisabeth, raising a long silver platelet over her head.

Elisabeth empties the chalice, raining a mound of Devil's powder onto the platelet. She gives the chalice away then approaches the steps. "Come, loyal servants," she beckons those of us at the bottom. "Receive our Lord's generous bounty."

The music sounds again as those around me race up the steps, all fighting to reach the top, slowing the gait of all.

I join their ranks, each step bringing me closer to the landing where Father resides. Not wishing to give away my presence, I shut my sight of him and will myself further up the steps.

The girl in front of me twitches with each step taken. "I need it," she whispers, more to herself than anyone near. "I need it, need it."

I follow her example, twitching my head, moving my shoulders in jerked motion so as to not stand out among the others.

Witches sated by Devil's powder retreat back down the hill, their faces awestruck. One stops, grabbing at my shoulder.

"Do you see?" she asks, showing me the back of her hand, turning it back and forth. "Do you see?"

Traces of powder linger beneath her nose and she laughs to herself, carrying on down the steps before I think to answer.

The line moves quick and soon I witness the tips of the Warlock's horns. Two steps further, and the whole of his bison skull looms within my sight. He and Elisabeth stand as one, the pair of them overseeing all who partake.

Each witch approaches only when beckoned. They kneel before the plate and snort a line of powder offered them by the waif.

I am but two witches from the line's end. Part of me wishes to descend the steps, vanish back into the woods, and trail the Warlock as he leaves.

My consciousness warns to leave now would be folly. That even if I should escape to the wilderness, I may not track the Warlock again.

I think of Father, how he endured his pain and welcomed the Warlock's blade to his throat without flinching.

My hand grazes his dagger.

I offer a silent prayer that the ancestors allow me a warrior's death. That I might die with my dagger in hand.

The next witch steps forward, leaving only one to separate the short distance between the Warlock and me. He shows the witches little regard, the tilt of his horns bidding me think him weary of the ceremony.

Alertness lives in Elisabeth. She turns at the approaching witch in front of me.

Drawing a deep breath, I twitch and reach inside my robe, a show to scratch my side. Instead, my fingers clasp tight around Father's dagger.

The witch kneels before the platelet.

I rush forward, drawing my blade.

Time slows.

I step atop the kneeled witch's back, using her to spring me higher as I fly toward the Warlock, blade raised over my head. The shriek of my war cry draws his attention.

He turns, too late for defense.

Using both hands, I plunge my Father's dagger into the Warlock's chest, the force of my fall sending us both hurtling backward. His ribs crack as I land all my weight atop him.

Screams invade my ears.

I do not allow them halt me, yanking off my hood that Cotton Mather might see my face and know me in our final moments.

"I am Red Banshee," I say. "Hear me—"

"D-De—" he sputters. "Deborah?"

The name halts me.

I clutch at the bison skull he wears, shoving off of him, revealing his face.

Isaac stares on me with dead eyes.

A lone clap draws my attention.

I wheel off Isaac's body, drawing Father's blade from his chest.

Elisabeth stands before a host of witches, all of them with daggers drawn. She lowers her hands, grinning. "I want her alive."

Her witches rush me as one.

I hardly have my second blade drawn when the first of them reaches me.

Her mistake is to not protect her legs.

I duck beneath her swipe, catching her heel, slicing and tossing her off balance.

Another dagger whistles over me.

I stand, catching the second witch in the throat with my blade, shoving her back to ward off the others. Yet for every one I fend off, others close in on me.

They taunt me with their blades, nicking my skin, bidding me turn to face them instead.

Their cackled laughter surrounds me.

I scream back, swiping my blades in wide arcs.

For each that backs off, another swoops in just after.

I realize their game before long—the same as a pack of wolves taking on a she-bear. Bit by bit, they seek to tire me with their numbers.

The Devil's powder grants them inhuman strength, their blows stronger than my own.

A weight falls on my back—a witch, snarling and hissing in my ear.

I duck to throw her off me.

Another spears my side, driving me to earth. Her companions catch my stabbing attempts. Heavy boots kick me in the ribs.

The witches cackle as I suck for air.

I roll to my stomach, attempting to draw my knees beneath me that I might stand.

A witch ventures too close.

I take her by surprise, catching her in the belly with Mercy's dagger.

She falls, screaming with it in her side.

Another pulls at my hair, jerking back to bare my neck.

"Pretty." Her craggy voice whispers, scratching her nails down my cheek, drawing blood. "So pretty."

I ignore her taunts. My gaze settles on the full moon and stars. I pray a witch brings a blade to my throat and that I may end my own life rather than allow them take me living.

None do.

My body weakens with each blow rained on me, though my resolve remains strong. I scream only when they wrench Father's dagger from my grasp.

The witches shriek back.

A knee to my face sets me tumbling back, my vision blinded, nose spurting blood.

The burn of rope ties my wrists together, siphoning off my blood flow.

I pull at it even still and receive another blow to my head in reward.

Black and red swirl my mind as the witches lift me under the arms, dragging me toward their mistress. They drop me on my knees before her, their strong hands keeping me from falling further.

"The daughter of Simon Campbell." Elisabeth gazes down on me. "Welcome."

I spit blood in her direction.

Elisabeth grins, wiping it away. "Shall we begin your breaking, child?"

She stands and claps her hands.

I close my eyes to right my mind from spinning and pray that I make an honorable death, as Father would. Yet when I look out on the world again, I face no dagger or noose. No hammer or axe.

Only the waif.

She kneels before me, holding the silver platelet aloft.

I blanch at the mound of Devil's powder.

"The Invisible World awaits," says Elisabeth. "Pray, let you breathe deep of our Lord's bounty and see spirits."

I grit my teeth, glaring up at her.

At her nod, the witches push my head down, forcing me toward the powder.

I blow hot breath at the mound, scattering much of it.

Elisabeth grabs a clutch of my hair and shoves my face well into the powder. "*Breathe.*"

I struggle to raise my head.

Elisabeth kicks me in the ribs, obliging me take breath.

Powder shoots up my nostrils and invades my lungs.

My body rages against the ambush, wracking me upon the ground. I gag at the bitter taste choking down my throat, its sand-like grains scratching my insides.

"Yes," Elisabeth coos. "*Breathe...*"

I hack at the burning in my throat and nose.

The witches release me.

My body seizes. My eyes feeling as though they pop from my skull.

Cackled laughter surrounds me, their voices like the stories of harpies Bishop once frighted me with. Their faces twist before me, melting like candles, their eyes glowing red.

I attempt to crawl away, my heart racing in panic.

Their laughter grows and turns deep, startling me all the more.

Elisabeth kneels in front of me. "Do you see?" she asks, her words slurring in my mind, as she lifts my hand.

Light pours from my fingertips in patterned waves. I sit on my heels, awestruck.

"Do you see?" Elisabeth asks, showing me her own hand, turning it over and around in sweeping movement.

I gasp at such beauty—all the colors of the rainbow dancing in her palm.

"The Invisible World," she says. "Within our grasp."

I reach to touch the vision in Elisabeth's hand, stopping short when my sister steps out of the crowd.

"S-Sarah?" I say.

Her hair gone, blood dripping down her forehead, a raccoon sits perched on her shoulder. "Why did you allow them take me, sister?" Sarah asks.

"Sarah," I cry. "I-I didn't—"

"*Sssssshame...*" The raccoon hisses at me. "*Sssssshame...*"

I scream at the sight of its blood-tainted fangs, and fall backward to the tune of more laughter.

"Why, Rebecca?" Sarah asks.

"*Sssssshame...*" Its voice follows me no matter where I turn.

Light touches race up my arms and legs like fingers grazing my skin.

I glance down—hundreds of spiders litter my body. They delve into my skin, moving in scattered, boiled lumps.

"Sarah, I'm sorry," I cry, rolling to my back, scratching to rid my skin of the spiders. "Father, save me! Father—"

The raccoon appears above me, perched on Sarah's shoulder, their eyes glowing red like all others in the crowd.

A demon approaches my sister, wrapping its arm about her.

"*Sssssshame...*" the raccoon hisses. "*Sssssshame...*"

My screams live on.

"Oh, yes," says the demon with Elisabeth's voice. "I will enjoy your breaking."

-fourteen-

TIME DOES NOT EXIST IN THE HELL ELISABETH KEEPS ME IN. No light to count the passing of day or night. No food or drink. She leaves me with only darkness and whispers.

"*Ssssshame…*" says one from the corner.

"*Why, sister?*" Sarah asks. "*Why did you allow them take me?*"

I clutch my knees close, resting my forehead upon them, hands clapped over my ears to shut out the voices. The cold of the iron manacles clapped round my wrists and ankles seeps through the whole of my body. The chains allow me but enough leave of the wall to reach the bucket her waif left me for my bodily waste.

I have grown numb to the stench wafting from it. For every use of the bucket, my thoughts drift to those overflowing in the cells inside Elisabeth's home and the memory of caged corpses. I think on the mad woman often, regretting I did not grant her plea, more in wonder how much time passed before madness overtook her.

I do not think myself near that brink yet, nor do I believe myself inside Elisabeth's home. Here the walls and floor are stone carved, ice-cold.

My shoulders twitch at the spiders continued crawl up my neck and into my cheeks.

"No…" I say to the dark, crossing my arms, turning my hands to fists beneath my pits, refusing the need to claw at my skin.

After a time, my skin feels raw from deep digging to pluck them free.

The spiders elude me always.

Hours pass. Or minutes.

My body continues seizing. I ball up upon the scattered remnants of soiled straw and scream my pain and fury.

Neither aids my cause.

No one answers. No one comes.

The all-consuming dark and whispered voices blur the lines of sleeping and wake.

A new vision visits me when a thick, wooden door swings open, the light blinding and yet a welcome respite from the dark. I cringe at the onslaught to my eyes and raise an arm to shield them.

A clamor of wood against stone echoes—the waif sets a chair near me—then her footsteps retreat to the doorway.

My eyes adjusting, I risk peeking out.

From where the chair is placed, I gather my chains will not allow me reach it.

"How fare you, child?" Elisabeth stands in the door, holding the torch aloft.

I scream at her, my chains pulling taut in a failed attempt to reach her.

"That well?" she mocks, resting the torch in a hook upon the wall. She walks to the chair, only several feet away. She looks around my cell. "I should have given you far warmer and brighter accommodations had you not stolen into my home."

Elisabeth reaches into her coat, removing the drawn portrait of my blood father, Simon Campbell. "Could it be you have forgotten the good doctor's face after all these years?"

My silence fills the void between us.

"Yes." Elisabeth says. "I thought so. You cannot have been more than a child when he was taken from you. Here"—she tosses the portrait at my feet—"let you keep it then. I have little need of such a thing. He lives in my mind, your father. His face never far from recall."

I push the portrait away.

"You scorn my gift?" she asks. "No matter. I bring another for you...and a visitor."

I look past her at the echo of approaching footsteps.

An unshapely shadow turns the corner into my cell, pausing in the doorway. Gasping at the smell, he pulls a kerchief from his pocket. He brings it to his nose in passing the waif.

"Mind your manners now, girl." Elisabeth draws my attention. "You sit in the presence of greatness."

"Come, dear," he says. "This one knows who I am. She came to find me...and I have so long waited to meet her."

"My Lord." Elisabeth bows her head, backing away. "The Reverend Cotton Mather."

Cotton limps into the room, more decrepit corpse than the demon I so long imagined him. Wincing, he groans in easing into the chair with Elisabeth's aid. His lips purse as he looks down his nose at me, the motion giving birth to several layers of fatty cheeks upon his neck.

I lunge.

My chains restrain me within inches of him. Their cold bite tears the scabs on my wrist anew. The warm of my blood staves off the cold as I stare on Cotton Mather.

"Indeed, this is a feral thing you have brought me, Elisabeth," he says, his gaze studying the whole of me. He turns to Elisabeth. "Pray, does it speak?"

My head pounds that the chains will not allow me bring him to his end.

"She will." Elisabeth leers at me. "In time."

"Ah, but will you fetch truth from her or lies, my dear?" Cotton asks.

"No doubt she will be like all the others come before her," says Elisabeth. "A shrieking hatchling at the first. A beautiful songbird thereafter."

I raise my chin, daring her approach.

Cotton sighs. "Would that it need not come to such torments." He coughs, hacking up bloody phlegm, spitting it at the last. "My body grows weary of this world."

"You will find a way, my Lord," says Elisabeth. "A means to fend off your sickness as you did the pox on all of Boston."

"No. Not this time. To say elsewise would be a lie." Cotton collapses back into the chair, dabbing his mouth with the kerchief, clearing his throat. "And lies are but the masks we don in public, a show for pretenders of likewise piety. None reveal their true face to the world."

I meet his stare that he might know I wear no mask now.

Cotton sighs. "Ah, but here"—he looks around my cell— "here we have little need of masks. The dark welcomes all secret truths." His gaze finds me. "And I know many of yours, Rebecca. Or should I name you Red Banshee?"

Fear wells within me at his knowing my names. I hide it deep within, keeping my silence.

"Your friends have lovely voices," says Cotton. "At least for one who knows how to tease such songs from untrained throats."

Elisabeth curtsies behind him, drawing my eye.

"I especially like your savage," Cotton continues. "*Ciquenackqua.*"

I bite my tongue, staring at the stone floor of my cell.

"But then, their kind has ever intrigued me most," he says. "They do not feel pain as we do. My studies prove this time and again." Cotton leans back, crossing one leg over the other. "I have witnessed them roasted over fires, turned slow like a hog upon a spit, and still they sing, even to their deaths. Truly fascinating specimens, the savages."

His easy tone sets my blood to boil, aiding me near forget the aching hunger coursing through me.

"Your friend, Ciquenackqua"—Cotton grins—"he fascinates me. He loves you, I think, as does Andrew Martin."

Elisabeth snorts. "Poor, deluded fools."

I grate my teeth as both speak of my friends easily, baiting me rise to their taunts.

"Aye," says Cotton quietly. "But then what man is not in the presence of such a wild beauty?" He folds his hands in his lap. "We men are simple beasts. Show us innocence and we corrupt it. Reveal a wild creature and we covet it. But a headstrong and wise woman"—he dips his chin to me—"what man knows what to do with such a creature?"

"You, my Lord," says Elisabeth.

"Aye." Cotton smiles. "But this one before me has no need of such gifts as I offer. She is headstrong already." He cocks his head. "But is she wise, as her father was?"

Elisabeth laughs.

"You mock her." Cotton's cheeks tighten. "And yet she slipped among your company and slew my favored son."

The scorn crossing Elisabeth's face bids me take some little joy.

"God is a cruel master, no?" Cotton sulks. "I long prayed for the prodigal son's return. Instead, He sends you to take the loyal one from me also."

Elisabeth steps forward, placing her hand upon his shoulder. "You yet have a daughter, my Lord. Loyal and ready for all that you command me."

"The world is not yet ready to allow women to hold sway, even those brilliant as you." Cotton pats her hand. "Indeed, I wonder if ever the world will be ready."

Cotton's eyes fall on me. "My, but you are a silent type." He laughs. "I were also for a time. God afflicted me with such stammering in my younger years that I should keep my prayers to myself rather than offer them up. My father taught it should teach me humility in the face of God." His lip curls. "Yours bid me rise up and take hold of destiny. Aye, he who aided me understands the curious nature of science and God. Secrets my father kept from me and the whole of mankind."

The rage with which he speaks of his father belittles the conflict in his eyes as he looks on me, his voice quieting.

"I loved your father, child. Aye, loved Simon so that I would have given him the whole world and a legacy for men to envy for the whole of time," says Cotton, his face pained. "And yet he scorned me. Why?"

I keep my silence.

"*Why?*" Cotton's voice rises. "I have long begged God provide some solace on the matter, yet He offers me no answer, nor even small comfort."

He leans closer toward me, though not within my reach.

"Pray, child," says Cotton. "Let you comfort me now and I will see you safely from this place. Teach me why your father abandoned me in our darkest hour, when I needed him most."

My shoulder twitches with the hunger.

"*Sssssshame...*"

Cotton follows my gaze to the corner. "You see it even now, the Invisible World, do you not?" He leans forward. "Pray tell me what you see. What do the voices say?"

My *manitous* sits in the corner, its beady eyes staring at me from behind the black-painted mask crossed over its eyes.

I sway back and forth, mumbling in answer.

Cotton leans closer. "What do they say?"

My chains snap taut as I lunge again. They draw my hands tight behind me, the pain in my shoulders bidding me cry out.

But no chains hold my neck.

I slam my forehead against Cotton's, our skulls cracking together.

Cotton falls back, moaning.

The heel of Elisabeth's boot breaks my nose and leaves me strewn upon the ground, blood pooling around me.

I crawl to my hands and knees, my gaze swirling.

Cotton holds his head, his face pale, breath labored.

Elisabeth steps forward. "Shall I loose her tongue, Lord?"

"No," says Cotton. "I will have my answer from her, but I will hear no false confession."

"She is a savage, Lord," says Elisabeth. "Aye, one who knows naught of the freedom that confession brings to the spirit. Mayhap we should teach her our Lord's grace for those who admit their transgressions and speak truth. A goodly example for her to model."

"Aye," says Cotton, after a time. "Bring her then."

I tense in wait for Elisabeth to approach me and release my chains.

Instead, the waif vanishes out of my cell.

Thoughts of my tortured companions dance across my mind. I steel myself for that to come, promising I will show Cotton and Elisabeth no emotion for whomever they bring before me.

I lose all such pretense when the waif reenters with a guest behind her.

Betty enters of her own accord, neither shackled nor any visible bonds laid upon her. She strides to Cotton's side, kneeling before him, and takes his hand in hers.

My anger wakes the shackles to strain my wrists from the pull I place on them.

"My child." Cotton places his hand under Betty's chin, bidding her look up. "How is it you come among us again?"

"This girl, sir," says Betty. "The daughter of Simon Campbell. She brought me here along with Mary Warren and the others I warned Elisabeth of. They desired your death at her hands, my Lord."

Rage seethes through me at her betrayal. Thoughts flood my mind as to when she turned on us, and how she sent word to Elisabeth.

"You are truly a goodly servant sent from God to stay their hands," says Cotton. "But pray, why should you keep such dark company as they?"

"I did not wish it, sir." Betty pulls away from him, her eyes pleading. "They brought me against my wishes. Aye, and under threat of my daughter's life if I refused them."

"Peace, child," says Cotton to Betty. "I wish you no harm

for your part in this. Where is your Susannah, now? It has been too long since last I saw her at a gathering."

"At my home, sir." Betty points at me. "With her brother."

I banish all thoughts of George, willing me forget him that it might prevent Cotton and his ilk from reading my face.

Elisabeth's grin bids me think it all for naught.

"Simon had a son?" Cotton asks, his voice a whisper.

"Aye," says Betty. "George, sir. He fell ill before our journey and she abandoned him to sickness. Vengeance is all that lives in her black heart, my Lord. Indeed, I think she should give her own soul if only she might take your life in trade."

"An unholy pact, if it be true." Cotton plays at disgust. "What tempts you to make such claims?"

"They be no claims, sir," says Betty. "Let you ask her why she kept Mary Warren in her company. Aye, and safeguarded Mary through heathen lands to bring her here."

Elisabeth kneels closer to Cotton's ear. "Betty speaks true, Lord. Mary Warren's loyalty ran deep to Campbell's daughter. Indeed, it took me far longer than I first credited Mary to tease such confession from her." Elisabeth turns on me. "Would you know the key I used to unlock her tongue? How Mary learned me all I should ever need know about you and your fellows?"

I quake at her words.

"Truth." Elisabeth grins. "You protected Mary only so you might betray her into my hands for furthering your own desires."

"Aye," says Cotton. "Just as Betty will now return to her home and deliver Simon's son to me."

My knees buckle at Betty's nod.

"How shall I tempt him here, sir?" Betty asks.

"You have your father's silver tongue, my dear," says Cotton. "I have little doubt you should find a way."

I spit blood at Betty, staining her dress. "Liar."

Betty ignores my taunt.

"Truth and love," says Cotton. "The greatest weapons in the Lord's arsenal. If you will not confess your father's secrets, Rebecca, perhaps we may yet convince your brother to speak in your stead."

"That man is no brother to me," I say. "Only another fool I convinced to follow me."

"She lies," says Betty. "One look upon his face and you will know him for Simon's son. He shares the same face as his father. Aye, even his eyes match, sir."

Cotton takes Betty's hand, bidding her stand. "Then go from here, good woman. Fly home and return with dear George. I would look on his face and see my old friend again."

"As it please you, sir," says Betty. She turns on her heel and strides from my cell.

"Liar!" I shriek.

"Well," says Cotton. "It seems this one speaks after all. Will you confess to your father's sins against me, girl? Will you answer for why he abandoned our common cause?"

"He was not my father," I say.

Cotton stands. "There is power in confession, child. Look you to Betty Barron just now if you would see my words true. She admitted her guilt and received forgiveness for her part in your murderous plot. Just as I should forgive you if—"

"No," I say, rising to my fullest stature.

"Your anger and pride keep you here," he says. "I, too, suffered from both once. Fasting and fervent prayer rid them from my soul and taught me humility." He glances around my cell. "Perhaps solitude will learn you such values also."

"And perhaps my gift learned you some notion of my fury," I say.

Cotton touches his forehead, wincing. "Aye. I do you too much credit. Indeed, now I think on it, mayhap Elisabeth has the right of it."

Elisabeth steps forward. "How so, my Lord?"

Cotton turns his stare on me. "She is a savage. A heathen who rejects God and His mercy."

"Then her soul is damned to Hell," says Elisabeth.

"Aye, but we may yet save her," says Cotton. "God's cleansing waters are ever open to those who seek Him out."

I like the look Elisabeth gives not at all.

Cotton strides from the room, accompanied by the waif.

Elisabeth waits until long after they are gone before she turns on me. "That were a foolish thing you did. He would have left you to rot in darkness, but now you are given over to me. Do you know why I stand before you now rather than any other of my Salem sisters?"

She slinks to Cotton's chair, her eyes shining in the torchlight.

"Patience," she says. "Cotton's death draws nigh and so he has little time for patience. In times past, he would have you starve. Now he asks me tease such confessions from you quick as to set his mind at ease before he leaves this world."

"And you will not?" I ask.

Elisabeth laughs as she reaches into her cloak and removes a vial of Devil's powder.

I stave off the moan my body would bid me give up for but a taste of the powder.

Elisabeth plays with the stopper, tugging it free. "Your father saw promise in me, just as Cotton does. My uncle saw it before either of them. Patient and calculating, your father considered my uncle his nearest equal, I think, far more so than those others he conspired with, Thomas Putnam and the Reverend Parris."

Elisabeth snorts the powder quick, her eyes widening. She brings the back of her finger to her nose, not wasting a lone grain of powder, and snorts the remainder too.

I despise the weakness in me that delights in her removing such temptation.

Elisabeth smiles. "Your father oft whispered such things to me that I keep still. 'A preacher to sway them, a soldier to fright them, and a doctor to teach them,' he said to me."

She settles in Cotton's chair, laxing her body, rubbing against the chair as if to scratch her back.

"Abigail was always a fervent liar," says Elisabeth. "Just like her uncle. And Mercy kept to the brutish ways Putnam learned her. But I..." She turns her hand over and around in front of her, eyes widening at the sight. "My uncle were a doctor and learned of pain, how to heal—" She turns her gaze on me. "And how to deal it."

I meet her stare.

"A challenge, then." she says. "I do so love those who seek testing me. But first, I owe you a gift in recompense for the service you did me."

She digs into her pockets again and produces a new vial. There be no Devil's powder inside, only crimson liquid.

"Here," she holds it in her palm, offering it to me. "Drink this and be free."

The hunger lurches in me and my shoulder twitches.

"You are a strong one, aren't you?" Elisabeth asks. "Already you feel the lack of powder. The glorious aching need to see spirits."

The spiders crawl through me at her words. It takes all my power not to scratch them.

"Take this, girl." Elisabeth places the vial on the floor, rolling it toward me. "Drink your pain away."

I turn my stare from the vial, glaring at her.

"I do not offer mercy lightly," she says. "Drink down my gift to you for clearing my ascent to power."

"No."

"Your murder of that poor, innocent, young man. Isaac, the Devil's Warlock." Elisabeth feigns sadness, the truth of it living in her eyes. "Say rather a bastard born of Mercy's whoring ways."

My pulse quickens at her words.

"Ah, she spoke of him to you, did she not?" says Elisabeth, her face drawn curious.

My gaze falls to the floor, my mind turning to Mercy's last conversation with Father. Her words of the child he put in her belly before abandoning her.

I choke back the bile rising in my throat.

Elisabeth stomps her foot, drawing my focus. "What did she say to you of Isaac?"

"She mentioned nothing," I force myself look on her. "One finds it hard to speak with their throat cut."

"Do not toy with me, girl." Elisabeth eases back into her chair. "I knew you for a liar the moment you stepped in my home. Even the basest of Mercy's servants would not dare cross into my domain and risk my wrath."

"Come closer," I say, my chains rattling as I stand. "And allow us learn whose wrath wins out."

Elisabeth scowls. "Wrath is an odd thing. Most who speak of it conjure righteous destruction. Hellfire and brimstone, blood and death." Her cheeks tighten. "Such drivel bores me. Quiet, patient wrath interests me far more. Salem taught me such lessons and they have served me well all the rest of my days. Perhaps I will learn you of the power in it before the end."

She motions to the vial.

"Unless you would rather drink of my mercy," she says. "I will not offer it again."

I pick up the vial, removing the stopper. Then I drain its contents upon the floor.

"So," she says, her grin widening. "You choose play."

"I choose life."

"Aye, you will keep that for now." Elisabeth laughs. "The good reverend would have me teach you humility, but he said nothing of the games we might play in the waiting time." She steps forward. "And we shall play many games, you and I."

I stand taller to spite her. "Mercy Lewis sought such sport with me, and Abigail Williams with my sister." I step close as I am able to her. "Both fed the worms led long ago. So it will be with you."

"Fool girl. Do you not know where you are? This *is* hell." Elisabeth cackles. "The worms feed on your corpse already. Aye, and all those you love dear. Think you spirits should speak if you were not one of them?"

"You lie." My tone belies my doubt.

"No," says Elisabeth. "This is but one of the many plains of hell and we its fallen angels. But there may yet be redemption for us if we are willing to serve."

"I will not," I say.

"You need not serve as others have," says Elisabeth. "You need only confess why your father abandoned our good Reverend Mather. Or else let you say that Simon Campbell were a true warlock. Aye, one who bewitched the Reverend Mather and made him seek out the Invisible World. Such confessions would suffice. You need only speak them to serve."

My shoulders twitch.

Elisabeth grins. "Already your body hungers, no?" She steps closer. "The ache your body feels now is but the first step of many, all of them descending into the abyss. Will you venture there and find your way toward light before madness overtakes you?" She reaches into her robes and produces a vial of Devil's powder. "Or confess and be healed?"

My gut twists with the hunger pains. The spiders scurry faster throughout my body.

"Why, sister?" the phantom voice of Sarah asks.

"Shame..."

Trembling, I grit my teeth and glare at Elisabeth. "The only thing I will serve your master is vengeance," I say. "Though you should not live to see it."

"Strong words," she says. "Shall we test their resolve?"

Elisabeth pushes the chair toward the door. She kneels in its former place, removing the vial stopper, pouring the small mound of powder upon the floor. "Your friends mentioned you as a hunter. Have you ever happened upon a trap and found your only prize a paw the beast gnawed off and left behind?"

I stare on the powder, my body twitching.

"What will you do, Rebecca"—Elisabeth reaches the door of my cell—"when the hunger takes full hold of you?"

Elisabeth shuts the door slowly, the groan of hinges matching the one my body makes in need of powder. She leaves me the torch upon the wall, the light from its flames furthering my torment by the powder that lay beyond my reach.

-fifteen-

I WAKE TO THE HUNGER.

The mound of powder Elisabeth left torments me from afar.

I pull at my chains, struggling to reach but a few grains to sate me.

Elisabeth knew her work well—the mound remains untouched as pain ravages my body, convulsing me at its whims.

For every small relief, the seizing overtakes me not long after.

"Sarah..."

"Leave me!" I scream to the voices and the pain.

"As you left me?"

I open my eyes, finding Sarah seated in the corner.

"S-sister..." I reach to her. "Sarah, please."

"You call her sister?" a familiar spirit whispers in my ear.

I wheel about, facing Mercy Lewis. My face twists. *"You."*

"Me..." Mercy smiles and raises her dagger.

I throw myself against her, screaming. Stealing her dagger away, I shove her against the wall and marry the dagger's blade to her throat, coating the wall red.

She falls at my feet, face down in a pool of her own blood.

I nudge Mercy to ensure her dead.

Her neck turns and her hair falls away, revealing not Mercy... but Sarah.

"Why, sister?" she asks me. *"Why did you allow them take me?"*

A weighted ball of fur lands upon my head, shrieking in my ears.

I glimpse its ringed tail and fight to rid myself of it, feeling the raccoon's nails dig into my skin, drawing blood. Catching hold of its leg, I fling it free of me, into the woods.

"Rebecca..."

I spin to the voices, singing my name in blissful harmony.

Sarah and Hannah stand upon the banks of some nameless river of blood. Bishop waits with them also, holding the hand of a woman I do not recognize by face. They wave as one, bidding me cross.

I start toward the waters.

A lone figure rises from its depths. Blood and blackness coat near the whole of his face and body, all save for his eyes. They glow white as he wades toward me, his presence barring me from joining the company of the dead.

"Shame..." the voice of Father fears me, growing louder with each step he takes. *"Shame!"*

I cower upon the beach. "F-Father...Father, please."

He opens his mouth, hissing at me.

Sand clutches my legs, sucking me into its depths.

I struggle against its pull. My fight serves only to sink me faster. I flail for Father.

The demon Black Pilgrim mocks my plight with the glow of his eyes.

"Shame..." he says.

Sand fills my nose, scratches my throat.

The night swallows me whole and darkness wraps me in its icy embrace.

I wake to a cold sweat. My body trembles with hunger, but not for powder. The whispers continue their call of me, now fainter. The number of spiders lessens, their bite no longer requiring me reach out to halt their scurrying in my flesh.

"I-I will serve h-him v-vengeance," I say to the darkness, willing myself take courage and continue beating back the visions.

Exhaustion casts me in dreamless sleep.

When I wake again, the voices and spiders have gone. Only a vision of Elisabeth's waif, standing in the door of my cell, remains. Several hooded men enter at her command. Their shoulders twitch as they release me from the wall.

I collapse into their arms, my mind reeling from the light.

They bear me out of the cell and up a dim, stony hall.

Through the bars of one cell, I glimpse a prisoner's battered and bloodied face. He lay on his stomach, his mouth gagged. Ropes bind his hands to his feet, keeping all aloft, forcing him arch his back and hold the position.

"A-Andrew," I say, struggling to free myself of my keepers.

Purple bruises litter his body and head, yet still he turns at my voice. Anguish floods his face the moment our eyes meet.

"Put her in the dark," says the waif.

One of her fellows raps me on the head, dizzying me anew.

Another throws a mildewed bag over my head.

My stomach heaving, I gag at the bag's odor and thank the ancestors there be no food in me to vomit.

The waif and her company drag me onward.

I count several flights of steps—some wood, others stone—before the air turns colder and my feet graze snow. My breath quickens at the whinny of horses and creaking of wagon wheels. My captors lead me step through drifts up to my naked knees.

"All right, lads," cries the waif. "Get her in."

Strong arms lift me from the snow.

In blind waves, I kick and punch as best my shackles will allow. My blows graze off their persons.

They heave me away.

My stomach flutters with weightlessness. I land upon a wooden base that steals my breath. Unknown hands chain me to a new wall whilst I suck for air.

Hinges and leather squeak. A door slams closed. Voices call out orders.

The floor jerks beneath me to creaking wheels and the footfalls of horses.

I tug the hooded bag off my head and find similar dark.

A rustled movement hails from the opposite corner.

"W-who are you?" I ask.

"A traitor, the same as you—"

I gasp at her voice.

"Though you, at least, have courage."

"Mary," I say, my bonds pulled taut as I attempt drawing near her. "Or are you another spirit sent to haunt me?"

"I am yet flesh and blood," she says. "Though I fear soon we shall both be two more souls given to the Invisible World."

"What cause have you to believe such things?"

"What cause have you not to?" Mary asks.

My gut wrenches with the thought.

The wagon continues bumping beneath us, bearing us away.

"They have no need to kill us," I say. "This is but more sport for Elisabeth only. No doubt she means to fear us with the unknown."

"The known fears me now," says Mary.

"Death?" I ask.

"Aye," she says. "But death would be a welcome release from the torture Elisabeth visits on me noon and night. Have you seen the others?"

"Andrew only," I say. "Bound and gagged, but living."

"And Betty?" she asks. "What of her?"

"Gone."

Mary sighs. "I saw them drag Ciquenackqua away days ago. The guards returned alone." Her tone drops. "Brave lad, he was. Aye, but he should have left Andrew and me when they came for us. God knows he could have slipped away in the chaos of it all."

My head leans against the wall.

"Why did he not run?" Mary asks, her voice shattered. "Foolish boy. He *should* have run, as any sane person ought do. Instead, he fought to save me. Just as Andrew quit his own fight on their promise to spare my life."

"Aye," I say, imagining Ciquenackqua leaping down the steps, his father's war club singing against the skulls of those invading the inn. "I imagine they both did."

"But why?" asks Mary. "I have asked myself that all these long hours since. I were no kin to them, nor even friend. Still they fought. Why?"

"You were among our company. Mayhap they believed you were true to our cause." I struggle with the words. "As I should have believed in you also."

The wagon rumbles beneath us, forcing me hold tight against the wall before leveling off anew.

"Forgive me, Mary," I say, after a time. "It were wrong of me to force your company all this way."

"I have wronged many in this life," she says. "No doubt their souls wait for me at the gates of hell. I would not add yours to their company for the wrongs I have done you."

"What wrongs?" I ask.

She keeps her silence for a time, though her sobs cut through the winds whistling through the cracks of our wagon, singing their cold song.

"I told." Mary sputters. "Confessed all your secrets but one. F-forgive me my anger, Rebecca, I beg you. I held such plans and plots of yours for days until Elisabeth told me of your intent to give me over."

I sit up. "I swear on my soul that I never meant to give you over, Mary. Only meant to draw her out with the promise of you."

"*Only*," she says. "If ever there were a word God should banish from our tongues it be that one. I only meant to join my Salem sisters at the dance. Aye, sought welcome among them and friendly gossip. All that has befallen me in my whole life came on account of only."

My chin dips at her words, the phantom voice ringing in my head. *Shame...*

"Such things matter little now, I suppose," says Mary. "We are both betrayers riding to our doom. I pray only that God allows me keep the last of your secrets before the end."

I straighten, tugging against my bonds. "What be that, Mary?"

"George," she says. "Elisabeth teased all knowledge from me, but his safekeeping."

Thoughts of my brother visit me as the wagon rolls along, bumping through the snow and over hill. His last words of placing my trust in others haunt me now Mary speaks of her loyalty to him. I ponder on whether to make known Betty's betrayal to Mary or no.

Her pride for safeguarding my brother bids me keep such knowledge quiet.

"You are a good woman, Mary Warren," I say. "A far better one than I ever credited you."

"A coward only," says Mary. "Craven as Judas himself. Even now, I know in my heart that I should give George up in exchange for my own life," she says through her tears. "And all after both he and Hannah ever showed me naught but kindness. Did George ever share with you the time he beat my husband to a bloodied mess?"

"No."

"Aye, he did," says Mary. "Beat him until he could not walk upon noting the bruises on my face, then warned my husband the next fist he landed upon me would be his death. Never in my whole life has such a man looked after me, as your brother did. Yet even now I think how I should betray him to save my own soul."

"And yet you have not," I say. "Nor will you."

"Aye," says Mary. "Only for distrust of Elisabeth. Were she an honest woman to make such promises, I have little doubt I should accept her offer."

"I do not believe that."

Mary barks a laugh. "You know me better than I know myself?"

"Not I."

"Who then?"

"George," I say. "He bid me put my trust in you before we left Betty's home. Asked that I believe in your goodness."

My voice cracks at hearing her cry. "Would that I had done then as I believe in it now."

"Only a fool would put their faith in me," she says, after a time. "I am a coward."

"You are not," I say.

"*I am,*" says Mary. "Have been the whole of my years. All know me as such. My master, John Proctor, knew I should wilt with only the threat of his fists, just as my husband did. Aye, just as your father saw fit to make example of me to the other girls."

"And yet it were you alone of all the girls to break from their company and speak truth to the people of Salem," I say. "You to name them liars."

"I did," says Mary. "And then all those innocent in Salem hung when I wilted anew, their necks stretched as I looked on."

"Those days were not this one, Mary," I say.

"Aye," she says. "This be the last of them."

The quiet grows between us as the wagon rolls on. I pray to the ancestors, begging them allow me make a brave end of my life and keep safe those of my friends who yet live.

The wagon rolls to a stop. A leather flap opens, revealing a clear night sky and Elisabeth's witches. They climb into the wagon, unarmed, approaching us slowly.

Mary struggles against them.

The witches taunt her when she cries out at their touch.

I give them no such pleasure. My gaze turns to the stars as the witches untie my bonds, freeing me of the wagon side, hauling me to the edge. I shrug off their clutches, leaving the wagon of my own free will.

A line of torches leads toward a stone bridge. Elisabeth waits at its middle, surrounded by her followers.

"Come on then," says the waif to me. "Haven't got all night, have we?"

My legs wobble for lack of use as my feet settle into snow. I cling to the wagon side, then force myself stand tall.

"Lead on," I say to the waif.

She grins and turns on her heel, waving us follow.

Witches surround Mary and me, jabbing us move forward.

The desire to fight them lives strong in me. A voice of reason tells me this lot should relish such an opportunity. I walk on.

The stars call back my gaze. Memories of Bishop's stories flood my mind, his words that stars were the spirits of good men and women, shining their light to guide us and ward off even the darkest nights. The thought of seeing him and Sarah again gives me courage to trudge the snowy path with my head held high.

The waif halts before we step onto the bridge, stopping us upon the banks.

The river lay near iced over save for a single, gaping hole, its waters black.

Mary's panted breath sets the frozen hairs on my skin to standing, her fear calling me join her in it.

I fight against such notions, willing my body not bend nor break.

Elisabeth strides forward, her gaze wavering between the pair of us. She stops shy of the bridge end, her focus settling on me. She grins. "Bring her."

My muscles tense in wait for the witches to take hold of me.

They take Mary instead.

"Rebecca," she calls, her feet stumbling as they drag her up the bridge.

"Stay strong, Mary!" I shout. "You can—"

The waif knocks me down with a rap of her baton to the back of my knees. "Shut your 'ole," she commands. "It's not your time yet."

Witches lift me from the ground, keeping their hold to stop me from falling again.

"Mary Warren," says Elisabeth, "you are charged with blasphemy against our Lord—"

"Lies!" Mary shouts.

"Conspiring murder of the Reverend Cotton Mather—"

"Elisabeth, please!"

"And practicing the dark arts," Elisabeth finishes. "Will you confess to these crimes and save your soul?"

"A-aye," says Mary. "I have done them all."

Elisabeth nods. "And did you sign your name to the Devil's book?"

"I did," says Mary. "The same night as you, Elisabeth Hubbard. The same as you all here have!"

I glance to the stars, praying Mary keep her dignity.

Elisabeth clears her throat. "Our sins are not those in question this night."

"I have confessed my sins," says Mary. "Is that not enough to save my soul?"

"You know the good book as well as I, Mary," says Elisabeth. "Confession is but the first step to salvation. Only those who are baptized may receive God's grace."

My heart pounds as two men move Mary near the bridge edge.

"Without baptism," says Elisabeth, "we are damned—"

"My soul were damned long ago," says Mary. "Not even holy water may save it now."

"If you will not save your soul, mayhap you would keep your life instead." Elisabeth cocks her head. "Such as it is."

"Aye, I would keep it," says Mary.

"Good." Elisabeth purrs before turning her gaze on me. "Are there any here among us who joined you in signing the Devil's book, Mary Warren?"

Mary's eyes flirt toward me. "N-no."

Elisabeth grins. "You know this game well, Mary. I cannot allow you go free if you will not confess all you know."

Mary meets my stare, her jaw trembling. "Th-those days are not this one, Elisabeth."

"What say you?" Elisabeth asks.

"The dead of Salem cry out for righteous vengeance," says Mary, her voice growing louder. "They sing our names even now, bidding a banshee carry us to the depths of hell."

"It will be you alone to visit there," says Elisabeth. "Unless you con—"

"I will not name her!"

"Pride cometh before the fall, sister," says Elisabeth. "If you will not confess, you leave me little choice as to how I might ascertain your guilt or innocence. Perhaps a test be the surest way."

My stomach pains as Elisabeth backs away.

"Mary Warren," she says. "You stand accused of many crimes, consorting with spirits and witchcraft chief among them."

"I am no witch," says Mary. "Only a fool who played at one."

"Aye, a fool who betrayed us," says Elisabeth. "We Salem sisters carried out the good Lord's work while it were you that confessed to witchery in the courts. This night we will have the truth of it."

At Elisabeth's nod, one of the hooded men knocks the wind from Mary.

Witches descend on her, binding her feet to her hands.

"No…" I say at the realization of what they intend for her.

"Quiet." The waif slaps the back of my head.

Mary pulls against her bonds, cursing.

The witches finish their chore.

The hooded men lift her to sit on the stone wall, keeping her balanced, halting her fall.

"Please, Elisabeth." Mary shudders, casting her gaze over the bridge side toward the gaping hole in the ice.

Elisabeth steps close. "Baptism is the only way to salvation, Mary."

"Not this way," Mary sobs. "Not like this."

"Leave her," I shout at Elisabeth. "I am the one you want."

Again, the waif silences me, rapping me harder.

My captors jerk me stand, overpowering me.

Elisabeth turns to her followers. "And as they went on their way, they came unto a certain water—"

"Please," Mary cries.

"And the eunuch said, 'See, here is water. What doth hinder me to be baptized?'"

"Elisabeth, I beg you!"

I bow my head, praying to the ancestors that Elisabeth performs all only in show. A display meant to fear me, or else give Mary cause to confess further knowledge.

Elisabeth's voice grows with each passing moment. "And Philip said, 'If thou believest with all thine heart, thou mayest.'"

"*Please!*"

"And he commanded the chariot stand still," says Elisabeth,

turning slow, laying her hand on Mary's shoulder. "And they went down both into the water, both Philip and the eunuch—"

"God save me!" Mary cries to the heavens.

"And he baptized him!"

Elisabeth sends Mary hurtling backward off the bridge, falling through the hole in the ice. A plume of black water rockets skyward and wets me on the shore.

The fight in me blossoms.

Several guards and the waif keep me from rushing out onto the ice.

I fall to my knees, retching air, spittle drooling from my lips, all whilst I watch the hole in the ice, willing Mary breach the surface.

Elisabeth stands upon the bridge, her arms raised to the heavens in praise. "And when they were come up out of the water, the Spirit of the Lord caught away Philip, that the eunuch saw him no more"—she gazes down at the ice-hole—"and he went on his way rejoicing."

Tuning out her voice, my stare remains on the water long after I know it all for naught.

A spark flames on the opposite bank. It passes on, lighting several others, revealing more of Elisabeth's followers. They step from the wooded depths, bearing a new prisoner between them, and cast him to his knees. One holds a torch near the prisoner's face that I might better recognize my father.

The followers look to Elisabeth on the bridge.

So, too, do I, finding she watches me.

Elisabeth grins. "Bring her."

-sixteen-

THE WITCHES BEAR ME UP THE BRIDGE, CASTING ME BEFORE Elisabeth.

Father watches me from the opposite bank, the bruise on his eye lessened, granting him full power of his sight. Naked save for a soiled loincloth, traces of the black tar yet line his skin. The remainder of skin be mottled red, scrubbed clean as if by a rake's end.

"A foul beast," says Elisabeth. "Isn't he?"

I look on her face. "Who is he?"

Elisabeth smiles. "Why must you persist with lies? I know all your secrets, girl." She steps nearer me. "Does it pain you to see the man you name father brought so low?"

"I do not know him."

"No? Well, let us pray the son of Captain John Alden knows you then." Elisabeth grabs a clutch of my hair, forcing my face toward Father. "Look to me, bastard!"

Steam pours from Father's nostrils, the violence in his eyes frighting me.

"Did you think I should not remember your face, Alden?" Elisabeth asks. "Even with your heathen mother's whore's blood there be no mistaking the Captain's traitorous eyes gifted you. Too long your family has held this new world back."

Father says naught in reply, though quiet rage lights his eyes.

Elisabeth leans close. "Do you think he loves you, dear?" she asks. "My Salem sisters believed he loved them also once, and such affections near broke our company."

Elisabeth releases her hold on my hair.

"Did Mercy tell you, Alden?" she asks. "Is that what drove this girl here? To find your bastard son and continue the line of savage-lovers and usurpers?"

The wind gives her more answer than Father or I.

"Odd that your son should have become one of us," she says to him. "Stranger still that your adopted daughter should see him from this world, not that I expect you should care of such news. You abandoned him just as you left my sisters to torment and grief. Aye, just as I warned both that you would. The hearts of men are fickle things, concerned only with what lay in their sight."

Father's gaze does not waver.

"Some insist blood runs thicker than water." Elisabeth strokes my cheek. "I wonder...will the sight of your torment loose his tongue, or will your adopted father keep his unrelenting pride?"

My eyes sting with rage. "Do your work, witch."

"I am no witch," says Elisabeth. "Only a servant to dole out the Lord's justice."

She steps back and hooded women approach me, tying a rope around my waist. Securing it, they fan out across the bridge, uncoiling the rope, taking up positions several feet apart.

The stars call me as Elisabeth's followers lead me toward the ledge and seat me upon the wall.

"Let us give thanks to God," says Elisabeth. "He welcomed Mary Warren into His fold this night, the truth in her words made known to all when she did not float to the surface."

I close my eyes as her followers lift their voices in thanks.

"Now, we bring to His judgment this new sinner," she says. "The spawn of a most evil man and minion of savages. She came seeking our destruction, but the Lord instead delivered her into our hands. Will she accept grace, as Mary Warren did, or will her pagan gods swoop down and free her of the saving waters?"

"Grace!" The followers shout.

"No," says Elisabeth. "It is not for us sinners here to decide her fate. For that we must trust in the Lord and give her over to His wisdom." She grins. "Unless, of course, she would confess her sins."

"You will not fear me as you did Mary," I say.

Elisabeth leans to my ear. "It is not your fear I seek. Only your breaking"—she glances at Father—"and his."

"You will have neither." I hiss.

Elisabeth faces her followers. "Truth and love—the greatest weapons in the Lord's arsenal. Tonight we weigh their worth." She turns to me. "Rebecca Campbell, we bid you abandon your savage ways—"

My chest pains at her words.

"Accept the Lord's salvation and welcome Him into your heart—"

I glance at Father as Elisabeth lays her hands on my shoulders.

"And let your soul fly to Heaven."

His pained face sticks in my mind as Elisabeth sends me tumbling off the edge.

The drop flutters my stomach, my body somersaulting end over end.

My back slaps hard on the water surface. A frozen blanket wraps the whole of my body, the frigid temperature yanking breath from my lungs.

Darkness and the scattered bubbles of my wasted breath swirl about me.

I twist and churn to free my hands from behind my back.

The rope bindings prevent it. So, too, do the chains shackling my ankles hold my kicks.

The weight of my chains sinks me deeper.

Thin tendrils brush against my legs, tickling my shins with their icy touch, wrapping round me.

I soon learn them no tendrils at all.

Suspended around her, Mary Warren's hair clears from her face in the wake of my panic. Her eyes lay open in deathly stare, her legs trapped up to her knees in the muck bed, her body tipped back and lain in the same muck my chains carry me into.

The muck sucks at my ankles, pulling me down.

I strive to push off it, swirling a cloud of dark.

The muck sinks me deeper.

I clutch at Mary's shoulders, attempting to leverage myself free.

My chest thunders for air, my mind popping spots of black and white.

The rope round my waist grows taut. It pulls me from the muck, angling me away, drawing me upward.

I give up my last breath.

The cold invades me. It shudders my throat, closing it full up, gagging me.

My muscles stiffen, my neck twisting in search of air.

The rope pulls harder.

I breach coughing, choking.

Elisabeth's followers continue their pull of the rope, hauling me onto the ice.

I collapse upon its frozen surface, vomiting stream after stream of water. The ice gnaws at my skin. I roll to my back and look on the stars, near weeping at the sight of them, as my body shudders at the blessed, replenishing air.

The waif and my captors lift me under my arms and bear me to the opposite bank.

I do naught to stop them, my toes grazing the ice all the way.

They fall me near Father, dropping me on my knees.

I welcome the pain of each stabbing breath, relishing the taste of air upon my tongue.

A withered hand grasps my chin, forcing me look up.

I glare into the eyes of Cotton Mather.

"None the worse for wear," he says, more to himself than I. "No doubt she will run free through the fields come spring."

Cotton releases his hold of me. "There," he says to Father. "You see, Alden? She lives. I have honored my part." Cotton draws a vial of liquid from his robes, the contents crimson in the torchlight. He pulls the stopper and extends the vial toward Father. "Now let you keep yours."

Father takes a deep breath, staring on me. He nods.

I glance between them, not deciphering his meaning.

"It appears this man loves you more than his own life." Cotton lifts the open vial to Father's lips. "Drink."

"*Father,*" I say in our native tongue, my voice panicked. "*What is this?*"

He opens his mouth, though not in answer to me.

Cotton puts the vial to Father's lips and upends it.

Father chokes it down. He coughs then pitches forward, gasping.

I lunge forward. "Father!"

My captors catch and restrain me.

The whole of Father's body seizes on the ground. Blood seeps from his nose, staining the snow. He reaches for me, his hand trembling.

"Father!"

He collapses, his body continuing its tremble.

"Interesting," says Elisabeth. "He lasted far longer than the others."

"Aye," says Cotton. "Perhaps on account of his savage mother's blood. Their species is not given to its power so easily."

"*Rise.*" I croak, my gaze fixed on Father's fingertips, inches from me.

Cotton clears his throat. "See Alden's son from here, Elisabeth. I would have Rebecca ride—"

"Murderer," I shout at him. "You are a murderer!"

Firm hands clap my ears and force a sweat-ridden gag in my mouth, tying it off behind my head. I scream curses at my captors as they bear me up the hill to a waiting carriage. Elegant and polished black with glass windows, the waif hurries before us to open the door.

The inside beams bright with lighted lamps and shades to cover the windows.

With great effort, my captors lift me inside and lay me upon a pillowed bench. They tie my wrists to a handle above my head and bind my feet to a post at the other end.

I continue my fight, knowing their work done well, my struggle all for naught.

They abandon the carriage quick.

Cotton climbs the step a moment later. He sits opposite me, his gaze studious, a grin teasing the corners of his lips.

The waif shuts the door then raps her knuckles against its side.

The carriage pulls forward.

"My dear," says Cotton. "You must be dreadful cold."

He slips off his outer robe and covers me with it, drawing it close to my neck.

"There," he says. "That should warm you."

I keep my quiet, willing my body not shudder at his lingering hand on my shoulder.

"My but you are indeed a beauty. Were I a younger man, I scarcely believe I could rebuke such temptation." Cotton retires against the plush backing of his seat. "Then again, you are the daughter of my greatest friend."

He crosses his leg and draws the shades as the carriage bumps along.

"You are cross with me," says Cotton. "I know the look well. My father oft wore such a face, though, admittedly, his were often more disappointment than anger. I believe he rightly saw in me a usurper to his legacy." He *tsks*. "But what is legacy in compare to the true love and affections of one's father?" Cotton smiles ruefully. "I speak of ghosts long gone now. And we two here but mortals yet."

He removes his white wig.

I stiffen, expectant he should move near me again.

Yet the old man only eases back, stroking his bald and splotched head.

"Vanity," he says, laying the wig beside him. "No matter how I fast or pray, God will not remove it, no more than He takes the other sinful lusts that live in me. Pray, Rebecca, do your pagan gods bid you strike such impurities from your heart and mind?"

I narrow my eyes in response.

"No," he says. "I should think not. Theirs is a simpler way of unlawful freedom. Better, mayhap. God demands obedience, despite harping on forgiveness and love. A duel nature to match the one He gifted us, His imperfect creation."

Cotton clasps his hands in his lap. "I have such a nature. In my heart I desire naught but to serve God's will, but my mind, Rebecca...mine has ever been a curious one, requiring answers to sate its unending questions." Cotton's chin dips. "Oh, that I should give my soul to live with the quiet ignorance your people embody."

He leans forward, his eyes wide like a child.

"I have often wondered what it must be like to forego knowledge of the Invisible World, aye, to lead an inconsequential existence as near all men do. Sadly, your father damned me to the madness of learning its secrets, even as he abandoned me to explore it alone." Cotton pauses. "Did he ever speak of me and our partnership?"

I shake my head, my spirit gladdening at the dismay that crosses his face.

"No," he says. "Of course not. In his life with you, he too lived out his duel-nature, safe in his alias and the knowledge no one of consequence should note his face or name. A bastard son of no one—your father's shame and his blessing." Cotton's lip curls. "Would that I were born of such lowly origins. No one expects them to rise above their station."

The wagon rattles as the horses lead uphill to judge by the pull tempting me roll back.

Cotton too feels it, resting his hands against the carriage side to brace himself before the pull levels off. He turns his baleful stare on me. "Was Simon happy in his quiet life with you and your family? Did he find peace?"

I blink in reply. *I will give you nothing.*

Cotton smiles. "I wished that for him, though I envied the notion he should have it." He pauses. "Do you understand why I speak these things to you, Rebecca? Why I bare my soul now?"

I shake my head.

"There is power in confession," he says. "The whole of time will grant me honor for a forward-thinker, a man beyond my years." He chortles. "Who could ever believe that to save a man from the pox, you must first infect him with but a small dose of it? That it were no grace of God, nor any pagan idol, but science only. Aye, the inner workings of the Invisible World living in the here and now, within the very grasp of those few minds who understood the obtaining of its secrets."

My mind warns the madness has taken him, his voice rising and falling as if I am not even among his company.

"But who should believe such heresy?" Cotton asks. "Who should consider the spectral evidence good men and women afflicted by witchcraft gave against such wretched hags as Goody Glover."

I straighten at the name of Bishop's wife, pausing Cotton from his rant.

"You know her name?" he asks. "How? She were dead and buried long before you could have been born into this world."

I work at the gag, attempting to use my tongue to push it free.

It relents no more than Cotton.

"Such things matter little now, I suppose," he says. "She were but one more lost soul given to the Devil's company. Had she confessed, mayhap she should yet live. Instead, she kept her pride, fool woman."

He dons his wig anew, straightening it upon his head as the carriage slows to a halt.

"Will you confess to me now, Rebecca?" he asks. "I beg you once more, answer me why your father abandoned my company. Allow me learn that peace before my death takes me."

I turn away from him, staring at the carriage ceiling.

"You believe you have suffered at Elisabeth's hands?" he asks. "Her torments of your mind and body are nothing compared to those I should visit on your soul. Tell me, do you think I should have truly killed the man you name father, Alden's bastard son, after I have so long sought him out also?"

I roll back.

"No." Cotton smiles. "He will die a thousand deaths before I finish my work. This night served only for him to trade your place. He would never relent for want of his own life. Only love shatters such spirit as his." He leans close. "And now that I have broken him, perhaps I shall break your brother in likewise fashion. Ah, but you, my dear," he pulls at a strand of my hair. "You, I will save for last."

Cotton raps his cane against the door.

It opens quick with the waif outside it. "My Lord?"

"Let her rot for now," Cotton says. "But see that she is kept alive, aye, fed and watered too. She will need her strength returned for that to come."

"Yes, my Lord."

The waif climbs inside, untethering my feet.

I kick at her face, striking her back.

She draws her baton.

I do not wilt as she cracks the end of it upon my skull, dazing me.

My hands fall free when she cuts them loose, her men dragging me out of the carriage.

One throws me over his shoulder and carries me toward an open door. Then he descends the stairs, bearing me back into the depths of hell.

—seventeen—

"HUNGRY?" THE WAIF SETS A PLATE OF STEAMING MASH BEFORE me.

My stomach grumbles at the smell, hating me for not devouring the mash on sight.

"Come on now," says the waif. "Want your health, don't you? Miss Elisabeth has big plans for you."

I kick the plate away, scattering the mash.

The waif grins. "Told'em you wouldn't eat, I did. Your kind never does. *Savages*," she says. "Miss Elisabeth says your lot has true magic in them. Not the sort Mister Cotton conjures."

"She knows nothing of my people," I say.

"Oh, but she does," says the waif. "Studied'em a good long while now. Her and Mister Cotton both say—"

The waif flies to the door at the echo of footsteps up the hall. Her smile pains my gut. "Big plans indeed," she says.

Elisabeth strides into my cell, passing the waif without acknowledgement. "I have a gift for you," she says to me, her eyes gleaming.

She stands clear of the door as two burly guards haul a hooded prisoner between them. They cast the prisoner to the floor and pin his shoulders with their knees.

Elisabeth steps toward the prisoner. "You scorned my last two gifts, girl. No doubt you shall enjoy my third." She kneels and takes his hood in hand. "Say hello to your brother."

His face cut and bloodied, George looks on me as one dazed to his surroundings. He mumbles with spittle drooling from his mouth.

"Come now, George." Elisabeth grabs hold of his hair, yanking up, forcing him look on me. "Did you not miss your dear sister?"

"That man is no brother to me," I say, forcing the lie. "Betty played you for a song, Elisabeth. The same as she played me."

"Did you, Betty?" Elisabeth turns.

My nostrils flare as Betty Barron and her daughter enter my cell. Cloaked in heavy robes to fight the cold, Susannah will not meet my stare as she shuffles in.

Betty shares no such qualms.

"Mary Warren is dead on your account," I say, drawing near to Betty as my chains allow. "Add her soul to the list of those waiting for you."

"No," says Betty. "You forced this recklessness upon us all, Rebecca. And I warned that I were well versed in this sport you play at."

Susannah draws her robes tight, folding her hands inside. "It is so cold in here, Mother."

"Patience, child," says Betty. "We will leave soon."

I glare at Betty. "You bid me trust you."

"And yet you did not," says Betty. "Had you listened well, no doubt you should have seen the wisdom in my words."

Elisabeth chuckles. "What wisdom do you possess? You hold no secret knowledge."

"My father taught me humble servitude is of the highest virtues. That kneeling before the master"—Betty reaches into her robes—"means you draw near him."

Betty sheds her robes, a blade in her hand. The tip of her dagger erupts through the neck of the guard nearest me. He falls clutching his throat, gasping.

Susannah gives her guard little time to respond, burying her hatchet in his back. She backs away as he screams, spinning in attempt to remove it.

The waif screams and flees my cell.

"Mother, the girl!" Susannah cries before giving chase to the waif.

Elisabeth screeches and lunges at Betty. "You traitorous bit—"

She falls to the floor—yanked down by George. He pulls her to him, climbing astride her, straddling her chest, wrapping both hands around her neck.

The guard trips with Susannah's hatchet in his back. He falls within my reach.

I waste little time in throwing the chain of my wrist shackles around his neck, pulling tight against them.

He grabs hold of my hair, yanking me close to him.

A woman's scream fills my ear alongside a deep, punching sound.

The guard gasps at each thud landed and gives up his final gasps not long after a few have fallen. His grip relents in death and I pull away.

Betty stands above me with Susannah's hatchet in her grip, dripping blood.

"Y-you saved me..." I say.

Betty drops the hatchet and flees the room.

"For my family." George's growl draws my attention.

Elisabeth flails beneath him, her mouth opening and closing without sound. She claws air to reach his reddening face.

"*For my wife,*" his voice breaks.

Elisabeth's eyes roll in her head, her head lolling in his grip.

George keeps his stranglehold of Elisabeth long after she grows still.

"Brother," I say. "She is gone."

His attention snaps to me, his face livid. It melts away when our eyes connect, and he paws at Elisabeth's body, not ceasing until he finds a ring of keys.

"George," I say. "How did you—"

"We have little time, sister." George scrambles to me and tries my locks with each of the keys. "Have you seen the others?"

The shackle around my left ankle unlocks.

"Mary is dead," I say as George frees my right ankle. "Andrew were somewhere here, last I saw. I know not what they have done with Ciquenackqua."

George curses at another failed attempt to free my wrists.

"Did Betty speak to you of Father?" I ask.

"Aye," says George. "We will—"

A shackle unlocks.

George frees the other.

I fall into his arms, clutching at his neck. "Forgive me, brother." I cry. "Forgive me all that has happened."

"I do," he says. "But we must go now. Can you walk?"

"I can run to escape this place."

George grins. "Good. Come then."

My heads swoons when he aids me stand. I fight the dizziness by glaring at Elisabeth's corpse. I fall upon her screaming, grabbing her hair, bashing her skull into the floor to ensure her dead.

"Rebecca!" George pulls me off her. "We must go. Now!"

"Wait." I pluck the axe from the dead guard and reach for the dagger in the other's throat.

George throws me toward the cell door ere I grab the dagger, then pushes me up the hall.

Betty waits at the far end, waving us hurry.

The rankling of keys in George's fist bid me hurry.

"We found Andrew!" Betty yells.

I follow her up the next hall toward a dying guard, clutching at the oozing hole in his belly. "K-kill me..." he begs.

I pause only to steal his dagger from its sheathe. Then I leap around his weak swipe and continue on, following Betty.

The guard cries out as George halts to end his suffering.

Susannah waits near the hall middle, knelt outside a cell door, her face blustery. "The girl, Mother. E-Elisabeth's slave," says Susannah. "S-she escaped."

Betty continues past her. She scurries to the hall end and lies in wait, peeking around the corner.

I reach the cell door. Different from the one that kept me, this door bears a grated opening near the top.

George pushes me aside before I can look inside. He tries the keys through the lock with maddening swiftness.

My gaze wavers between his efforts and our sentry, Betty.

"Hurry, George," says Susannah. "Hurry."

Anger swells in me at the approaching echo of footsteps and shouted voices from around the corner. I stalk to join Betty, my hands relishing the handles of both dagger and axe in my palms.

I throw myself at the wall beside her. Keeping careful watch of the approaching shadows, I count three on the opposite wall.

"Hurry, lads!" a guard calls. "They must—"

I lurch around the corner, frighting all three men. My dagger finds its home in the throat of their captain. I shove him back into the arms of his companions, then sweep Susannah's axe around, burying it the cheek of a guard.

Betty saves me from the third man, fearing him back with wide, arching swipes.

The guard drops his flintlock and flees back down the hall.

I fetch up the flintlock and train its aim. The shot thunders in my ears, filling the hall with smoke. When it clears, the fleeing guard lies sprawled at the hall's end. My blood surges in the aftermath.

"That were a fool thing to do," she says. "The sound of your shot—"

"The waif escaped," I say, dropping the flintlock. "No doubt she rallies more to come even now."

I dash back to George and Susannah, finding the door gaped open. Inside, George feverishly works his dagger through the ropes binding Andrew's wrists and ankles over his back.

"Andrew." Susannah cradles his head in her lap, stroking his hair. "My love, what have they done to you?"

"George," I say.

"I know, Rebecca…"

"The guards—"

"I know!" George cuts the last rope strands.

Andrew moans as his arms fall across his back and his legs slap stone. "M-my legs…I cannot feel them." He looks on George. "L-leave me."

"I will not," says George, squatting to slip his hands under Andrew's neck and knees. Grunting, he lifts Andrew off the ground and shoulders him.

Andrew cries out.

George turns to me, his face blustery red from the weight of Andrew. "Guard us well, sister."

I grab Susannah's arm and pull her out of the cell. "The guards walked you in here," I say. "Now lead us out."

Susannah lingers on Andrew's face.

I thrust the axe back into her hand, drawing her attention. "Lead."

Susannah takes the axe then flies up the hall.

"Where is Betty?" George asks.

"Gone ahead." I pause beside the dead guards, slinging a loaded flintlock about my shoulder and drawing the captain's pistol from its holster. Then I race to catch them.

We hurry down the steps, wheeling around corners, sprinting down a new hall.

Andrew cries out at each step taken, his face wincing, body bouncing on George's shoulder.

"What is your plan?" I shout to George.

"Trust...the others"—he labors to balance Andrew—"to do their work."

"Others?"

A salty breeze fills my nose as we descend a second stairwell.

Betty waits for us at the bottom of the steps, crouched behind a wagon, waving us stop.

George and Susannah hesitate in the stairwell at the echo of ominous bells and shouting men across the yard.

I move on, skulking low, sidling next to Betty. The night sky and shadow embrace me as I sprawl on my belly and peer underneath the wagon.

Our freedom lay not fifty yards of barren ground between us and an open gate.

War rages beyond the pike-tipped barricades. Several guards lie dead outside their wall. Others fall in clouds of smoke, all attempting to reach safety inside the fort as a train of blazing wagons rolls toward the gate.

Voices shout orders. The square fills with more soldiers. A few rush to swing close the wooden gates. Several more bear a wooden beam between them and slot it through holds to further guard the gate.

More men line the wall. Their rifles bark fire and smoke on those below, all to the tune of women's screams and those in death's throes outside.

"We must move," I say, pulling Betty back to the steps.

"What now?" Susannah looks to George. "We cannot escape this way."

My brother frowns.

Fear swells in me at the number of guards filling the fort square.

"George," I whisper, "we cannot hope to skirt their attention for long."

A gull flutters to land on the wagon. It cocks its head at me, then flies again at the echo of another volley from the guards. The bird's flight draws the attention of a guard captain across the square. Our eyes meet and he shouts to halt his fellows. All turn and bring the aim of their rifles to bear.

"*Run!*" I hiss to the others.

Shots whizz past me, shattering stone and splintering wood around us.

I kneel and unsling the flintlock. My sight locks on the captain as his fellows doctor their rifles for a second volley.

My shoulder jerks back, my aim firing off kilter.

"Rebecca." George flings me up the steps. "Go!"

I drop the rifle and trail Betty and Susannah up the stairs.

"S-save yourself, George," says Andrew.

"No," George pants.

The second volley rips through the steps behind us.

We sprint down the hall and up the next flight.

"There!" voices echo behind us. "Halt!"

More shots fly past me.

Betty turns at the top of the steps. "This level is the last."

"Find a window," yells George. "We cannot go back."

I swing around the corner and flatten my back against the wall.

"What are you doing?" George asks.

"Waiting." I raise my dagger.

George grabs me by the arm and hauls me away. "I did not come to see you killed now, sister."

"There is a room at the end," Betty shouts.

George thrusts me ahead.

I rush down the hall and join Susannah and Betty inside a corner room. A pair of windows on either wall floods the room with clean air. I fill my chest deep with it, savoring the salty taste.

George sets Andrew to rest with his back against a cannon, then moves to bar one of the doors.

I take the other, latching it closed and bracing it with a wooden beam. Then I survey the room—a guard post storeroom of sorts. A stack of cannonballs stands near one window, food provisions and water near the corner, and rifles line the walls.

"Andrew." Susannah pets his face. "My God, what did she do to you?"

"K-killed me, I think," he says.

"And still you breathe." George steals a rifle off the wall and checks it for powder and shot. "Do not give up so easily, Andrew."

I move to the windows, leaning out of each, taking in the surroundings. No guards line the wall atop us to either side. Distracted, I think, by those drawing their fight outside the gates. Craggy rocks and a furious sea lay beneath the southern windows, whilst sand and marsh sit below the eastern.

My heart pounds at the drop distance. I punch my fist upon the brick wall.

"What is it?" Betty asks.

I move about the room and yank the tops off all the barrels, finding mostly salt pork and fish. Those Andrew rests against hold darker contents, grainy to the touch. I dip my hand inside and sift it through my fingers.

Susannah's eyes widen. "Devil's powder."

"No." I pull the barrels down, spilling the gunpowder across the floor.

"What are you doing?" Betty asks.

"I will not be taken again," I say.

"Nor will any of us." George nods to the cannon.

We strike toward it as one. But where I move to position it, George works to untie the rope end securing it to the wall.

The door nearest me pounds. "Open up!"

"Rebecca," Andrew says. "F-forgive me."

I ignore him, unwinding rope from around the cannon as George frees the first bit of rope and moves on to a second knot.

"Th-they overheard me in the tavern," says Andrew. "F-followed me to the inn."

"It matters not," says Susannah.

The door pounds again. "Open this now!"

"It does," says Andrew. "I am the drunken fool your mother knew me for."

"Done," says George to me.

I kneel and take up the uncoiled rope in my arms, tossing the end of it out the eastern window.

"Unworthy of love," says Andrew.

"You are deserving," says Susannah.

George grabs the rope and puts his feet on the cannon, leaning all his weight back to test the line. It holds.

I lunge to the window, estimating the dangling rope end near ten feet above the ground.

The second door sounds, harder than the first.

"They have a ram," says George. "Betty, go."

"Not before my daughter," she says.

Susannah looks up. "I will not leave Andrew."

"He will be right behind you," says Betty, taking her daughter's arm. "Come."

"Aye," says Andrew to Susannah. "I-I will."

"You will not," Susannah weeps.

George grabs her by the waist and yanks her away screaming.

"Andrew!"

"Go now, damn you!" George pushes her to the window and thrusts the rope in her hands.

"Daughter, please," Betty urges. "I beg you."

Both doors thunder in succession then again and again, the brace beams thudding against their holds.

Susannah swings her legs out the window. Panting, she descends the rope, disappearing from sight.

Betty wastes no time in following her out, nor do I in stepping to the window after her.

"George," says Andrew, his voice withered. "George, I am done for."

"You are not," says my brother. "I will carry—"

"No," says Andrew. "Y-you will not."

The doors shudder in the twin onslaught against them.

I hesitate, not knowing whether to leave or remain to aid them in the fight to come.

"Andrew," says George. "You—"

"I have been a weight round your neck since first your family took me in." Andrew's shoulders heave. "M-my father taught a debt not repaid is a sin. Allow me pay mine now."

The slam against the doors resounds, the brace beams near fully cracking.

"George," I say. "We—"

My brother silences me with his glare then looks back on his friend. "You owe no debt, Andrew."

"I do. For Sarah and Bishop"—Andrew's gaze wavers between George and me—"and Han...*Hannah*." His face wilts. "You named me brother before...but now—"

George grabs Andrew under the arms and hauls him to his feet. "You were my brother then," his voice wavers. "You are my brother always."

My vision blurs as Andrew rests his forehead against George's, his body quivering.

"Care for her," says Andrew.

"I will," says George. "Susannah—"

"Not Susannah," says Andrew, pulling away, looking on me. "*Her*."

The doors thunder again, the beams cracking.

I step to Andrew and lean my face to his, our lips brushing in soft caress. I pull away, my head swooning, and stare into his eyes.

"G-Goodbye, my love," he says, his voice scarcely above a whisper.

"Goodbye, Andrew."

He chokes at my words, opening his hand to receive the captain's pistol.

George guides me to the window and forces me take the rope.

I swing over the ledge, gazing on Andrew's anguished face one last time, wondering if we may yet save him.

"*Go,*" he says.

I descend the rope.

My heart flutters with each new handhold and soon my feet touch naught but air. I slide to the end of the rope, burning my palms, and drop the remainder of the way, rolling when my bare feet touch sand.

George gives me little time to scamper away from his landing upon me.

My gaze lingers on the window above whilst the sounds of battle echo across the night sky. George lifts me to my feet and shoves me close to the fort wall. We turn the corner and sprint to the brush line where Betty and Susannah wait.

I fall down the sandy bank and crawl north with the others.

An explosion to dwarf a hundred flintlocks echoes from the tower.

George claps his hand over Susannah's mouth to silence her scream. He rolls atop her and me to shield us from the brick and wood shrapnel raining nearby, forcing us take shelter against the sandbank.

I squirm free of George and peek over the bank.

A pillar of black smoke rises and orange flames lick the shattered husk where the tower stood. The bells continue ringing, their song joined by men shouting for water buckets to fight the flames that fan out in greedy reach for the yet untouched wooden barricades.

George muffles Susannah's cries, holding her tight against his chest, the whole of her body seizing in his grasp.

I dip my chin, steeling myself against the sadness that consumes Susannah, praying Andrew's sacrifice will not be in vain.

-eighteen-

BETTY CRAWLS NEAR US. SHE REACHES OUT TO SUSANNAH. "Come, daughter. We need rejoin the others."

Susannah fights to remain in George's embrace.

"Who are these others, George?" I ask. "You spoke of them—"

"Daughter," says Betty. "Come."

"No!" Susannah says. "You despised him, Mother, and said he were no good man."

"Aye, I wronged him," says Betty. "But that does not mean—"

"You hated him."

I glance over the sandbank, watchful of the guards putting out the tower fire. My heart races at the sight of their banding together, each attempt more successful than the last.

"Susannah." George forces her look on him. "Andrew would not wish you weep for him now. He would have you live."

"But how can I without him?" she asks.

I move close to them. "Make your sorrow a song." I thrust my hatchet into her grip. "And this your instrument."

Susannah takes hold of the hatchet handle, her face hardening, knuckles clenching white.

Betty gives me an ill look.

"Come," says George. "The guards will fan in search soon. We should be gone from here well before then."

"Aye," I say. "But to where?"

George takes hold of Susannah's hand. He ducks low and traipses through the sand after Betty.

That he does not answer my question plagues me as I bring up the rear.

We keep to the shoreline, headed northwest toward the city and the wharves.

Betty abandons our course, turning west, looping us around a southern hill. We dart across an open, dirt road for the cover of trees and brush. We keep to the shadows, passing several homes with candles lit in their windows, chimneys belching white smoke.

A whistle sounds from a darkened barn.

The others halt.

My fingers clench around the dagger hilt.

George touches my arm. "All is well, sister."

I keep my grip of the hilt when Betty enters the barn.

At the slap of reins, a black-stained and gold-trimmed carriage led by a pair of roan geldings pulls from the dark. Dressed in a richly fashioned black cloak, the driver tips his hat to us as he brings the carriage to a halt.

Betty sits inside. She opens the door and waves us enter.

Like its driver, the interior shines of wealth to match the carriage Cotton held me in. Candlelit lamps illuminate the inside and flowing drapery covers the frost-paned windows.

George places his arms about my shoulders, urging me follow Susannah.

I glance at him, my fears plain in the look I give.

"Trust," he says.

I swallow my pride and climb the step to enter the carriage. With Susannah beside her mother, I sit opposite them, nestling into the cushioned seats.

George scoots next to me and closes the door.

Betty draws the shades over the windows then eases back and raps her knuckles against the wall behind her.

The carriage pulls ahead.

"Where are we going?" I ask.

"Where you should have from the start," says Betty. "Is this how you treat one who has saved your life?"

"Aye, my life." I belittle her. "What of Mary Warren's? Andrew and Faith, or—"

"I had naught to do with Faith's death, nor their capture." Betty folds her hands in her lap. "Andrew said himself Mather spies heard his plots in the taverns, as I warned someone might."

"Mother, please," says Susannah. "Let you speak no more ill of him."

"Aye," George sighs. "We cannot change their fates now."

I glare at Betty. "You came back for me to clear your conscience."

"Enough, Rebecca," says George.

"She betrayed me to Elisabeth!"

George looks from me to Betty.

"Aye," says Betty quietly. "She speaks true."

Susannah blinks. "Mother?"

"What should I have done?" Betty asks me. "Followed you to that gathering and been captured also? Shared a cell with you and the others?" She brushes sand from her dress. "No. I will not say pain were not wrought on you for my actions, but without them you should be there still."

"You cannot fathom what pain she wrought on me," I say. "What things she forced me witness."

"No more than you can those your father inflicted on me," says Betty. "But unlike me, your hate led you to that ill place."

"My hate?"

George rests his hand on my leg.

I bat it away. "Do not silence me, brother."

"You have a right to anger," he says. "But let you be grateful also. Without Betty and Susannah, we should never have found you."

"She played us all for fools," I warn. "Aye, and warned me of her skill at this sport I play at." I glare at Betty. "Now I see you true."

"Rebecca, let you remember—"

"No, George," I say. "Let you."

"What?" he asks.

"Her demands," I say. "She desired me banish Mary from our company and warned Andrew she would not allow him marry Susannah." My voice trembles. "She spoke of her distrust in them the same as she did her loathing of *savages*." I spit the word. "Does it not strike you odd, brother, that all of them are dead and gone now?"

George sits back, concern drawn over his face.

Betty meets my stare, though she keeps her silence.

"Mother?" Susannah says. "Let you say something against her claims."

"Aye," says Betty. "I distrusted the lot of you, but never did I wish death on your companions. No more than I wished you the pain you sought."

"I never—"

"You did," says Betty. "Only one with similar guilt would recognize it as such." She leans forward. "I, too, know of the darkness, Rebecca—the insatiable blackness of self-loathing that seeks the devouring of our very souls. And it does for those who allow their guilt roam unchecked. Only by God's good grace were mine washed away. Aye, and all my hate with it."

"My hate is all I have," I say. "I would not see it taken from me also."

"Much and more is what you still have, Rebecca." Betty motions to George. "Do not let the haunted call of those sent to the Invisible World deafen you to the voices of those who yet walk in this one."

George puts his arm around me, squeezes my shoulder. "Whatever demons you hold, let you forget them now. I beg you." He squeezes my hand. "These are good people, sister. I have little doubt I should be dead if not for their care. Aye, and you also."

Susannah blushes at his words.

The wagon rolls to a halt then jostles as the driver leaves his seat. The door opens, revealing we sit outside a manse far grander than any other home in Boston. Though the gates stand open, the iron bars around the property warn me tread lightly and keep outside their perimeter.

The carriage driver sweeps his gloved hand with dramatic flair. "He waits for you."

"All is prepared?" Betty asks.

"Aye, Madam," says the driver.

I give George a questioning look as Susannah and Betty leave the carriage.

He urges me follow them out.

I step out of the carriage and onto frigid, cobbled stone. A walkway lies before us, cutting through ice and snow in a cleared path from the road to the house.

"Miss, your feet," says the driver. He rests his hand against the carriage then pulls at his heel, plucking off his boot. "Pray, let you take mine."

I try it out, the warmth of its inside a welcome respite. My foot slips out before my heel touches earth. "Thank you, sir," I say. "My feet are too small."

"Then allow me carry you, Miss," he says.

My face hardens. "I will walk."

And so I do, before he or George object.

A plump, elderly man opens the door before we reach the midway. He rubs his bare head, devoid of the frivolous white wigs worn by near all the other well-to-do men I met in Boston. He waves us move faster as the wind picks up.

"Come in," he says, ushering us across the threshold. "The night wanes and we have precious little time."

My feet sink in the thick, rug in his entryway. I huddle close to George and Susannah, shivering in the tattered and stained dress Elisabeth left me.

"Blasted winter," the old man says, shutting the door and locking it. "Is it not enough God forces age upon me, but I must suffer this cold too?"

His grumble reminds me of an old bear, newly awakened from the winter sleep. The reminder serves truer still when he turns and looks on me, his eyes gleaming. "So, you are the one who began this mess, are you?"

I step toward him. "I came to end it."

His eyebrow cocks. "You look near at an end already." He sighs. "Half-starved and near naked. No doubt the sight of you should set Cotton to laughing himself to death."

"Rebecca," says Betty. "This is Judge Sewall."

"Aye, call me Sam," he says. "But you knew that already, girl, did you not?"

I nod.

Judge Sewall studies me then *tsks*. "Betty, dear. Go fetch her some proper clothes and shoes. If she dies this night, I would have her be warm at least."

Betty bows her head, then leaves out of the room.

"Come," says Judge Sewall. "And fill your bellies as well. I gather the others are still arriving."

We follow him through the home, my gaze wandering over each regal corner—artwork painted by the hands of masters, vases depicting odd cultures, furniture shining of polished mahogany.

Judge Sewall leads us to a sitting room. A table stands at the middle, filled with a silver tray of cheeses and fruit, and a tall, vat of steaming stew. I ladle stew into one of the bowls hardly before the Judge's invitation to partake leaves his lips. The taste of boiled cabbage and carrots, potatoes and beef, covers my tongue, each scalding spoonful forcing me draw breath to cool my mouth.

Betty returns with shoes and a folded bundle of clothes.

I gulp down the last of broth in my bowl then go with Betty to don the clothes in a separate room. She closes the door behind me and I shed the dress, near weeping at the pronouncement of my ribs and extended belly.

"Here," says Betty, averting her eyes from my nudity and handing me the bundle of folded clothes. "They belonged to my sons. I thought perhaps a dress, but your brother...well, he supposed—"

"They well suffice," I say, my gaze drawn to the crimson shirt.

"I thought you should like the color," she says.

"Aye."

I hold the clothes to my nose, breathing deep of the lye scent. Then I don the long-sleeved shirt quickly and pull on the leather leggings.

"Do the boots fit?" Betty asks.

"Aye." I say, pulling them on and testing their size. Then I tie my hair in a bun and take Betty by the arm, turning her around.

She gasps at the sight of me. "You look a whole different woman."

"I feel one." My chin drops to my chest as I draw a deep breath and release it just as quick. I glance up. "My thanks to you, Betty Barron. Thank you for my life."

She wipes her cheeks. "I am sorry only that I could not come sooner."

"And I for my mistrust of you. Forgive me."

"I do. Now come," she says, taking my hand. "The others wait."

Betty leads me back to the sitting room, devoid of Judge Sewall's presence.

The food sings to me again with its savory scents.

I resist its temptations, though my belly rumbles for more. I will it instead hunger for vengeance.

George stands at the ready, swinging a new-forged axe.

"Where did you get that?" I ask.

"A gift," says Judge Sewall, entering from the opposite room. In his hands, he bears another. "I bring one for you also."

I accept the hilt and step back, testing the weight of it, slicing through air. "This is well-made."

"It must be," says Judge Sewall, his face souring. "For it to end the life of such a man as Cotton."

"Why do you do this?" I ask. "I heard it said you and Cotton were friends once."

"Aye, once," he says. "Some name time a cruel master, dividing friends and family from one another. I call it a mirror, revealing the truth of such bonds. My kinship with Cotton ended the day my brother, Stephen, relayed the confessions of a little girl sent to him for safeguarding."

Judge Sewall glances at Betty. He sighs.

"Lies," he says. "Were it those acts alone, I might have prayed God forgive Cotton, but to use children as his weapon?" His face twists. "A sin of the foulest sort to blacken the good names of many."

Betty steps to him. "You yet have a good name, Sam—"

"Damn my name." Judge Sewall thunders. "I care as little for it as my own life. Young folk think of the future. We old men have only the past to dwell on."

Judge Sewall waves us follow him out of the sitting room. He leads us into another and halts beside a pantry door then reaches into his pocket and removes a small ring of keys.

"I have confessed my sins before God and men"—he fits a gold-plated key into the lock—"but words alone have ever rung hollow in my court. I shudder to think mine own should ring hollow come the day God passes his judgment upon me."

The lock and knob turn easily and the door shudders open.

A lantern hangs from a metal rung, lighting a flight of wooden steps descending into an elsewise black cellar.

A cold wind harrows up the steps, whistling as if the dead sit in wait for us to join them below.

Judge Sewall takes the lantern from the rung. Using his other sun-blotched hand for balance against the wall, he travels down the steps.

When George and the others hesitate, I plunge ahead after the Judge.

The steps groan under our combined weight, cautioning me not follow too close. Our shadows lengthen upon the wall and my palms sweat, loosening my grip on both axe and dagger.

Judge Sewall coughs as he touches down at the cellar base. "Had God chose me for a reverend, I might forgive Cotton and give over the decision of his guilt or innocence to the Lord and the Invisible World—"

I gasp when he turns his lantern light on the remainder of the cellar, the whole of it stretching near the entirety of the house above.

"But I am a judge," says Sewall. "And I will have justice served in this earthly court."

A swarm of seedy individuals of every station and age, gender and color gather at the far end, standing round a black hole with shattered brick remains littering the floor.

The crowd shifts at our approach and the Judge's lantern shines off the metal of those who carry blades. Still more bear wooden shanks. Most look feared.

"Who are these people?" I ask.

Betty steps close to me. "I promised you a shield. Let these folk serve as a testament to my words."

"This is your shield?" I ask her as George sidles next to me. "They have the look of farmers and beggars, not soldiers or warriors—"

"Aye," says Judge Sewall. "And others sailors, whores, and still more professions. Do you deem them less for it?"

"No," I say. "Only that I do not understand how they should be of use to our cause."

"What good is a shield without a blade in the other hand to strike down the opponent?" Judge Sewall asks. "It is true most here be no soldiers, nor warriors. That does not mean they are powerless to lend their aid."

My gaze sweeps over their faces. "But who are they?"

"Witnesses." Judge Sewall walks among them. "To the crimes of Cotton Mather. These are the sisters and brothers, sons and daughters, mothers and fathers of those once held in sway to his desires and given to Devil's powder. Some speak for those who no longer can, others attest with their own voices."

The crowd shifts at Judge Sewall's claims. Some speak their names loudly whilst others whisper.

I believe them introducing themselves at the first. Only when Betty adds her voice to theirs do I understand their true intent.

"Abigail," says Betty.

George swings his axe beside me, drawing approval from the crowd. "Hannah."

"Andrew." Susannah wipes her cheeks.

"Bishop," I say, my hopes rising from the rage in their voices. "Deep River and Sturdy Oak. Aye, and Mary Warren too!"

The crowd cheers at my yell.

"*Sarah!*" I raise my axe high over my head and scream a war cry.

The crowd roars back at me. One of the men snatches the Judge's lantern and dashes into the tunnel.

The others surge over the brick remains after him.

George follows them in and Susannah after him, shrugging off Betty's woeful attempts to stop her.

I, too, rush forward. Brandishing my axe, I leap inside the tunnel maw and allow its darkness consume me.

-nineteen-

THE TUNNEL COLD KISSES MY SKIN, COOLING NOT A LITTLE OF MY anger as we continue our course.

Footsteps not mine own echo behind me.

"Wait," Betty cries. "Susannah, wait!"

I hesitate, though her daughter does not.

Betty reaches me, a dagger in her hand. "I warned her our part is played in this," she says, reaching me.

We two continue up the tunnel, chasing the lantern light ahead.

The tunnel narrows, forcing all move closer together. We catch them soon enough.

"You should have remained behind, daughter," says Betty to Susannah. "As you promised me you would."

"And you knew I would not," says Susannah. "This is my fight as much as any here tonight."

"Your fight?" I ask.

"Aye," Susannah says. "I were once given over to Devil's powder. Despite my mother's preaching, Mercy and Elisabeth convinced me to see spirits. I should be a slave still were it not for Mother."

I glance on Betty, her face set in sternness, dagger pumping at her side in keeping pace with us.

"Never in my life have I witnessed such a change in one person as the night Mother came for me." Susannah grins. "As she stands with me tonight."

"Neither of us should be here," says Betty, her eyes searching out the shadows dancing across the tunnel walls. "I want no further part in this."

"You are a brave and goodly woman," says George.

"Aye," says Susannah. "There be none greater."

Betty sidles closer to Susannah. "Bravery has naught to do with any of this."

I keep my silence and careful watch of the lantern light. We pass more than several tunnels. None give any clue as to how deep or long each of them run.

"Cotton and his followers have long used these tunnels to move about the city, undetected," says Susannah. "Mercy led me down several one night. More fall into rubble and ruin every year with no one deeming them worthy of repair. Judge Sewall bricked his over for fear Cotton may send spies into his home. He opened it only this morning to allow us entry."

"And he should wall it back up now." George glances over his shoulder. "Had I anything to my name, I would wager we are not alone in these tunnels."

His words quiet us for a time, our footfalls falling over stone the lone noise to give us away.

Our tunnel widens into a round and arched ceiling. The lantern leader of our group pauses near the middle. Like spokes on a wheel, several tunnels spindle off the room.

"Where now?" someone asks.

"Aye, which way?"

I put my back to George.

"I like this not at all, sister," George voices my shared thoughts.

I raise my blades to chest level, their ends twitching in wait.

Susannah starts forward toward a tunnel mouth. "I have been here before."

"Wait." George follows her. "Susannah!"

A cackled echo rises from one of the tunnels, its sound herding our group close.

"Aunt Mercy showed me." Susannah traces her fingers over a stone pillar. "Secret runes of the Invisible World."

A second cackled laugh sounds—this time from a separate tunnel.

"George," I say.

"Aye, I hear it." He rushes to Susannah. "Come, we are—"

Shrieks surround us, drowning out his words.

"Trap!"

Black-cloaked and hooded figures swarm us from all sides. Snarling and scarred faces cloud my vision, their bodies twitching.

I swipe and duck, parrying and striking, all to the din of clashing blades, cackled laughter, and war cries. Blood flies around me, painting my face and others crimson-black in the pale lantern light. I step over the dead and dying, forgetting friend and foe alike, ever moving toward where I last saw George.

"Rebecca!" His roar gives me hope.

I glimpse him felling one witch and fending off another. Susannah stands with him, dispatching those that fall at George's feet.

"Mother!" she cries. "Where is Mother?"

A brute steps between us, his arm in full swing to bash my skull with his mace.

I step aside and thrust my dagger, sheathing it in his ribs.

His arm clamps over it and he sends me reeling with a backhand across the mouth.

I stumble to the ground, rolling away as he again attempts to end me with his weapon.

I scramble for my feet.

His boot catches me in the chest.

My dagger lost, I hold my axe aloft by blade and handle to ward off his blows.

His mace rains against the axe handle and he kicks at me to relent. Each of his strikes grows stronger, filled with the lust of battle and blood or else swayed by Devil's powder.

My arms warn I cannot sustain his attack much longer.

I wait for his next assault then kick his knee.

It twists under him, its pop near louder than his scream. He falls back, clutching it to his chest.

I ease his pain with my axe.

"George!" Susannah calls above the din. "Mother!"

Her voice calls me home. She stands alone, separated from George by a haggard witch.

"Susannah," I cry. "Watch—"

Wind whistles over my head. A rope draws tight across my neck, stealing my breath.

I gasp for air beneath its choke.

"Rat," the waif hisses in my ear.

I stumble amid the chaos, pulling at the rope to loosen her grip.

"The rats come up from the tunnels again." The waif forces me against the wall.

I struggle against its wet surface.

"Yes, I told her, sir, but she won't listen." The rope tightens. "Never listens, that one."

My eyes bulge wide, my life waning. I dig at my throat, drawing my own blood in hope of loosening the rope.

"Now, now, dearie, don't let them up," the waif cackles. "They're rats!"

My foot brushes a small ledge. I kick at it, sending us both stumbling back, me landing atop her.

The tautness round my neck loosens.

I gasp a breath and shove my elbow back into her ribs.

The waif cackles louder, oblivious to pain. "Rats!" she says. "*Rats!*"

I roll off her and crawl toward my axe, each breath stabbing my lungs.

The waif pulls me back, her nails digging into my skin.

My weak kick glances off her forehead.

"Rats." She comes on, her face and shoulders twitching.

My fingers graze the axe hilt, fetching it close at the last.

The waif grabs my ankles and flips me with inhuman strength. "Rats!"

Using the force she turns me with, I lunge at her and bury my axe edge through her neck.

The waif falls off me, gurgling on blood as she cackles.

"Rats..." Her eyes roll back. "Raaaatssss..."

I lay on my back, sucking air, my head pounding. I close my eyes, savoring each breath, despite the battle around me.

"Rebecca!" Susannah calls. "Over here!"

I climb to my feet and hurry for the tunnel where she stands.

"My mother," she asks. "Have you seen her?"

"No." My head acts a swivel in search. "Where is George?"

"There!"

A scrawny, but quick, roguish man knocks George's axe from his grip.

Barehanded, my brother catches the rogue by the wrist with

one hand and then by the throat with his other. He lifts the man off the ground and batters him against the tunnel wall before tossing him aside, easy as a toddler with a straw doll.

A witch appears behind him, dagger raised.

"George!" I cry.

The witch screams out, felled to her knees, slumping dead.

Betty looks on me, her face coated in blood. "Susannah, take her!"

A hand takes hold of my shoulder.

"Rebecca, come." Susannah fetches up a fallen lantern and races down the tunnel. "Come!"

I hesitate. "But George—"

"The others need him more," she says.

"I need him," I say.

"They are the shield," says Susannah. "And you the dagger. Now come!"

I follow her up the tunnel, fleeing the battle.

"How do you know the way?" I ask.

"Runes." Susannah winds us around the tunnels. She stops at the mouth of several, feeling around the stonework before dashing down the next.

My heart pounds in wait for another ambush. I near knock Susannah over when she halts outside a dilapidated entry with steps leading into shadow.

"Here," she says, feeling around the edges. "This one! This is his home."

I glance back.

"Go," says Susannah. "End this for all our sakes. I will bring the others."

She shoves me on.

I swoop into the entry. The dark leaves me feeling my way forward, hand over hand. Each step taken bids me wonder if it will be my last. I push aside thoughts a witch stalks me for sport, the sight of me plain to creatures given to shadow.

The clammy stone walls turn to rough wood and then to metal.

My fingers grasp hold of an iron ring. I push my shoulder against the door to no avail. Breathing deep, I pull instead.

The door groans open.

I slip around it, following the scent of sweeter air and find myself in a cellar near the size of Judge Sewall's. Yet where his lay barren, this cellar holds tables with open glassware, charts, and sketches strewn across them. I rifle through the papers—portraits of men and women in various stages of decay with notations and dates in neat, legible script.

Closed jars of varied size and animal remains line shelving in the corner. I near retch at the sight of human remains mixed among the animals. Even glassed in lidded jars, a putrid stench hangs near them.

I force myself away and on toward the stairs. Leaning hard against the wall, I take each step slow, testing the boards for any hint of weakness.

They hold strong under me, not a one giving any sound to warn of my presence.

I nudge open the door.

A low-burning hearth fire greets me as I slip out of the cellar. All expectations of opulence vanish the moment I set foot inside the kitchen. Were it not for Susannah's insistence and the waif's presence, I should almost think myself in the wrong home.

I venture further in, finding each room near vacant as the

next, all given over to ruin and disrepair. I tread over worn rugs and pass broken furniture. Those that yet stand of their own accord give me little confidence they could have sustained even the waif.

A set of tall, doublewide doors bids me pause.

I approach them slow, noting the open sliver between them and the orange glow from inside. Peeking through the slit, my gaze falls on row after row of books against the far wall. I prod open the door, awaiting any surprise.

Nothing comes.

My axe raised, I whip around to check behind both doors and find naught but shadows.

The fire burns bright, recently tended, or so I gather from the poker that yet lies in the hearth, its tip red with heat.

I keep close to the wall of books, my nose filling with the scent of crisp, old paper and bound leather. I break from it to make for the large, oak desk at the room's center.

My blood turns cold at the sight of who lay hidden behind it.

"Ciquenackqua…"

twenty

UNCONSCIOUS OR DEAD, HIS HEAD RESTS AGAINST THE WALL, tethered by a collar with tiny blades pinching his neck. A silver platter with a mound of Devil's powder upon its surface lay within his reach, untouched.

I rush to his side and place my hands against his cheeks, finding him feverish. "Ciquenackqua," I say. "Say something."

He groans and his eyes flutter before sagging shut again.

I study the collar, wondering how best to remove it without cutting him.

Behind me, a pistol clicks ready for fire.

"I told you he fascinated me…"

I wheel around.

Cotton stands not twenty feet from me, his aim trained at my chest.

I have no time for Cotton though, my heart breaking at the guardian shadow patiently waiting by his side, cloaked in black, his stare vacant as a corpse.

"Father," I say.

My voice does naught to stir him from his post.

"Father!"

Cotton grins. "The son of Alden is sworn to the Invisible World now, girl." He reaches into his cloak and draws a vial of the crimson liquid. "His mind given to those who have unlocked its secrets."

"What have you done to him?" I ask.

"I offered him a choice," says Cotton. "You stood upon the banks and witnessed him trade his service for yours. He drank my creation of his own free will. Now that will belongs to me."

"You lie," I say.

"Alden," says Cotton to Father. "This whelp has no humility. Pray, let you teach her some."

Father reaches for a coiled leather whip, dangling at his side. He takes the whip off his person and frees the coil, the long tail of it falling limp at his side. Its tail dances at his side then sings, slicing my cheek.

My hand flies to the fresh wound, my fingers wet with blood. Rage pulses through me, tempered by a deep churning in my gut that fears this lash be the first of many he means to sing me.

Cotton grins. "Now bring her to me, Alden."

"No," I say as Father raises his wrist again. "Let you—"

The whip cracks loud, the tip whizzing past my ear. It sounds again a second later, wrapping round my ankle. Father yanks up and fells me to my back.

I scarcely think to raise my axe before his shadow falls upon me. The ferocity in his attack fears me to my soul. "Father!"

He relents only to grab hold of my axe. Ripping it from my grip, he tosses it away.

I punch his face. "Father, stop—"

Snarling, he grabs my shirt and knocks his head against mine. The room spins as he draws me up off the ground. He knees me in the stomach, stealing my wind, and then throws me across Cotton's desk.

My body tips the chair and I crash to the ground, coughing.

Loose papers flutter around me and ink pools upon the floor.

I crawl toward Ciquenackqua.

Father drops his knee to my back, forcing me cry out. He unwinds the whip from my ankle then flips me to my back.

"Father," I choke. "Please...stop this."

He does his work mutely, binding my ankles and wrists as one out in front of me.

Ciquenackqua's eyes flutter open.

"*Wake, brother,*" I call to him in our native tongue as Father steps behind me.

Then I scream at feeling my scalp near torn off.

Father drags me across the wooden floor, me mauling at his wrist. He stops and yanks back on my hair to force me gaze on Cotton.

"The mind is a powerful tool, no?" Cotton asks. "Simon knew that better than any. His Devil's powder were a wondrous gift to our cause. Did you know he learned of its secrets from the natives? They too use its properties to see spirits. Such knowledge bid me wonder what other secrets lay hidden in savage lands throughout this world."

Cotton changes his focus to the vial and its crimson contents.

"If only Simon could have witnessed the day I learned of the borrachero tree and its beautiful flowers, the Angel's Trumpets." He shakes the vial. "Devil's breath, I call it. A marked improvement to the work he first revealed me."

Cotton removes its stopper and hands it to Father.

"Drink this, Alden," he says.

Father obeys without question.

"You see?" Cotton asks me. "Simon's powder made others our servants, for a time, but we could do naught to eliminate their will. Your friend, Mary Warren, taught me that in Salem when she broke from the fold. Aye, and your savage friend proved again the flaw in your father's work. Look you to the powder he refused for the truth of it."

Pride stirs in me at the proof Ciquenackqua would not relent.

"But my work"—Cotton takes the empty vial from Father and flings it toward the fire—"my Devil's breath, removes all trace of will. I shudder to think what further legacy Simon and I might have left were it made known to us in our younger years. Alas, it will not grow here. That vial were the last of my stores." He pats Father's back. "Ah, but what a specimen it created."

Father yanks back on my hair when my chin dips but a little.

Cotton walks to one of the shelves, his fingers running over the back of the book spines. "Girl, have you ever heard of the Greek hero, Achilles?"

My silence is my answer.

"You would have liked him, I think." Cotton pulls a worn book from the shelf. "Full of rage, that one. A lust for battle and glory."

He opens to a page marked by a red ribbon. "Prophecy warned the son of Thetis would live either a long life, surrounded by loved ones, or else find his life cut short though his name live on for all time."

Cotton closes the book and shelves it anew. He motions to the others. "These tomes are filled with such desire for legacy." Cotton fingers the book spines. "Caesars and kings, gladiators and learned men, all hoping their names echo through the ages. Achilles was but one of the few who succeeded in the task."

I glare back as he looks on me.

"God deems pride a sin, though He instills it in us." Cotton stares on his books. "I, too, longed for my own name and deeds to fill such works, yet now my deeds are done, the whole of my life writ, and I stand tormented."

Cotton steps away from the books, moving toward me.

"Why, Rebecca?" he asks. "Your true father could have forged such a name. Why did he abandon time when near all other men will die for it? For all my learning and study, I cannot understand this decision. I once thought Salem turned Simon mad, but I knew him for a brilliant mind."

My lip curls as Cotton kneels to look me full in the face.

"Simon must have found something there," says Cotton, his voice barely above a whisper. "I beg you tell me now, what secret knowledge did he possess and not share with me?"

I spit on him. "Go to Hell and ask him yourself."

"They asked me, you know." Cotton wipes my spit away. "What should we do with those in Salem convicted to die? Simon thought hanging a cleaner death, one that should allow us convict more before the crowd turned. Still, I oft wondered if the old ways were best."

My gut turns as he glances toward the hearth fire.

"Give me the answer I seek," says Cotton. "Or taste of the hellfire that awaits you."

I resign myself to silence.

"It seems I must go to God with more prayer," Cotton sighs. "Cast her into the fire, Alden."

Father scoops me into his arms, lifting me from the floor.

"No!" I struggle against my bonds and his hold. "Father, stop!"

He does not, approaching the fire with me fighting all the while.

"*Black Pilgrim,*" I say in our native tongue.

Still he walks on.

"Priest!"

My back grows warmer with each step he takes. I lurch up, biting his arm.

Blood pours from my nose when he elbows my face.

The move releases his hold for but a moment, my upper body swinging to earth, upturning my view.

The flames lick the hearth, flickering like fingers that bid me join them.

Father grabs hold of my shirt, pulling me back up despite my struggle.

I glimpse his family dagger, sheathed in his belt.

"Cast her into the fire!" Cotton demands.

I strain to reach the hilt, my fingers grazing its top.

Father grunts, kneeling under my weight to lift me onto his shoulder.

It is enough.

I draw the dagger from its sheathe and plunge it between his ribs.

Father cries out, dropping me on my head as he backs away.

Heat engulfs my body as I near roll into the fire, stopped only by the hearth lip.

"Alden!" Cotton shouts. "Kill her!"

Father winces as he draws the dagger from his ribs, blood staining the blade.

I struggle against my bonds to no avail as he turns his glare on me.

"*Kill her!*"

Father strides toward me, dagger at the ready, his blade tip turned down to end me.

I lean to the fire and fetch the glowing poker in hand. My skin hisses and I scream closing my fingers around it.

"Alden!"

I roll away, swinging the poker free of the fire.

Orange and yellow sparks fly from the embers and into Father's face.

He stumbles back, dropping his dagger, hands flying to his eyes.

"Wake, Father!" I lay the poker end against his chest and hold it tight.

Father howls under its searing touch. He bats the poker away, rolling toward the fire.

"Father!" I reach out, unable to halt him.

The flames lick up his back and the logs roll beneath his frantic waves and screams. He escapes their clutches, his cloak singed and smoking, raising his skin in bubbled white boils. Father shakes on the ground, his breath rapid.

"Arise, good servant," says Cotton. "Finish your work."

I watch in horror as Father climbs to his knees, gasping for breath. He blinks in search of the room, pausing on Ciquenackqua then Cotton.

"Rise!" Cotton commands.

"F-Father," I say.

His head turns slow, his body wavering like stalks in the wind, holding to its roots, unrelenting. His eyes flicker.

"Father..." I say. *"Come back to me."*

"Rise, Alden," says Cotton.

Father obliges, wincing as he does. He stumbles toward his dagger.

Cotton steps closer to me. "Now finish her."

I bow my head at Father's approach, unable to look on him.

He kneels beside me and his fingers touch under my chin, bidding me look up.

My bonds fall away.

I meet his gaze, tears streaming down both our cheeks. *"Father."*

He places the dagger in my hand, then collapses.

Blood stains my palm as I tighten my grip of the hilt.

"Alden?" Cotton says.

I throw the dagger at Cotton, its tip burying in his stomach.

His eyes widen as he falls back, his pistol shot firing into the floor.

I wheel to Father. Grunting, I haul him to a seated position.

His breath labored, he places his hand on my cheek. "Rebecca…"

"Father," I say, kissing his knuckles. "You came back to me."

His grin melts at Cotton's groan.

The old reverend crawls toward his bookshelf, a trail of blood in his wake.

"Go." Father grips my shoulder tight, his face pained. He motions to Cotton. *"Go."*

I step away from him, stalking toward our enemy.

His shirt stained red, dagger yet in his belly, the old man chuckles at my approach. "M-my thanks to you, girl," he says. "A swift death has been my fervent prayer for…many a night now."

"It will not be swift." I point to the dagger. "I would have aimed higher if meaning to offer such a gift."

"A gift nonetheless." Cotton coughs blood then wipes the

traces from his lips. "I have long waited to experience the Invisible World. N-now I shall see it plain."

"R-Rebecca..." Ciquenackqua calls.

I twist my head around only to witness him collapse once more.

"Yes," says Cotton. "Look on him and learn your truth...the veiled legacy Simon and I leave this world."

I face him that he will know the face of Red Banshee.

Cotton grins. "Did you not wonder why I had your savage delivered here to my study?"

"You are the savage," I say.

"History will argue elsewise." Cotton coughs. "They will debate my triumphs and failures, but none should ever recognize that"—he points at Ciquenackqua—"my finest contribution to this new world." He groans. "Though I shall not live to see it played out. Such is the f-fate of great men."

"There is no greatness in you," I say.

"Aye, not me." Cotton shakes his head. "All my finest works... stolen from the minds of men greater than I. Simon...and even the Iroquois."

I step back. "What do you know on the people of the longhouse?"

"Their confederacy be six nations strong now." Cotton raises his hand, his fingers open. "What happens when they come together as one?"

Cotton grins as he closes his hand, forming a fist.

"So it will be with this new nation I have fathered." His voice cracks. "For what are these new colonies but nations unto themselves, full of fear and doubt? They act as children now, but each year their defiance grows. In time, they will strike against those who seek to control them from across the sea. A new Rome... such is the world I envision this nation to be. All thanks to the fear Simon and I unleashed in Salem...a show to reveal the awesome might wielded by the powerless when gifted opportunity."

I point to the dagger in his belly. "Let that be your proof of those who seek control over others."

I rise and leave him to a slow death.

"Aye, so it is," says Cotton. "So it shall ever be. But like the phoenix, a new power will rise from my ashes and the world shall tremble in its wake. All th-thanks to my work."

I ignore his taunts, fetching up my hatchet, venturing to Ciquenackqua's side.

"Re-Rebecca," he says.

"Easy," I say. Sawing through his bindings, my eyes light on the silver platter and Devil's powder. I free Ciquenackqua of the collar and remaining bonds.

Father ambles toward us. He touches me light upon the shoulder, then motions to the opened entry doors.

Those who stood with us in Judge Sewall's crowd into the library, pointing and whispering at Cotton. Susannah stands among them, her pale face painted with the blood of others.

My heart drops when she runs across the room and flings her arms about me.

"What is it?" I ask.

"George...he—"

"No..." I say, my lip quivering. "Let you not say he is—"

"He saved us," she gushes. "George saved us all. I wanted to come for you, but he...Oh, forgive me, Rebecca, for not coming—"

"Where is George?" I shake her.

Susannah points to the entry. "There."

I find my brother and Betty the last to enter through the doors. He leans on her, limping as he walks.

I run to him, flinging myself into his arms. "George, I thought you—"

"Dead?" His grin broadens. "I came not all this way to die, sister."

Again, I hug him close, reveling in his returned embrace.

"Ciquenackua?" George pulls away and kneels beside Susannah. "Is he—"

"He will live, I think," she says. "Though we should see his wounds nursed soon."

"Rebecca..." Betty points to the crowd, gathered round Cotton.

George stands, his face grim. "Is he dead?"

"Not yet," I say.

My brother starts forward.

"Wait," I say.

"No," says George. "He does not deserve breath for the pain he has wrought."

"Cotton will die soon enough. Why should he not live a while longer?" I pick up the tray of Devil's powder. "Wait here."

George narrows his eyes. "For what?"

"For me to call your name."

Father leads me on, the crowd parting before his stare. They whisper as I pass them, some wondering why I carry the powder, others retreating at the sight of it.

Cotton pants as I bear toward him.

"Would you see spirits, old man?" I ask stopping shy of him.

His lip curls. "I-I will be one soon enough."

"But what of the answer you sought?" I ask. "Do you not wish to know why Father abandoned you?"

"I-I do," says Cotton.

"Then let you peer into the Invisible World now. Perhaps you will find your answer."

At my nod, Betty and Susannah fall to restrain Cotton.

I kneel before him, raising the plate to his face.

"No," he says. "Cease this now!"

Father grabs Cotton by the hair. The wig pulls off in his hand.

"Leave me my dignity at least," Cotton pleads with him. "For God's sake—"

Father shoves Cotton's face into the powder, holding him there until the old man chokes.

Cotton pulls away, gasping, his eyes widening, shoulders twitching.

I expect the crowd to taunt him and jeer.

They say naught as Cotton shrinks like a frightened child.

"Mercy, spirits," he says. "I beg you, have mercy."

"George," I say.

Cotton's eyes widen when George appears in the crowd. "Simon," Cotton's chin wavers, his tears a river. "Simon, my old friend!"

George steps back, looking on me with question.

"No, Simon," says Cotton. "Do not go! Do not leave me to darkness again."

George glances at me.

"Simon, why will you not speak to me?" Cotton asks. "Why not comfort me with the answer I seek?"

"He cannot," I say, kneeling beside Cotton. "His soul has moved on."

The old man draws away from me, wincing. "Wh-who are you, spirit?"

"I am Red Banshee," I say. "Come to sing the final song."

Cotton gulps. "Pray, spirit. T-tell me why? Why did he abandon me?"

My thoughts turn to Sarah and her beliefs, her teachings of the life before and strict adherence to them. One such verse plays in my mind as I place one hand behind Cotton's head, the other upon Father's dagger. I lean close, whispering.

"No man can serve two masters. For either he will hate the one, and love the other, or else he will hold to the one and despise the other," I say. "You gave your life's pursuit to legacy, Reverend. Simon turned from such a path to save his soul. None will know his name, but his soul will fly to heaven."

I twist the dagger.

"Yours is damned," I say as he trembles in the throes of death. "I swear on my soul that my tribe and others will fight to stave off this dream of yours. We have our own legacy to forge, a proud people who will not go silently into the night as you do now."

The grimness of those around us catches within me, my spirit moved to give them some revenge also before he passes.

"F-forgive me," Cotton gasps.

"They will not," I say. "Look well on the faces of those around you now. None will forget your trespasses. They will see your name stained, old man." I whisper. "Aye, the legacy of Cotton Mather, linked to Salem forever more."

I pull away and join the others, the lot of us witnessing his last, gurgled breaths.

No one cheers when at last Cotton gives up the ghost.

Several weep and whisper the names of their loved ones. Most wander away, vanishing out the doors.

I remain, my stare lingering on Cotton.

"What do we do now?" Susannah asks behind me.

Glancing back, I watch George place his arm about her shoulders and pull her close. "We live."

-twenty-one-

MY BREATH STEAMS ON THE COLD AND CLOUDY MORN.

"You are certain she lay in this direction?" George asks.

Father nods.

Seated between them, I clutch the leather pouch around my neck as George drives the Barron's wagon up a lonely street. My gaze darts up every alley we pass, and I look to each window, never sighting a single soul. "Where is everyone?"

"The funeral procession," says George. "Judge Sewall expects the whole of Boston will gather to pay their final respects this morn. I pity the man."

"Cotton?" I ask.

"Sewall," says George. "His position requires him make an appearance. Some say he may even speak on Cotton's behalf. I know not how Sewall lived two lives all these many years, but I am grateful for his aid."

I glance back into the wagon, smiling at the sight of Ciquenackqua sleeping. Fresh bandages wrap round his head and his body covered full up with blankets upon the straw bales.

"Betty also," I say, turning my focus back to the road.

"Aye," says George. "Would that she and Susannah might have stayed with us a while longer in Sewall's home."

Father's grin sets me to laughing.

"You mean Susannah, rather," I say. "You will see her again soon enough."

George shifts in his seat. "I should think to see her for longer than a brief stay. Betty thinks her husband will take a liking to me." He pauses, chewing his lip. "Aye, and might be intrigued in my managing his trade here in Boston."

I sink deeper into the bench. "You would stay then?"

"Aye," says George, pulling on the reins, driving the horses west. "Though I did not come to the decision easily. Priest and I spoke on the topic long last night around the fire. He agrees."

I glance to Father and find his gaze elsewhere. "But why, George? Why would you—"

"Naught but pain awaits me in the wild, sister," says George. "I am sick and to death of warring tribes, the fights between French and English. My post is gone, both my wife and partner dead. I have naught to my name. But here," George sighs. "Here, at least, I may find some hope of life again."

He turns his gaze from the road, looking on me.

"Do you not wish that for me?" George asks.

"I do," I say quietly, moving closer to him, resting my head against his shoulder. "Though I will miss you sore."

"Aye." The weight of his head rests against mine. "And I you."

I keep my hold of George, drinking in his scent, as he drives us through the streets of Boston. I close my eyes, listening to the cry of gulls and the creaking wagon, losing all sense of time.

"Whoa," George says to the horses after a time, pulling on the reins.

Our wagon rests at the base of a hill with the sea in sight.

Crossed, wooden markers and stones litter the snow-covered pasture ahead.

George jumps from the wagon and retreats to the back as I climb down after him. He returns a moment later, shovel in hand.

We wait for Father to lead us into the cemetery. Though his gait be stilted and slow, he marches with purpose through the drifts.

The contents of the leather pouch drag heavier with each step I take.

I stave off my tears, promising them their time comes soon.

Father halts before what looks only a large stone, its top covered with snow.

I kneel beside it, sweeping off the snow, and gaze on the name crudely engraved in it. The first tear of many caresses my cheek. "You did find her."

Father nods.

I wipe the tear away then dip my hands into the snow bank, pulling it toward me.

George joins in my effort until our fingers strike naught but earth.

I sit back as George plunges the shovel end, splitting up the frozen ground, and then tossing each scoop behind us. Each time its blade scratches earth, my thoughts go out to all those we loved and had no time to bury, praying they forgive us.

George quits his work. "It is ready, sister."

I kneel again to the fresh hole. Untying the leather string that holds the pouch, I offer my voice in song.

Come, fair lass, just you and me.
We're bound for them colonies, far o'er the sea.

I gaze out to the cloudy sky and grey ocean waters, its waves rumbling into whitecaps.

> *'Augh, no,' she said. 'You stubborn old fool.*
> *I've heard of those lands, and them savages cruel.'*
> *So the Lord took pity and sent me some cheer,*

I lay the pouch inside the hole, holding it at the last, not wishing to let go. My voice quitting, tears flooding down my cheeks.

George kneels beside me and pulls me close to his side. Then he takes up my song.

> *Rebecca's her name, the pretty little dear.*

George weeping alongside me, the pair of us sing together.

> *'Come, lass,' says I. 'Let you not fear no witches.'*
> *Your grandpappy's here, and—*

I clap my hand over my mouth, my body seizing in George's embrace. My brother pulls me close, kissing my forehead.

The snow crunches beside me, Father kneeling with us.

"Rest easy, old friend," Father whispers, sweeping a mound of dirt to cover the pouch holding Bishop's ashes.

My sorrow breaks, a memory of Bishop's coughed laughter in my mind.

I cannot say how long we sit at the grave of Ann "Goody" Glover, listening to the bells toll and sounds of the sea. I do know my brother and Father will not stir until I do. Leaning forward, I pat the mound of dirt and smooth it over.

"Goodbye, grandpappy." I kiss the stone. "You are with your Annie again."

George helps me stand then plucks his shovel free.

I lean on Father, safe in his shadow, as we tread our way back. Rather than sit in the driver's bench with Father and

George, I venture instead to the back, climbing inside next to Ciquenackqua.

George waits for me to settle before slapping the reins.

The wagon bumps forward, headed southwest to leave out the Boston neck, and head for the Barron homestead.

Ciquenackqua stirs on the straw pallet.

"You look well," I say, stroking his brow as his eyes flutter open.

He grins. "I had a good nurse."

I smile, taking his hand in mine.

"Are we leaving?" he asks.

"Aye."

"To where now?"

"The wild." I say, my spirit soaring as the sun peeks through the clouds, warming my face. "And freedom."

Acknowledgments

IT'S BEEN A WILD RIDE, FOLKS.

The Salem trials have fascinated me for as long as I can remember, which made researching the players involved and the time period a true joy. While this story painted the Reverend Cotton Mather in a less than favorable light, I encourage you to read more on his genius—specifically his influence on American science.

In truth, I'm not a little sad to bid farewell to Rebecca, Priest, and all the rest. Good, strong characters are hard to come by and I'm just as thankful they allowed me tell their story as I am to you for reading along.

In regards to this novel, (and trilogy), I could not have done without my coven: Annetta Ribken, Jennifer Wingard, Greg Sidelnik, and Valerie Bellamy. Thank you all for lending me your many talents and knowledge to shape *Salem's Legacy*.

To Karen, my wife and first reader, thank you for loving me and believing in me, especially seeing as I don't write kissy-kissy books, provide the endings you hope for, or change the fates of characters even when you demand it.

To my parents, siblings, and the countless family and friends who have followed my crazy antics all this way, my thanks for your continued support.

And thank you, dear reader, for continuing this journey with me.

About the Author

Aaron Galvin runs the creative gamut.

He cut his chops writing stand-up comedy routines at age thirteen. His early works paid off years later when he co-wrote and executive produced the award-winning indie feature film, *Wedding Bells & Shotgun Shells*. In addition to the Vengeance Trilogy, he also authors the Salt series, a YA urban fantasy praised for a unique take on mermaids and selkies, and the middle grade mystery/fantasy novel, *The Grave of Lainey Grace*.

He is also an accomplished actor. Aaron has worked in everything from Hollywood blockbusters, (Christopher Nolan's *The Dark Knight,* and Clint Eastwood's *Flags of Our Fathers*), to starring in dozens of indie films and commercials.

Aaron is a native Hoosier, graduate of Ball State University, and a proud member of SCBWI. He currently lives in Southern California with his wife and children.

For more information, please visit his website: *www.aarongalvin.com.*

Now, here's a sample chapter of Book One
in Aaron Galvin's SALT Series

SALTED

Available for purchase at most online retailers

LENNY

LENNY DOLAN NEVER ASKED FOR A SALTED LIFE.
No one smart ever did.

But unlike those poor wretches stolen from the surface and dragged into the depths, Lenny didn't have anything with which to compare his Salt existence. Born in the realm beneath the waves, he knew of no other life until his owner raised him up and gave him a profession.

None of Lenny's fellow catchers bothered to stir when he woke screaming from a night terror, two hours past. Each recognized the cries associated with guilt's icy stabs and the shaded memories of those they hauled back into lives of Salt slavery.

Lenny shivered in his hammock crafted of worn trawler nets. *Fear is for runnas not catchas. Don't run from it. Become it.*

He tossed the molded blanket aside and swung his stunted legs free of the bedding. Lenny winced at the cold onslaught when his bare feet grazed the cavern floor. He did not pull away. Once his feet numbed, he slunk through the maze of sleeping bodies.

Lenny had grown quite good at slinking over the years, admittedly not hard for one of his stature. He tested the hinges of the rotted driftwood door. It threatened to fall off but held. He thanked the Ancients for their mercy and slipped out of the shack.

Morn had not yet graced Crayfish Cavern. Some might have risked a torch to ward off the near absolute dark and light their way to the docks. Lenny did not. Doing so would only attract unwanted attention from whichever taskmaster had drawn the early watch. Not to mention the accompanying ten lashes for being outside of quarters without leave. Instead, he used the glittering stalactites, high in the stony ceiling, to guide him. Like countless glittering stars, they winked at him as if to warn they kept watch where taskmasters' eyes could not follow. Declan Dolan had taught his son the use of them as a pup. They had yet to fail him.

Lenny caught a dank smell in the air, rife with the blended stench of body odor, vomit, and excrement. He recognized it for a fresh slave crop come down the Gasping Hole. Not for the first time, he wondered why the taskmasters didn't have the newest catches cleaned upon their arrival. Soon enough the lucky amongst them would earn a Selkie suit. The others...

He snorted the scent away and continued on. Even now, with no one to see, he avoided the boardwalk. Bad habits led to accidents and Lenny sought no more of those. He waddled alongside the boardwalk, trading the slave stink for that of seaweed hung to dry from the tops of six-foot racks.

Barrels lined the dock, each of them brimming with fresh ocean crops—Atlantic cod and haddock, littleneck clams, mussels, and oysters. All awaited surface delivery for the Boston fish markets.

Lenny's stomach grumbled at the sights and smells of the fresh and untouched food. He hurried past, lest temptation overpower his sensibilities, not stopping until he reached the oldest dock. Its wooden beams remained in drastic need of a repair that would never come. He hopscotched over the barren spaces toward the dock edge, leaned over the side to look down.

The cavern ceiling gave the ocean waters an eerie, greenish glow. Three-foot waves struck the thick, barnacle-encrusted pillars. Lenny felt a giddy rush as they shook the rickety wooden pier. The receding tide beckoned him come hunt, then another series of waves rushed to shake the pier anew.

Lenny reached behind his shoulders for the soft and fuzzy hood draped down his backside. Smoky grey and adorned with white circles of varying sizes, it hung from what Drybacks would say resembled a one-piece wetsuit. Donning the hood, he pictured the Salted form given to him—a tiny Ringed Seal.

Lenny's transformation began.

He felt the hood elongate, covering his face, blinding him. His sleeves and leggings tickled past his bare feet and hands, warming them. The sealskin grew further, cocooning his legs into a single tail. He knelt and lay prostrate before his upper body weight toppled him. He felt his feet splay sideways, toes curling to form two hind flippers.

His already pudgy stomach bulged and grew into a fat, seal belly. The white circles of his former hood scattered across his back like a light touch meant to tickle. They shifted in size—some grew to the size of dish plates, others shrank to the size of coins.

He felt his sleeves cover and tighten against his human hands like mittens. They morphed into fore flippers and sprouted nails from tiny digits at the end. His nose and mouth grew into a cat-like muzzle. Whiskers burst from his cheeks. His ears retracted to leave two holes on either side of his seal head.

Lenny opened his seal eyes as the transformation from human to seal completed. He dove into the near freezing North Atlantic water headfirst. The water should feel frigid, he knew, but his seal body's blubbery layer kept the cold at bay.

A school of cod drifted nearby. Lenny gave chase. One he nipped in his mouth before the doomed fish recognized him for a threat. The others he swam down, hooking them with claws sharp enough to hack through glacier ice.

The school unnaturally changed direction.

Lenny halted mid-swim. With a shift of his head, he spun to face whatever predator stalked him now. He saw a chimney of bubbles churn below frothy white circles near the surface where he entered not moments ago. *Looks like I'm not the only hunta this mornin'.*

He caught the scent of his owner's seahorses on the current. The thought occurred to him one might have escaped, but their stable door beneath the docks remained tightly latched.

His seal instincts suggested he surface and head for shore. Lenny dove deeper.

Slap!

The noise came from the surface; a sea otter, floating on its back, used its tail like a paddle to propel it forward.

Endrees. Lenny realized his mistake too late.

A grey shadow with light rings across its back sped up from the depths. Its skull collided with his stomach stealing his breath away.

Lenny swiped at the other Ringed Seal.

His opponent batted away the weak attempt. It weaved behind, collared him by the nape with its pincer-like jaws.

Felt like an early mornin' swim, huh? a man's hard voice growled in Lenny's mind like one of his own thoughts. *Against the rules and five lashes for a first offense. How many times ya done this now? Eight?*

Ya've only caught me eight, Lenny directed his thoughts to the other seal.

Eight times too many.

The sea otter dove to their depth and swam circles around the two seals.

Get away from me, Endrees, said Lenny to the otter.

It replied with a series of trills. Then it flipped to its back and swam alongside him, just out of reach.

Endrees, Lenny's captor spoke. *Go to shore.*

The otter stuck out its tongue but obeyed the command and swam away.

Good riddance, Lenny said. *Ya oughta drown that sea rat.*

The other seal bit down harder. With a quick tug, it dragged Lenny inland. *A catcha watches...waits in the shadows to make sure the goin's safe. Otherwise he's the one bein' caught. Ya supposed to have at least two ways of escape. Ya forget that?*

I was in the water, Lenny argued. *There's a thousand different directions I coulda swum.*

If ya got no plan of where to go it don't matta. Ya neva gonna be big Len, so ya gotta be fasta—

—or smarta if ya wanna live, Lenny interrupted. *I haven't forgot.*

The other seal said nothing more as they neared the shoreline shallows.

Lenny poked his head out of the water to learn who his captor had wrangled to release them both. A pair of sausage-sized fingers grabbed his upper seal lip before he could see anything. The fingers yanked up and then swept the entire seal head backward like removing a costumed mask. The seal head changed to an average hood again before draping down Lenny's backside.

He felt his seal claws retract into fingers as the flippers melted back into sleeves. His tail split in two, the remains of it shrinking up and against his ankles. Lenny shivered, now without the seal's blubber to shield him. He glanced up to see who had released him.

Paulo Varela, a bred-and-born product of slave owner selection. The crayfish tattoo on his neck marked him as belonging to August Collins. Its claws seemed to reach for his jaws as he yawned. His normally dark-gold Selkie coat glistened black, now soaked by ocean water. Paulo wiped the last bits of sleep from his eyes. "Heya, Len. Did you have to get up so early?"

Lenny ignored him, just as he ignored Endrees hissing at him from atop a nearby boulder. He waded up the stony shore as Paulo went deeper to release the other Selkie.

"Don't walk away from me, son," the captor's voice transitioned from thought to spoken word.

Lenny turned around.

A grizzled, middle-aged dwarf had replaced his seal opponent. The little man stood no taller than Paulo's waistline and, like Lenny, wore the smoke-grey suit with embroidered white circles marking him as a Ringed Seal. His hardened, lumpy face appeared marred by a drunken chiseler who had left the numerous scars for sport, and the corners of his hazel eyes wrinkled into crow's feet the longer he stared at Lenny.

Declan Dolan pointed at his son. "How many times ya gotta see others whipped before ya smarten up, boy?"

"Pop," Lenny said. "We're catchas—"

"That don't make ya no betta than those bound for the Block," Declan said. "Ya still a slave! Master Collins can do with ya what he wants. That includes sellin' ya."

Paulo snorted. "August would never do that. Lenny's the only thing that keeps you from running."

"Oh, yeah?" Declan said. "So what if Master Collins decides the lash isn't keepin' his catchas on the straight and narrow? Maybe he takes one of Lenny's ears to remind him how important it is for slaves to listen. Better yet, Paulie, what if he takes ours to make sure *we* keep Lenny followin' the rules? How'd that be?"

Paulo instinctively reached for his ears and massaged the crystal-studded earrings.

"Sorry, Pop," Lenny said. "It won't happen again."

"Mistakes and apologies don't keep ya safe in the Salt, boys. No more than they will on land," Declan said. "Now come on, the both of ya. Ya been called up."

Lenny straightened. "Did someone run off in the night?"

Both young catchers looked to Declan for confirmation. Neither received an answer. The elder Dolan limped alongside the boardwalk with his pet otter close on his heels.

Lenny noticed Paulo's earrings twinkle just before the thought transmission came through. *We're going out.*

Made in the USA
Charleston, SC
22 February 2016